DIRTY SCORE

ROUGH RIDERS HOCKEY SERIES

SKYE JORDAN

1

R afe Savage was going to get laid tonight. Laid good. Laid hard. And laid by an extremely hot chick. Too bad it wasn't the woman he'd wanted to fuck since he'd been eighteen.

He finished drying off in the locker room shower and tugged a towel around his waist, knotting it at his hip. Wandering back toward his bench, Rafe found most of his Rough Riders teammates already showered and dressed. And while they were planning various ways to celebrate their win on home ice tonight, Rafe's head was still pounding from his last hit against the boards.

At his space among the heavily lacquered wooden benches, he pulled ibuprofen from his duffel bag, popped a few, and downed them with cold water.

"Mia's going to be bummed when I show up without you." Tate Donovan wandered to the bench next to Rafe's and sat. "She just texted to say she's sorry she missed the game. She's waiting for us at Top Shelf with a few of the other girls."

That made Rafe smile. He could see Mia catching up with the wives and girlfriends of teammates at the bar. Tate's sister was as much a part of the Rough Riders as any of them. Maybe even more so. Wives could be divorced, girlfriends dumped, but sisters were blood.

Which was exactly why he'd never touch her. But that was only one of a slew of reasons. Those thoughts stole the smile from his face. Rafe could weather a lot—the hardest hit from any NHL player, the most grueling training schedule, new strategies thrown at him on the fly. What he couldn't face was another concrete demonstration that he and Mia would never be more than friends.

"I'm sure I'll catch up with her while she's in town," Rafe lied, scrubbing a dry towel over his head.

Every time Mia had come to see her brother over the last year, Rafe made some excuse to avoid her. But the longing never faded. If anything, it only got worse. She still texted him, but he rarely responded. She still called, but he never answered. And just knowing she was in town made him hurt. He fucking missed her.

And that was the problem. He shouldn't care enough to miss her this badly.

He spread a little gel through his hair, wondering how *she* was wearing her hair now. What she looked like now. What perfume she was using. What new clothes styles she'd helped create and started sporting. Man, he could talk to her for hours about what she'd been doing in New York. Missed hearing her crazy stories about the characters she met and worked with in the fashion industry. Missed the way she made him laugh.

God, he *hated* it when she came to town.

"You okay?"

Tate's question helped Rafe refocus on the night ahead and the stupid dinner he'd been roped into. At least the chick who'd won the charity auction and chosen Rafe as her companion for the evening was hot. He was hoping this puck bunny would be able to distract him from the fact that Mia was relaxing just blocks away from the restaurant, enjoying time with their mutual friends.

"Sure," Rafe lied again. He pulled on his suit pants, wincing at the aches pulling through his body. "Just want this headache to go away. It's not the head I want throbbing while I bang the hell out of someone."

Tate snorted a laugh. "Just because she's hot and she chose you for the dinner doesn't mean she wants to fuck you."

"Of course she does. She didn't choose me for my excellent breeding or outstanding intelligence."

His buddy grinned. "I see your point."

That brought some laughter from the others in the locker room—because it was true.

"All right." Beckett Croft, the team's captain, tossed his duffel over his shoulder and walked toward Rafe on his way out of the locker room. "You've been milking the hell out of this damn dinner. Let me see her picture."

Beckett had once been Rafe's womanizing wingman. The two of them had been able to make more women swoon than a half a dozen karats from Jared's. The bruise developing around Beckett's left eye would have had women swarming around them in the old days. Before Beckett's five-year-old angel of a daughter had been dropped on his doorstep and put a wrench into his bachelor lifestyle. But Rafe loved Lily. And he also liked the woman Beckett had recently swept off her feet too.

"I'm gonna tell Eden," Rafe said, referencing Beckett's fiancée as he picked up his phone and tapped on the photo of the season ticket holder who'd won the auction.

Ashlee Covington was the woman's name, and she looked every bit the young, sexy puck bunny Rafe bedded on a regular basis. He handed the phone to Beckett and started on the buttons of his dress shirt.

Isaac Hendrix, their second-line right wing, glanced at the phone past Beckett's shoulder and whistled through his teeth.

"If her body is even half as nice as her face, you've got a twelve on your hands there."

Rafe chuckled, hoping it didn't sound as forced as it felt. "My thoughts exactly."

He tucked in his shirt and fastened his belt. Beckett handed off the phone to Ty. "Don't drool on it."

The phone made the rounds through the locker room—for the tenth time since one of the team's administrative assistants texted Rafe Ashley's photo.

"You suckers were all pitying me last week when I got picked for this. But now, while you're out shooting the shit like every other boring night at Top Shelf, I'll be eating a five-hundred-dollar dinner and drinking a couple three-hundred-dollar bottles of wine from Bellissimo's with that beauty, then moving up to her hotel room to get showered with sexual appreciation."

The guys tossed out a variety of fake condolences and envious sarcasm that made Rafe smile.

"You're so full of yourself," Tate told him.

Yep, he was working his playboy image hard. It was the only tool left in his mental arsenal to fight thoughts of Mia.

"You have to be the luckiest shit on the planet," Isaac said, handing his phone back. "Out of all the season ticket holders who could have won, what are the chances you'd get a woman like that?"

"Normally, I don't believe in luck. I believe in skill." He pulled his silk tie around his neck and wound it into a French knot. "But in this case, I've got to agree with you, because the probability of having a young, hot chick win this dinner out of a pool of rich old men has to be pretty low. I think the universe really wants me to get laid."

"Probability?" Tate said, lifting a brow at Rafe. "This from the man who couldn't pass high school stats without tutoring *and* cheating?"

"You say that like it's a bad thing," he told Tate. "I learned a lot from both tutoring and cheating."

Like where my loyalties lie. Fucking the most important woman in Tate's and Tate's father's lives would hardly be considered showing appropriate gratitude for all they'd done. A great reminder of why Rafe hadn't rescheduled this obligatory dinner when he'd found out Mia would be in town.

Beckett shifted his duffel to the other shoulder with a wince and glanced at Tate. "See you guys at Top Shelf?"

A few of Rafe's other teammates left with Beckett. But Tate stayed, waiting for Rafe to pack up his duffel and put on his shoes.

"Dad's coming into town while Mia's here," Tate said. "He wants to take us all out to dinner."

Shit.

How was he going to get out of that?

The hell of it was, he didn't *want* to get out of it. Joe had treated Rafe more like a father than his own dad. But Rafe knew how he'd feel if he had to sit through dinner with Mia. The same way he'd felt last year when she'd brushed him off for another man—like a mule kicked him in the gut.

"I'm sure he wants to spend time with you and Mia," Rafe told Tate. "I'm not going to get in the middle of that."

"What's wrong with you?" The irritation in Tate's voice signaled his friend's suspicion, which meant Rafe wasn't hiding his misery as well as he should. "Why don't you want to see Mia or Dad?"

Shit. Now he felt like a selfish, ungrateful asshole.

He shrugged into his blazer and looked at Tate. "It's not that I don't want to see them. But they don't get to come all that often, and our game schedule is really tight while they're here. You should be their focus. They're your family, not mine."

"Stop acting like a prick." Now Tate was angry. "They've been as much your family as mine since we were kids, and you never had a problem hanging out with them before. Where is this coming from?"

The locker room was emptying out, and Rafe's muscles were tightening with the direction of this conversation. "Look, I've gotta go. If I'm late to dinner, management's going to bench me."

"We're in the fucking playoffs. You could spit in Tremblay's face and he wouldn't bench you. All Dad and Mia will talk about if you're not there is *why* you're not there."

Tate shook his head, disgusted. He pushed to his feet, true frustration and disappointment darkening his eyes. "I moved my interview with the ESPN journalist tonight back a couple of hours, but I'll still be leaving Mia alone with a bunch of puck heads at Top Shelf. If you're not fucking this other chick blind all night, maybe you could at least check in with Mia and make sure she's okay."

Tate started to turn, then swung back to face Rafe. "You've become a real ass over the last year, you know that?" His eyes narrowed and searched Rafe's face. "I thought it was a phase. That it was the stress of the game, the job, the travel, the growth. I thought it would pass. But, to tell you the truth, I'm getting pretty sick of waiting."

And Tate stalked out of the locker room.

Rafe's eyes closed. A rock bottomed out in his stomach. "Fuck."

Guilt spiraled through him, from the top of his head to the bottom of his feet, but he didn't have time to think of the way his life had veered off course.

After dropping his gear at his apartment, Rafe grabbed a taxi to the Bellissimo, a hip, upscale hotel, restaurant, and bar.

"Have you been to the Bellissimo before?" the friendly taxi driver asked. "I hear it's very nice."

"I haven't." Rafe stared out the window, distracted by the conflict brewing inside him.

"Pretty expensive, no?"

"Very. Luckily, I'm not paying tonight." This dinner was on the team's dime. Rafe only had to provide the entertainment. And now he was sure as hell hoping this woman was as hot as he'd been building her up to be, because he needed a full-scale distraction tonight.

His phone pinged with a message. Rafe pulled it from the pocket of his blazer with a sigh, but when he found a text from Mia, his heart jumped to his throat.

You're not coming? WTF? I haven't seen you in almost a year! Frowning emoji.

Emotions whirled in his gut. Emotions Mia had been the only person, the only woman, to ever stir inside him.

He blocked those feelings and texted back: *Team PR commitment. Sorry.*

Really. Scowling emoji. *Tate says you're ditching us to get laid.*

Anger spiked. "Tate you—"

"I'm sorry?" the taxi driver asked.

"Nothing. Just talking to myself." He texted Mia back. *Your brother is a dumb shit.*

That doesn't make him wrong. Fine, go get laid. I'm going to do the same.

A carnal image of Mia, naked, in the throes of sex, flashed in Rafe's brain, and his blood ran so hot, sweat broke out over his upper lip. He closed his eyes, wiped a hand down his face, and groaned.

He couldn't remember exactly what her boyfriend looked like from the last time they'd visited. Hell, he couldn't even remember the guy's name. Even before Rafe's affection for Mia had grown beyond platonic, he'd liked very few of her boyfriends. But this last one...

He shook the thought from his head. It didn't matter. His opinion didn't matter. The fact that he wanted to be the one to fulfill her need to get laid tonight *didn't matter.*

Tate didn't tell me you brought your boyfriend with you, he texted.

That's because I didn't.

He lifted one brow. *You're stepping out on your starched suit?*

I'm done with starch. I'm ready for something different. Very different. And I think I've just found it.

Rafe's brows snapped down. *What does that mean? And how could you have found anything? You just got into town.*

I work fast. Gotta go.

Rafe pulled in a breath. *No.* But he clenched his teeth around the useless word. Dropping his head back against the seat, he covered his eyes with one hand and bit out, "*Shit.*"

Emotions roiled so quickly, Rafe was on the edge of insanity when the driver pulled up to the Bellissimo. When the car stopped, Rafe rolled his head toward the ornate entrance and prayed to God this woman was as ready to be fucked as he'd portrayed to his team. Because he had to get the thought of Mia doing some other guy just blocks away out of his head if he wanted to stay sane.

He paid the driver and took a minute outside the hotel, in the thirty-degree weather, to cool down and get his head on straight.

Mia was out of bounds. Off-limits. No amount of wanting her would change that fact. And this *"I'm ready for something different"* was surely just a phase she was going through after yet another breakup. The woman went through men like her brother put away pucks.

He forced the thoughts from his mind and walked up the marble steps toward the hotel's entrance with the cool late spring wind whipping the edges of his blazer open. Greeting the doorman, he passed through the glass entry and sauntered into the grand lobby.

Rafe paused, slid his hands into his pants pockets, and scanned the plush sofas and chairs of the foyer. A few couples dotted the space. Off to the left, the hotel's registration desk stretched across one wall. On the right, the bar opened up to the lobby. Already in full swing, music and chatter and laughter spilled into the space and echoed off marble.

Man, he was so not in the mood to socialize now.

Movement near a bank of elevators drew his gaze as Ashlee strolled into the lobby. Her body was even more gorgeous than her headshot. She was definitely a fifteen on the one-to-ten scale. Tall, leggy, slim, tight. She wore one of those dresses that looked like they'd been painted on. It was deep pink, starting low on her chest and ending high on her thighs. Her breasts were obviously fake, but fake tits felt just as good against his cock as real ones. Sometimes even better.

Ashlee lifted her eyes from her phone, cast one look through the lobby, and her gaze froze on Rafe. Her face lit up like a starburst. The stress in Rafe's gut eased. A smile lifted his lips.

Yes. This was exactly what he needed. This was exactly the kind of woman who could make Rafe forget all about Mia out somewhere getting it on with a stranger.

He met Ashlee in the middle of the lobby, pulled up his best smile, and held out his hand. "Hi, Ashlee—"

"Oh my." She took his hand, but not to shake. She laid her fingers in his while her gaze roamed his body, shoulders to toes. "Don't you look mouthwatering. Is that Armani? I do believe I remember reading that you are one of the sharpest dressers on your team, and I couldn't agree more."

Then she met his eyes, took another step closer, into his personal space, where her extremely feminine scent touched his nose. Her eyes were blue. Almost otherworldly blue, thanks to her obviously colored contacts. But that didn't dim the heat there or the sly edge in her smile. "I certainly hope I'll get to see the legendary Savage beneath all this glamour tonight."

Yes.

Rafe almost laughed with the surety of this score. His grin was wide as he wrapped his fingers around her hand, smoothly turned toward the restaurant, slid his other arm low on her waist, and walked her that direction. "Let's talk that over during dinner."

A short dinner, if he had anything to say about it. The quicker he could get his mind off Mia and how badly he wished he were walking toward a long-drawn-out night with his best friend's little sister, the better.

2

Mia stuffed her phone into her purse, picked up her wine, and finished off the glass, then signaled the bartender for another.

Anger burned through her chest, but it almost immediately mellowed into hurt. A deep, frustrating hurt. One that made her eyes tear up.

Faith, girlfriend of Rough Riders' center Grant Saber, turned from listening to the guys talk over the game and asked Mia, "Is he coming?"

"Nope." She thanked the bartender for her fresh glass of wine, then took a drink. She laughed, but there was no humor in it. "Maybe I'll just move across the country without telling him. Let him hear it from Tate."

She shook her head, her mind combing over the last year for clues to the change in their relationship. But she came up empty like always.

"I don't get it. I just... We've been friends for *years*. Good friends, you know? If it weren't for Tate, I'd say we were best friends. I know I'm his best girl friend. Or I was. Why would he just brush me off like this?"

"Maybe he's going through a phase," Faith offered, her voice compassionate. "Grant says he's always hooking up with someone new. When I'm with the guys after the games, he eats up the puck bunny attention. He's a good guy, but he's not worth the aggravation, Mia. You have enough to think about right now."

Faith was right, Mia did have a lot on her plate. The problem was, she needed one very big thing off her plate to make room for the rest, and that thing was Rafe. But she couldn't do that if he didn't cooperate.

But she wasn't going to waste her time with friends bitching over it.

"You're right. Screw him." Mia stuffed the hurt and pulled up a smile. She reached out, tugging at the extra fabric on Faith's boxy top. "Sweetie, don't take this wrong, but is that the best jersey you can find?"

"Right?" She exclaimed, eyes wide, hand open and gesturing to the front of her body. "I said the exact same thing when I put it on tonight. I told Grant these women's jerseys are so boring. They're just like the men's, just a little better fit. But nothing fun, nothing cute. If they're going to go to all the trouble to design a whole line of women's wear, it should be more than just a slimmed-down version of the men's."

"Sparkles and glitter," Mia said in agreement. "And they ought to show some skin."

"While we're on the subject, I hate you for looking so ridiculously hot in that dress. Tell me where you got it."

"Mmm," Mia said around a sip of wine. "I made it. One of many I designed during this last apprenticeship."

"No. Way." She scanned Mia again, mouth open. "I really, *really* hate you now. Unless you'll make me one. Then I won't hate you quite so much."

She lifted her brows. "Do you have a sewing machine?"

"Me? Ha. No." Her face brightened. "But Beckett's mom

does. And I'm pretty sure his sister Sarah does too. In fact, I bet she'd love to talk to you while you're in town. She's gotten really into making things for the girls. She's always altering patterns and doing really fun outfits."

"I'd love to. I really want to see the girls. They grow so fast. Let me see how the week goes. I imagine I'll have time on my hands. Maybe I can whip a dress out for you."

Faith squealed and lunged at Mia to hug her. "Oh my God. I'm going to have an authentic Mia Leighton dress? I'm going to tell *everyone*."

Mia laughed at the way Faith made her sound like a designer. Someday, Mia hoped she would get there, but she was a long way off. That kind of thing took a lot of cash, and she wasn't ready to dig herself into debt or shackle herself to partners.

After all, according to her exes, she was a commitment phobe.

Faith leaned away, smiling. "You're so lucky, headed into the glitz and glamour of Hollywood. I'm going to stalk you on Instagram and Pinterest and Facebook and anywhere else I can find you, so you'd better be taking and posting pictures of *everything*."

"Will do," Mia promised. "I hope you can make it out west for a visit once I get a place. Maybe in the off-season or when the guys play the Ducks or Kings."

"Absolutely." Faith squeezed her hand. "I'm going to miss you so much. But I'm so excited for you. This is a great time in your life. Young and free and working on a Hollywood set. You're going to meet so many famous people."

"You mean like these guys?" she said sarcastically, gesturing to the players still signing autographs and taking pictures with other customers, and felt another twinge of frustration over Rafe.

Faith laughed. "Not exactly what I had in mind."

"I think that's one of the things the producers liked about me. That I'd grown up with this, knew all these guys, and it didn't faze me. I guess they wouldn't get much done with someone fangirling over everyone all the time." She drew a deep breath, trying to quell the roll in her stomach. "Gah. Every time I think about it, I still get nauseous."

"That's excitement."

Partially. But there was a lot of other shit going on inside her. Once she got this thing with Rafe behind her, she'd feel better. Mia tipped her head, smiled, and drank more wine.

"It's not excitement?" Faith narrowed her eyes. "Is it Sam? Are you having second thoughts?"

"You mean about the guy who called me emotionally unavailable, detached, and afraid to commit, then broke up with me and left me without a place to sleep? That Sam?"

"Right. Screw him. You just haven't found the right guy," Faith said. "When you do, you'll jump in with both feet. Maybe he's in California."

Maybe. Either way, she was going to make sure that when she got there, she was completely unfettered and ready to take on anything. "It's an amazing opportunity. I think the nerves stem from the fact that I don't have much of a choice but to take it at this point. Anything else would leave me stagnant or send me backward in my career. Lack of options is scary."

"Transitions are always hard. Once you're there, you're going to love it." Faith picked up her beer and glanced toward Grant, where he talked with teammates. "Uh-oh." She refocused on Mia. "The new guy's locked on to you."

Mia glanced around at the team standing or sitting in small groups or milling among friends. The new guy was Cole Kilbourne, a trade from Calgary to give the Rough Riders more offensive power in the playoffs. According to Tate, he was an arrogant asshole who thought he was a one-man team and hurt more than helped them.

"I can see the problem from here," Mia told Faith. "He's too handsome for his own good." All the guys were well built and fit, but they didn't all have the best faces. Cole's blond hair and chiseled features belonged in a Calvin Klein ad. "That alone probably made the guys hate him on sight. Does Grant dislike him as much as Tate?"

"Grant doesn't love him, but you know Tate, he leans a little toward the extreme on most things he believes in. Though, I have to admit, every time Cole opens his mouth, he digs his own hole a little deeper."

Cole stepped away from the edge of a circle of guys who weren't including him anyway and started toward Mia and Faith.

Mia sighed. "Incoming." Then an idea popped into her head. "Does Rafe hate him as much as Tate?"

"Oh God, yes. Cole and Rafe ram heads on a regular basis."

Her devious side perked up. "Well, if Rafe won't come to me, I might just have to go to him. And maybe I'll bring a friend."

"Oh no." Faith laughed the words. "Remind me not to make you mad."

Cole came up to them, greeted Faith, then turned to Mia. With his hand held out to her, he said, "Hello, beautiful." When she shook his hand, he enclosed it in both of his. "I'm Cole Kilbourne. It's normal to be intimidated by me, but try to get over that, because I have a feeling we're going to be very, *very* close."

A little laugh huffed from Mia's lips. Then the fact that he was totally serious hit, and full, rolling laughter burst out.

"Oh, I can see why you're such a favorite." She pulled her hand from his and patted the stool on the other side of her. "Come sit, Cole. Let's get to know each other."

When Cole moved to her other side, Mia winked at Faith,

who grinned, rolled her eyes, picked up her drink, and wandered to her boyfriend's side.

Before Mia had fully turned back to Cole, something flew over her head, bounced off Cole's forehead, and landed on the bar. A balled-up napkin. Frowning, Mia glanced over her shoulder and found Tate stabbing the air in their direction.

"Sisters are off-limits, Kilbourne. Touch her and you'll wish you'd never heard of the Rough Riders."

That. That right there had governed so much of her childhood, she couldn't even see how or when it had insinuated its way into the fabric of her life. She and Rafe might never have taken their friendship to the next level even if they'd been left to follow their hearts, but Tate's fierce protective streak made just the thought an absolute impossibility.

That, plus the fact that Rafe barely even acknowledged her existence anymore, along with all the stress built up from this new job, was pushing her over the line tonight.

She opened her mouth to tell Tate to grow up and stay out of her business, but Cole touched her jaw and brought her gaze around to his. "Ignore him. I'm way more interesting."

Mia let her frustration toward Tate ebb. Tate wouldn't change. Rafe wouldn't change. The complex relationships between their bizarre, makeshift little family wouldn't change.

But Mia could change. Mia had changed. And what she needed most right now was to stay focused on her primary goal: getting her heart unhooked from a ridiculous fantasy she'd held on to since adolescence—her romantic feelings for Rafe.

Once she accomplished that, everything else would fall into place.

And since Rafe was pulling his new normal tonight and avoiding her, Mia was going to have to take more desperate measures. What the hell? She didn't have anything better to do. And she sure didn't have anything to lose either.

So she leaned into the bar, smiled at Cole, and said, "Tell me about yourself."

3

An older man in a staff uniform smiled as they approached the entrance to the restaurant. Rafe opened his mouth to tell him what name the reservations were under but Ashlee spoke first.

"Reservations under Savage," she said. "Rafe Savage. I called down earlier and spoke with the restaurant manager, Dennis. He said he would reserve table twelve for us." She glanced at Rafe. "Twelve is our lucky number, right? Your jersey number and the number I picked to win this dinner? It's okay, isn't it? I know hockey players are superstitious and all, but I figured if your number was twelve, you couldn't have superstitions against it, right? Now, thirteen, definitely. And if there had been a table numbered sixty-nine, well, you know I would have jumped on that one first, but of course there's not. Could you imagine how big a restaurant would have to be to have sixty-nine tables?"

"This way please." The older man was trying—and failing—to hide his grin when he turned away and started into the restaurant.

Ashlee followed.

But Rafe stood there frozen for a long second, mouth still hanging open at the babble that had rolled out of the woman's mouth in mere seconds.

How much trouble would he be in if he turned and walked out? Really? What could they do to him? Tate was right about benching him. In the normal season, he'd definitely be risking missing out on playing time, but not with the playoffs.

"Rafe?"

Her voice cut off his hopes of running. He refocused on her. She stood about twenty feet away, between two tables of diners, looking back at him over her shoulder. Her silky straight blonde hair swept over her bare, tanned skin revealed by the open back of her dress. And damn, the woman had an incredible ass.

An image of her riding him while he gripped that ass and hauled her into his thrusts flashed in his brain. His blood drizzled south and his cock tingled. Unfortunately, not as much as he preferred. Or needed.

But Rafe took a deep breath, straightened his shoulders, and sighed. She was probably just nervous. After a drink or two, she'd relax. After a drink or five, he wouldn't care what she said. "Yep, right here."

He pulled out the chair facing the wide windows, showcasing a gorgeous view of Capitol Hill for Ashlee.

"My, what a view," she said. "You can just never get tired of that, can you? I love touring and walking all the neighborhoods of DC. No matter how many times you do it, you always see something new. And the museums... Can you believe they're all free? That just amazes me. I don't know how they manage that, what with their displays changing all the time..."

Rafe had long since taken his own seat on the other side of the table with his view of the bar, where people his age were actually having fun. And he had to fight not to roll his eyes as Ashlee continued to talk.

And talk.

And *talk*.

The waiter held out a tall, thin menu toward Rafe. "We have an extensive list of wines—"

Ashlee cut him off with a sparkling smile and, "We'll have a bottle of Mondavi's 1996 Opus One, please."

Rafe's breath caught in his throat. He felt the skin of his face chill. He didn't know why. It wasn't his money. But when the waiter turned his gaze from Ashlee to Rafe with the slightest lift of his brows, Rafe said, "Actually, let's make that a bottle from 2012." He smiled at Ashlee. "In honor of—"

"Your second hundredth goal with the NHL, and of course our lucky number—"

"Of course." Rafe smiled, but his satisfaction came from knowing he'd just saved the team twelve hundred freaking dollars on a bottle of wine only Ashlee would be drinking. Rafe already knew he'd need something much, *much* stronger. "And could I get Patron?" he asked the waiter. "Best you've got on the shelf."

The older man nodded, took the wine list, and retreated.

"I never dreamed you'd be even better looking in person." Ashlee rested her elbows on the edge of the table, clasped her fingers beneath her chin, and sighed with a dreamy look on her face. "This is just so exciting. You should have seen me when I won. I don't know if you saw that video clip of me when I picked the number twelve in the lottery, but, oh my God, when I saw the prize, I screamed like a girl. I mean, of course I *am* a girl, but I've never sounded more like a girl than I did in that moment. My heart was just bruising my ribs. Kinda like it is now. I'm not normally a nervous person..."

A server brought water to the table, and the waiter returned with the wine and Rafe's Patron. Ashlee never shut up. Barely even paused to take a breath. While the waiter uncorked and poured the wine, Rafe swallowed the rich, luxurious tequila he should have been sipping. And when the waiter set the wine bottle back on the table, he offered the empty glass.

"Another, sir?"

Before Rafe could answer, Ashlee said, "If his glass is empty, just assume he wants a refill." Then to Rafe, "I've read about your love for Patron. An elegant drink, if you ask me. Sexy. Suits you perfectly. I had a little extra time after I checked in earlier —I'm staying here at the hotel, by the way. I thought that would be easiest. No pressure or anything, I just like to be prepared. And it gave me time to look over the menu..."

Rafe mentally checked out while she continued the nonstop monologue over food. When the waiter brought Rafe's second Patron, he had to force himself not to hammer it back. He was sure she would have at least slowed down by the time she had a glass of wine in her, but she just kept talking.

Right through the salads.

Straight into the main course.

"...in fact, my mama says my husband is going to be a very lucky man. She trained at the Le Cordon Bleu before she met my father and puts on the most amazing dinner parties, and she's been grooming me since I was knee-high. My father is constantly entertaining. Real estate at his level is such a fussy business, but I so enjoy meeting and chatting with his clients. Recently, he represented the ambassador to Kenya, and the man brought his eight children with him. Eight. Can you believe? I mean, I love kids, and I want a big family, but eight? Anyway, I pitched in and entertained the kids while the ambassador and his wife toured properties with my father, and oh, those children were so precious..."

The waiter quietly replaced Rafe's empty glass with a refill. His fourth. Rafe knew he couldn't drink it. He should have stopped after one. Too much alcohol would dehydrate him. The aftereffects could dull his reaction times in tomorrow's game. And the realization was truly painful.

Rafe tilted his head back and met the man's eyes. They held gazes a moment. And a very clear understanding passed between them. The waiter gave him the slightest nod of sympathy before he placed a comforting hand on Rafe's shoulder and drifted away.

Rafe cut a piece of prime rib and lifted it to his mouth. Chewing, he met Ashlee's gaze to give the illusion of actually listening, then slid his focus slightly left, where he could watch the customers at the bar again.

Ashlee giggled at something she'd said. She was three glasses into the bottle and now seriously tipsy, bordering on drunk. Rafe wished he were as lucky. While he was definitely feeling the Patron, he wasn't near as numb as he wanted to be. And this dinner had the horrible potential to go on forever, especially considering Ashlee was talking too much to eat.

He picked up his water glass instead of the alcohol and tipped the glass back. His gaze skimmed over the bar again, and he caught sight of a new couple sliding onto stools at the end of the bar bordering the restaurant.

The man caught Rafe's attention. Tall, blond, well-dressed, good-looking— Cole Kilbourne. The Rough Riders' new trade from the Calgary Flames. *Prick* was the first thing that came to Rafe's mind. It was no secret that Kilbourne wasn't any happier about the trade than the Rough Riders were.

The guy was in his early twenties and needed to have that hot-shit chip smacked off his shoulder in a big way. He might be good at getting the puck in the net, but he lacked so many other crucial skills to pull a team together, Rafe thought they were better off without him. Kilbourne had nothing but a bad attitude since he'd arrived, he was too arrogant to even attempt to try and work with the other players, and lacked even the most basic respect for teammates and coaching staff.

"...and when I have children," Ashlee was saying, "I'm certainly not going to have a nanny raise them. I'm going to raise my own babies, the same way my mama raised me. But I will definitely have a planned babysitter because I love to work out. I believe it's important to keep fit for mind and body, not to mention a healthy sexual relationship..."

Rafe shifted his gaze to Ashlee again. How could someone so physically beautiful make him so viscerally miserable? If he had to listen to her drone on any longer, he might just stab his steak knife through his heart. Or maybe he could just stick his cock in her mouth.

When the thought made him wince, Rafe corralled his wandering mind and started strategizing how he could use Kilbourne to get him out of this. His gaze traveled back to the bar, where Rafe's new teammate now stood very close to a woman he'd guided into a seat. Her dark hair was cut in layers and curved softly to her shoulders. She was slim, wearing a stylish, fitted dress that showed great curves. It was going to be hell getting him away from her.

Rafe was wondering if he had Kilbourne's cell number in his phone. Wondering what he could possibly offer the guy to come over here and make an excuse to get him out of this.

Kilbourne put his hand on the back of the woman's chair and leaned close to say something to her. She turned toward him, tilted her head back, and laughed. Her hair fell off her face and, *wow*, she was...

She was...

Shock stole his breath.

Mia.

The reality of it hammered his gut with fire.

She was *Mia*.

Emotions whipped through him, colliding at the center of his body—excitement, happiness, desire. They mixed, creating a physical yearning to reconnect with her.

In that moment, looking at her from a distance for the first time in a year, he realized that *not* talking to her and *not* seeing her had only made him want her *more*, not less. And knowing he couldn't have her, knowing he couldn't break the trust he'd built with Tate, or the loyalty and respect he owed Joe, felt like a knife popping the balloon of joy in his gut.

Then Kilbourne's hand slid across her shoulders, jolting an angry sensation straight into the pit of Rafe's stomach. Mia's earlier text filled his head: *I'm ready for something different. Very different. And I think I've just found it.*

Oh no. No, no, no.

She was *not* going to be fucking Kilbourne while Rafe was still alive and breathing. No way was Rafe going to look at Kilbourne's ugly mug every day knowing he'd had Mia in a way Rafe had fantasized about for years.

He put down his fork and pulled his phone from his pocket, pretending he'd gotten a message. "Excuse me just a minute," he murmured over Ashlee's babble, tapping into his text messages. "It's my agent. Go ahead, I'm listening. I'll just text him."

"Oh, no problem," Ashlee said. "I do that all the time, carry on several conversations at once. You know, with cell phones and social media nowadays, everyone's always communicating with someone..."

He tuned her out again, his mind suddenly stalling on what to say and how to say it. He had no right to tell Mia what to do or who to do it—or not to do it—with. After all but shutting her out of his life for an entire year and bailing on her tonight, Rafe knew he was the last person she would listen to.

He'd have to go at this an entirely different way.

4

Mia would give Rafe ten more minutes to act, because ten more goddamned minutes of Cole Kilbourne was all she could stomach. Unless Rafe was truly enthralled with the Baywatch babe sitting across the table from him—not exactly a surprise—he couldn't have missed Kilbourne. She had put herself and Cole directly in his line of sight.

While Mia had arrived with a come-hell-or-high-water determination to royally fuck Rafe Savage out of her life, the moment she'd seen him, she'd had second thoughts about the out-of-her-life part. Then she'd gotten a good look at Baywatch, and her hopes for the royally-fucking part dwindled to nothing.

Now, as she cast a covert gaze their direction, she was planning more of an intervention. Because if Mia couldn't get him into bed tonight, she was going to do her best to make sure no one else could either. Yeah, she was pissed. She had an entire year of pissed to whip out and wield against the man.

"Are you going to come to watch me play against the Kings tomorrow night?" Cole's question drew Mia's gaze back. His hand slid over her shoulders, his fingers toying with the skin exposed in the openings of the dress she'd designed.

Mia swiveled a little more, bumping his arm loose. She used her knee to push at his thigh, giving her another inch of space. "What makes you think I'd come to watch you play when my brother's on the team?" she asked with matter-of-fact congeniality. "Or when I know the other twenty-three guys like family, but when I just met you?"

Cole wasn't looking at her face. His gaze was on her breasts. Her dress was modest by club standards, but definitely sexy. She had, after all, come out tonight with a purpose.

"I thought we connected tonight," Cole said, lifting his pretty hazel eyes to hers, his mouth quirked in that lazy little half smile all hockey players mastered somewhere around age twelve. "Thought we had a little, I don't know, spark going."

Mia sighed. Cole was still with her only because once he'd started talking to Mia at the bar, everyone else had seen their chance to escape. And that was fine. It fit her agenda. If it hadn't, she wouldn't have had any qualms about leaving him to fend for himself.

As for Cole's motives, she was pretty sure he was sticking with her simply because he didn't want to be alone. Despite his flirtation, she didn't get the feeling he was really attracted to her, and Mia had experienced that lost sort of loneliness enough to recognize the look of it on his face.

He ordered a rum and Coke for himself and wine for Mia, but he was already three sheets to the wind.

She lifted her hand to his cheek, tapping it to get him to open his lids a little wider. "You know you shouldn't be drinking so hard before a game."

"I'm fine. Doesn't affect me."

"Right, I forgot," she said with honest sincerity. She'd learned to love these idiots over the years. "You're an invincible, granite-headed hockey player."

Cole's brows pulled a little. He got a confused look in his clouded eyes. "Was that meant as a cut?"

"No, honey. You'll know when I mean something as a cut." Her cell vibrated twice in her other hand, and Mia's pulse jumped. But she kept her gaze on Cole and didn't immediately look at the message. "Sports should be coming up soon. Why don't you watch to see if they talk about you?"

Worked like a charm. His attention diverted to the television, and Mia lifted her phone to glance at the message. When she saw Rafe's name, she had to dig her fingers into her palm to keep from pumping her fist in success.

The message read: *Save me.*

That was a surprise. Definitely not what she'd expected. But she stuck with her original plan and looked up and around the bar, as if she didn't know he was sitting a few hundred feet in the other direction. Then she pressed her hand to the base of Cole's spine—which faced Rafe—and slid it up his back.

When Cole looked at her, she smiled. "Anything good on the news?"

"Nah. Want to get out of here?"

"Nah. Keep watching. It's not over yet."

Her phone vibrated again. *Leighton, stop groping the puck head, get your ass in the restaurant, and save me the way I saved you from the Cody Matthews fiasco at prom.*

All the anger she'd been holding on to for the last year instantly softened. She didn't know how one memory could wipe away all the hurt and frustration she'd suffered from the phone calls he hadn't returned or her visits to DC he'd missed. But images from those rough high school years flashed in her head again now—how excited she'd been to get invited to prom when she'd only been a sophomore, and by one of the most popular seniors. How she'd told *everyone* Cody was taking her. How she'd worked extra jobs for neighbors, and her mom had paid the electric bill late so Mia could buy a dress.

Only to be stood up at the last minute. Worse, to be stood

up so Cody could take an older girl, a prettier girl, a more popular girl.

Mia's chest still pinched, remembering the humiliation. Still remembered crying all day, sure she'd never be able to show her face at school again. Sure she'd lose all her friends and be the laughing stock for the next two years.

And then of Rafe showing up at her door, in a suit he'd borrowed from Tate's father, carrying tickets to the prom he'd bought with money he'd earned working at the skating rink. All after he and Tate had been swearing off prom for months. The fact that Tate had been pissed he had to spend prom night alone instead of hanging with his best friend confirmed it had been Rafe's idea, not Tate's or Joe's.

"Dammit," she said softly, a smile lifting her lips despite her best efforts to stay angry at Rafe for more recent events.

"What's wrong?" Cole asked without taking his eyes off the television.

She didn't even bother answering, because Cole wasn't paying any attention. She heaved a sigh and pushed sweet memories of Rafe to the background. That had been a long time ago. He'd been a good friend. A best friend—as best as a boy could be. And then, last year, without warning, he'd dumped her friendship like a hot rock. After all her attempts to piece it back together, she had to admit it was over. A thing of the past. She had to let the nostalgia and her feelings for Rafe go. And she had to do it now, before she tried to make another hard transition.

So she typed: *What happened to getting laid?*

Not in a million years with this chick.

Too bad. My options are looking rather promising. This puck head is way hotter than Cody Matthews ever was.

She pushed to her feet and leaned into the bar, which also put her closer to Cole.

Kilbourne? Promising? How much have you had to drink? You

could do so much better. And you shouldn't be fucking Tate's team-mates. Especially not during the playoffs.

God, it was always hockey. Hockey, hockey, hockey. Mia loved her brother, she loved hockey, and she respected Tate's and Rafe's careers. It was one of the many reasons she'd never made a move on Rafe. But she was done living her life around Tate and Tate's hockey. It just didn't work for her. And it didn't *have* to work for her anymore.

Thanks for the lecture, she texted back. *Find your own escape.*

Mia. Please.

Excitement built low in her belly. Excitement and...something else. Something sad. Regret? Guilt? Loss? She'd used the fantasy of Rafe as an escape for a long time. The way one of her coworkers had dreamed of traveling through Europe, Mia had dreamed of being loved by Rafe. She'd used the thought as a light at the end of the tunnel. Her fantasies were a way to get through a boring day or a packed subway ride or the stress of meeting a deadline. She might have wished it would happen, but in her heart of hearts, she'd known it never would.

And then Sam. Sam and his *"If I didn't know that you worked too much to be seeing someone else, I'd swear you were in love with another man. It's like your body's with me, but your mind and your heart live somewhere completely different. If there's someone in your past you haven't told me about, you have to get over him, because there's no room for anyone else."*

Mia had instantly realized that Sam had been talking about Rafe without knowing it.

She'd also instantly known how utterly ridiculous it was to allow one-sided feelings for a friend hinder her adult relation-ships. And as soon as she proved that to herself, she'd be free. She'd just have to find another fantasy to dwell on to get through rough times.

She shook off the nerves and realigned herself with her goal, then texted Rafe. *Seriously?*

SERIOUSLY, came back immediately.

Mia took her sweet time straightening, then turned and scanned the restaurant, purposely skipping over him several times before she finally let her gaze settle on Rafe.

Until now, she'd only taken quick, sidelong glances. And for the last year, the closest look she'd gotten of Rafe had been video clips on television or a rare postgame interview. Now, even from where she sat, as soon as their eyes met, she felt the solid snap of their connection in her belly.

The warm sizzle both thrilled and angered her. She'd always downplayed her feelings as a lingering schoolgirl crush. But there was nothing lingering or schoolgirlish about the desire that flared white-hot low in her body or the softening in her chest. These feelings were present and passionate. And just like every other time she'd considered confronting him over the years, the sweetness she felt for him bubbled to the surface, blurring her good sense.

There was no room for sweet now. He would twist sweet into hurt. He'd done it dozens of times over the last year, and if she was going to get over him, she was going to have to stuff the sweet, take what she needed, and walk away.

Finally walk away.

Just like he had.

Then, in future relationships, maybe she wouldn't be accused of things like being more interested in hockey than sex. Or scheduling their vacations around the Rough Riders' travel schedule. Or living vicariously through her brother.

Or being in love with a ghost.

Rafe did that barely visible *get-the-hell-over-here-and-do-something* head-tilt thing. The familiar movement reduced the year between them to a day, making her feel like all her hurt and frustration was unreasonable, petty, childish. Suddenly, she wasn't so sure she had the strength to do what she needed to do.

Mia licked her lips and typed: *Just leave if you want to leave.*

Rafe replied: *You know I can't.*

Technically, he could. He could stand up, put one foot in front of the other, and walk out the front door. But she knew Rafe's heart wouldn't let him. If he walked out on this woman, he would be showing not only disrespect for her, but for the Rough Riders fans. Specifically, the season ticket holders. And ultimately, his action would reflect poorly on the whole team.

Rafe was nothing if not dependable—to his team, to Tate, to Joe.

She glanced at the woman across from Rafe. Baywatch was still talking. Even though their food had been sitting in front of them for at least twenty minutes, even though Rafe had finished half his dinner before abandoning the meal, the woman with him hadn't touched hers. Though she did manage to sip down quite a bit of wine in between words. Which might account for her lack of irritation over Rafe's texting and inattentiveness.

Mia took a breath and typed: *You'll owe me.*

Fine. Anything you want. I'm dying here.

She bit her lip. *Anything I want?*

Yes.

You're sure?

Mia. ANYTHING.

"Okay," she said to herself in a be-careful-what-you-ask-for tone.

Mia turned, picked up her pineapple mojito, and pounded the remaining half of the drink. She took two full minutes to put a plan together, then turned to Cole and put her hand on his arm. "Hey, look, Rafe's here."

Cole's gaze drifted from the television, his frown immediate. "Who?"

"Your teammate? Rafe Savage? Let's go say hi."

"No way." He pulled away from her touch. "That guy's been a jerk since the day I walked into the locker room."

"You've been doing this a long time. You know it's no fun getting a new guy at the end of the season."

"But I was never an asshole."

Right. It's always someone else's kid. "I'm sure you weren't. But you understand the stress, and look, you're stuck with the Riders, right? And admit it, you were pretty miserable at Top Shelf tonight. If you want to make friends and enjoy this phase of your career, you're going to have to make some kind of effort. With the more resistant guys, like Rafe, you might have to take the high road and make the first gesture."

Her phone vibrated with a message. She glanced down to see Rafe's *What is this? A fucking conference? Just walk away from the guy.*

She growled and hammered out a return message. *Stop being an asshole or I'll leave you with the babbling Baywatch babe until your ears bleed.*

After she sent it, she cut a hard you're-pushing-your-luck glare at Rafe. When he lifted a scowl from his phone and saw the look on her face, he rolled his eyes and refocused on his plate.

She looked at Cole. "If you don't want to make the gesture, how about grabbing the girl?"

"What?"

"The girl. His date. Rafe's dying to get away from her."

Cole's gaze darted to Baywatch. "She's a walking wet dream, but there's no way Savage is going to let me near her. He couldn't shut up in the locker room about how he was going to be fucking her all night."

The knife in Mia's gut twisted. She was about ready to ditch her fuck-him-and-forget-him plan, bail out of this godforsaken hotel, hail a taxi, and catch the next flight to Bermuda.

Fuck men. Fuck her career. Fuck life, for that matter.

Barefoot in Bermuda, sans men and all the trouble they brought, sounded like one damn good plan.

Her phone vibrated, and Mia closed her eyes. So help her God, if Rafe said one more wrong thing...

She took a breath, opened her eyes, and focused on the phone.

I'm sorry. I'm exhausted and sore and my ears won't be the only thing bleeding soon because I'm pretty sure my brain imploded half an hour ago. The first thing I should have said when I saw you is how beautiful you look and how much I've missed you.

Her gut squeezed, everything inside her twisted, and tears burned her eyes. Goddamn him. He always knew exactly how to yank her chain.

You're such a suck-up, she typed.

Normally, yes. But this is true. If you really want to get laid by that puck head, I'll stay here and drink until there is no possibility my mind would ever work well enough to even imagine you two together.

This was exactly the shit that sucked her back in. One comment like that and Mia would be on the hook for another five years. She'd never have a life unless she got to a point where comments like that didn't affect her.

She grabbed the front of Cole's blazer to pull his attention back to her. "I'll get you the girl, but you have to follow my lead, got it?" He looked like he was about to argue, so she jerked on his jacket. "Do you want the hot chick or not?"

"Sure, but I don't see how that's going to make things better between me and Savage."

"Trust me on this. I've known these guys a lot longer than you have." Mia slipped her hand around Cole's forearm, pulling him into step beside her. "No matter what I do, don't question me. Think of me as the coach. Do you question your coach?"

"No," he said resolutely. "Never."

"Exactly. Just trust me like you trust your coach, and you'll end up in bed with that Baywatch babe tonight."

Despite the anger rising in Rafe's face as she approached with Cole, Mia pulled up the social butterfly she'd developed while working in New York's fashion industry, along with the smile she used to dazzle, and held Rafe's gaze.

But the closer she got, the harder it became. Their year apart had helped her forget how damn good-looking he was, how sexy he looked fresh out of the shower after a game or practice. Oh, but that wasn't all. She'd forgotten about the crinkles at the corners of his eyes, the fullness of his lips outlined by an unshaven jaw, the intensity of those gray eyes rimmed in long, thick, black lashes.

Her throat grew tight. Her stomach balled into a fist. And for the first time, she was starting to realize she might just never get over the man.

Before she and Cole were within ten feet of the table, Baywatch's monologue reached Mia's ears. "...that's just one charity I'm involved in. I've considered cutting back on my interior design business to take on another. I mean, we're so fortunate, don't you think? I love to give back. I've seen you doing a variety of charity work with the Rough Riders, and I'd love to talk to you about coordinating some efforts to support those organizations. Wouldn't that be fun? And a great way to spend more time together, what with your travel and practice schedule and my work schedule..."

"Excuse me," Mia said in her most conciliatory voice as she stopped beside the table. "I'm so very sorry to interrupt." She turned her smile on Baywatch and offered her hand. "I'm Mia."

"Ashlee," she said, confused.

Mia shook the woman's limp hand, then gestured to Cole. "This is Cole Kilbourne. If you're a Rough Riders fan, you'll be seeing a lot more of him. He's the newest team member."

Ashlee's eyes widened, and she lifted her hand to Cole's.

"Oh my. Yes. Yes, you came from the Calgary Flames, didn't you?"

As the two shook and Cole did what he did best—talked about himself—Mia turned, wandered behind Rafe's chair, and pressed her hands to his shoulders. They were wide and as solid as the marble bar. His hair was too long and curling at the ends. And he smelled great, that recently showered fresh scent with an edge of spice. Just standing this close to him made Mia's chest hurt. So many emotions whipped up and around, she didn't know how to feel. She was having serious second thoughts about this plan.

He tilted his head back and looked up at her with those beautiful silvery-gray eyes, begging her to get him out of this situation. Mia put up her best shield to protect against the fact that this was a fantasy, pretend, a temporary spoof, not the real thing. Nor would it ever be the real thing.

She forced a smile, slid her hands over his chest, and bent until her cheek pressed his. Her belly fluttered with nerves, but her heart floated in bliss. She'd never made such a forward move—not with any man she wasn't already involved with, and most definitely never with Rafe. Her headfirst dive into the act unnerved her far more than she'd expected. So she did the only thing she could do short of abandoning the ruse and running for the nearest exit. She forged ahead, hoping to develop enough momentum to carry her through to the end.

He was warm and rough, and Mia thought the familiar scent of sandalwood and Rafe might just make her orgasm all by themselves.

"Hey, baby," she purred. "I'm glad you two are having such a great time. I'm just really tired. I hope you don't mind if I start home ahead of you."

God, he smelled like heaven, but he felt even better. With her hands stroking all the hard ridges of his abdomen, she turned her head, pressed her lips to that tender spot just beneath the ear, and an involuntary moan drifted from her throat.

His skin rippled with gooseflesh beneath her lips. The fine hair at the nape of his neck rose. His reaction to her touch set off a grenade of heat between Mia's thighs. She pulled back enough to look into his eyes, surprised to find what looked like real heat in them.

"Don't stay out too late," she murmured. "You've been so hard to get ahold of, I swear it feels like I haven't seen you in forever."

One of his big, warm hands closed over hers. The heat of it tingled up her arm. Then he gave her a squeeze, and his hand slid up her forearm, her biceps, her shoulder, and he shocked her by pushing his fingers into her hair. The way he cradled her head coupled with the look in his eyes made Mia feel like everything around them had vanished. Like she and Rafe were the only two people in the restaurant. Like his feelings mirrored hers.

Only she knew that wasn't true. Knew it for a fact. The last year had proven it.

She started to pull away, but his fingers tightened, and his gaze held hers. "It does feel that way," he said, his voice rough and soft. "And it's *damn* good to see you."

The following moment seemed to float, extend, and expand. Mia was trying to figure out if he was just playing the part or if there was a hidden meaning behind them when Ashlee spoke.

"You—" she started. "I didn't—"

Mia pried her gaze from Rafe's, relieved to break free of the look that caused so much turmoil inside her. She met the other woman's eyes and offered a smile, but she didn't let go of Rafe. This might not be real, but it was the only time she'd even get to pretend, so she stayed there, loving the warmth of his chest, the strength of his hand in her hair, the way he held her close.

Then he blew her mind—he turned his head and pressed his lips to her throat. Mia pulled in a little breath, and all her attention hyperfocused on the feel of his mouth on her skin. Heat skittered over raised nerve endings, spread into her chest, and tightened her nipples.

Mia drew every shred of strength she had together into a fragile string. "He can be captivating," she managed. "I know."

"But I..." Ashlee's brow dipped in confusion. "There's nothing anywhere to indicate he has a girlfriend."

Rafe opened his mouth against her throat and scraped his teeth along her skin. Mia sucked a breath of surprise, of titillation. He was getting way too into this role. But that was what she'd wanted, right?

She mentally slapped herself out of her stupor. This was just a game. One of many he'd been playing over the last year. And Mia didn't like it. She didn't like any of it. And for the millionth time, she wished she didn't care so much. That would make it easier to tell him to shove his games. Make it easier to walk away. To turn her back and let go.

Only that wasn't who Mia was. And it certainly wasn't how she felt about Rafe.

But she was angry, so she grabbed for the careless role and laughed. "Someone's had a little too much to drink. He's always frisky when he's been drinking." She slapped his chest. "Stop that, naughty boy. Save it for the bedroom." To Ashlee, she said, "We've been trying to keep our relationship quiet. Media is such a headache."

She tried to straighten, but Rafe didn't let her go. And when she turned her head and met his gaze, the heat there punched her gut. His eyes were stormy and hot. And the emotions floating there seemed to encompass everything from shock to *finally*.

"I'll warm up the sheets for you." Mia stroked her hand

across his cheek. "Wake me when you get home. You know how I like it."

The fire that flashed over Rafe's face was sure to keep Mia warm for a decade to come.

With every inch of her skin tingling, she pushed to her full height, forcing Rafe to release her. But she kept one hand on his shoulder and used the other to comb at the hair over his nape. Mia smiled at Ashlee, ignoring the way Rafe grabbed her wrist like she was abandoning him in the middle of the ocean.

"It was good to meet—" Mia started.

"Oh no." Ashlee pushed her chair back. "I'm so sorry. If I'd known I would never have kept him so long. Rafe, thank you for an absolutely wonderful evening. You've been so gracious to let me go on and on and run well over the two-hour time allotment—"

"You know..." Mia cut her off, glancing at Cole. His big hazel eyes were locked on Mia and Rafe with that just-slammed-against-the-boards look. "Cole, are you free for a little while?" She glanced at Ashlee. "I mean, if you don't mind the company of two handsome Rough Riders tonight instead of one, I bet Cole wouldn't mind staying to chat for a bit." Mia beamed at Cole. "Would you?"

"Really?" Ashlee's big blue eyes grew round and latched on to Cole.

Cole diverted his attention to the walking wet dream. "I'd love to." Then darted a cautious look at Rafe. "If it's okay with you, I mean."

Now Rafe did that just-slammed-against-the-boards thing, and Mia wanted to pound both men with a dinner plate. Instead, she pinched the skin of Rafe's neck.

He flinched out of his shock. "No. Yes. I mean, fine. Fine with me."

He stood so fast, he nearly toppled Mia right along with the chair. But he used the hand still on her wrist to drag her against him and caught her around the waist with the same speed and grace he used on the ice.

One second, Mia was cool and in control, the next, she was up against Rafe, looking into his steel-colored eyes, her brain scrambled by the sheer hardness of him, the raw heat of him.

Rafe's gaze slowly lowered to her mouth, then lifted to her eyes again before he murmured, "Let's hit those sheets, beautiful."

5

After living with the physical discomforts hockey wrought on his body all his life, there was little that really bothered Rafe. But having a hard-on for his best friend's little sister? Yeah, that seriously bothered him.

He kept his arm tight at her waist as they passed through the restaurant, the bar, and finally into the lobby, trying like hell to ignore how damn perfect she felt at his side. The way his heart skipped and jumped at the reality of being close to her again.

They stepped beyond view of Ashlee and Cole, where the other Rider had taken Rafe's place at the table. Rafe cut a look around the lobby for familiar faces. When he found none, he steered her to a corner, released her abruptly, and forced himself to put distance between them. Fast.

He paced a circle, trying to collect himself. But he'd had too much to drink, and all the emotions and desires he'd tucked away for so long didn't want to get stuffed back in their box. With his back toward her, he rubbed both hands over his face. But, shit, he couldn't get the feel of her lips off his skin or her husky insinuations out of his head. In fact, Rafe was fully, painfully hard.

Down, boy. It's not real. She's off-limits.

Rafe pushed all ten fingers through his hair, took a deep breath, and dropped his arms on a heavy exhale. "Jesus, what a night."

Bracing for the sight of her, Rafe clenched his teeth and turned. She stood several feet away, arms crossed, one hip cocked, head tilted, a look of irritated contemplation carving a tiny V between her brows. All that thick, luxurious hair the color of bittersweet chocolate was tousled in a way that made him crave the sight of her in the morning.

Naked.

After he'd fucked her ragged.

All night.

But... No. No, no, *no*.

She was *Mia*.

So perfectly Mia, it hurt.

He should hug her. He always hugged her hello and good-bye. But he was honest to God afraid to touch her again. Afraid he wouldn't let go. Afraid he'd do something inappropriate like he'd done at the table when he'd kissed her throat.

And, God, she'd tasted good. Her skin was so soft. And she smelled like Mia, like flowers and vanilla...

Stop. Stop, idiot.

He forced his eyes to the floor and planted his hands at his hips. *Breathe. Hold yourself together. Think of Tate. And Joe.*

Okay. That helped cool the fire.

He dropped his hands and lifted his head. But shit, she was still Mia. And he hadn't seen her beautiful face in way too long. Her cheeks were flushed, her lips pursed, her eyes sharp. She was the same Mia he'd always known—at least on the outside. But something was different. Something intangible. And Rafe got the distinct impression that he was at a disadvantage.

"I bet that was a first," she said in that flippant, irreverent, matter-of-fact tone he loved. A snarky little smile tilted her lips, but she didn't look pleased. She flipped her purse open and pulled out a thin wallet. "Finding a woman that gorgeous with a mouth that made you desperate *not* to sleep with her."

He wasn't going to touch that. He couldn't think about another woman while Mia was standing in front of him anyway. Had never been able to. His gaze fell to all her curves covered in a slinky dark silk slip of a dress. The sexy cutouts across her chest and shoulders showed all her smooth skin. The short skirt exposed toned, tanned thighs. Her heels were black velvet. Four inch. With one elegant silver strap at the ankle.

He didn't understand how she could make such a simple outfit look so hot, he wanted to strip her to the skin. Like, *now.* "That is one amazing little black dress."

She smiled, but her dimples didn't show, and her grin didn't reach her eyes. "It's not a little black dress. It's a *get laid* dress." She pulled a card from her billfold. "And I agree, it has been quite a night. In fact, it's been quite a month, hell, quite a year. For me, anyway. Hopefully, it's all about to get better."

"I should let you go, then." He forced the words out, trying to wipe the idea of Mia with another guy from his mind. "I'm sure there are a dozen guys who'll take you up on that, and they'd all be better alternatives to Kilbourne."

Rafe glanced toward the bar. He needed alcohol. Large quantities. Right now. But he'd have to find it somewhere else, because no amount of liquor would erase the sight of Mia picking up another guy. She'd never been a pickup type of girl. Sure she'd had a ton of boyfriends, men Rafe had occasionally met when she'd brought them into town—and God, talk about twisting the knife, every meeting had dug into Rafe like a talon —but she'd never been known to do the one-night-stand thing.

Rafe didn't know which was worse to imagine—Mia giving

her heart and her body to a boyfriend, or Mia giving her body to a stranger.

His guts were a turbulent mess. He needed to get out of here. Away from her. "I'm sorry I couldn't make it to Top Shelf tonight. Maybe—"

"You had a sure fuck waiting," she said, cutting off his offer to get together another day. She returned her wallet to her purse and met his gaze. "I get it. Priorities."

A raw stab of guilt hit. And yeah, even shame. But he knew Tate would never have repeated locker room talk. "Where'd you hear that?"

"I was at a bar with a dozen drunk Rough Riders. Where do you think I heard it?" Attitude snuck into her voice. "Secrets are not bragged about in a locker room. You should have learned that when you got busted for shoplifting at ten, screwing Tina Jenkins under the bleachers at the homecoming football game at fourteen, landing your first threesome with members of the dance team at sixteen—"

"Stop." He issued the command a little too harshly, but he didn't need her bringing up every last indiscretion from his life right now—most of which had been his way of pushing Mia from his mind. A few other people in the lobby cut looks of concern at them. He lowered his voice and asked, "What's going on with you?"

"Me? Oh, well, that's a *really* long conversation." Her eyes roamed his body in one hungry glance—the way other women looked at him, not Mia. And she started toward him in a slow, fluid stroll. Her dress ebbed and flowed over all her curves, making Rafe's mouth go dry. Making his palms sweat. And when she kept closing the distance, Rafe lifted a hand to stop her before she was pressed against his body, but she was still way too close.

She tipped her head back and met his gaze directly. Her warm, delicious scent made a deep hunger roll through his body. A repeat of the ravenous streak that engulfed him when she'd pressed her lips to that hot spot behind his ear. His brain hazed at the edges. Thick desire collected low in his gut.

"And talking," she said, her voice soft and sultry, "is the last thing on my mind."

"*What's* going on, Mia?"

Her hands pressed against his abdomen, and the contact shocked Rafe, shooting electric awareness across his skin. Then her hands moved up his chest, tightening the skin all along his torso and spreading heat deep into his body.

"I'm collecting a debt." She reached out and tapped the Up button on an elevator. "That's what's going on."

He cut a confused look at the glowing button, then narrowed his eyes on her. "Are you drunk?"

That made her laugh. "Oh no. I want every moment of tonight crystal clear in my memory."

The elevator doors opened.

"What are you doing?" Rafe asked.

"Going up to my room."

He felt like his brain was in a game of Pong. "I thought you were staying with Tate."

"Not tonight."

She stepped back, and Rafe was caught between holding on to her and letting her go. He wasn't ready for her to disappear. But he knew by the uncontrollable gnawing ache swamping him from shoulders to toes, he wasn't ready to dive back into a friendship with her again either.

Mia fisted a hand in his shirt and pulled him toward the elevator.

His brain flipped to full-scale alert, and his body put on the brakes. "Whoa." The farther he stayed away from any private spaces with her, the better. "I'm not going upstairs."

Her smirk was hot and knowing and sure. "Oh yes. You are."

A zing of *holy-shit* zapped his spine and spread fire through his groin. This wasn't the Mia he knew. And this wasn't the kind of relationship they had. This was a puck bunny scheming him into bed. And if this were any other woman even half as gorgeous as Mia, he'd already be upstairs with his head under her skirt, eating her out while she writhed and moaned.

His mind instantly put Mia in that position, and desire flashed through him, buckling his knees. He put one hand against the wall and pressed his other to her shoulder to keep him on his feet.

"What the *hell*..." He gripped her biceps and swung her out of the path of the elevator. When she didn't seem the least bit fazed, he gave her a little shake. "*What's* going on, Mia?"

She laughed, the sound hot and lazy. The elevator doors slid closed, and Mia reached out again, hitting the button.

His heart pounded like a goddamned jackhammer. Darting another look around, he bent his head and lowered his voice. "Where is this coming from?"

She got that gleam in her eyes again. The one that made his stomach squeeze and flip. The one that made heat collect between his legs. She reached into her purse and lifted her phone.

"Right here," she said.

He glanced at the phone but shook his head, growing frustrated. "I don't understand."

Mia tapped her screen, entered her password, and turned the phone toward him, showing their text messages.

You'll owe me, she'd told him.

Fine. Anything you want. I'm dying here.

Anything I want?

Yes.

You're sure?

Mia. ANYTHING.

His stomach somersaulted, then dropped to his feet. His

blood turned to ice one second, then melted in a firestorm the next.

"I didn't think I'd need to explain," she said, "but obviously, I do. My *anything* is you, me, upstairs, now. Is that clear enough for you?"

A fireball burst in Rafe's gut. His mouth dropped open. He was dreaming. He had to be. It was so like one of his dreams to do this. To taunt him with the idea of being with her only to wake him before he'd so much as kissed her, leaving him in a moody funk for a week.

But, he didn't wake. This was no dream.

"What the *hell*?" His words came out too loud and too pissed. A family of four standing near the elevators looked over, clearly concerned.

Mia raised her brows at him in the most goddamned adorable little smirk. "Be careful," she sang. "You don't want this to turn up on the news, do you?"

His mind shot to Tate. Then Joe. And Rafe's blood ran cold again.

He reached out and stabbed a finger against the Up button. "I'll go up to talk about this. But *that's it.*"

Holding on to that smirk, Mia looked down at her phone. To clear his head, Rafe watched the numbers on the elevator and strategized how he planned on keeping the woman he'd wanted for years at arm's length. A woman who looked good enough to fuck a dozen different ways every day for a week straight without coming up for air.

"Look at that," she said, pulling his gaze from the numbers. But Mia was still looking at her phone. "Dictionary.com defines 'anything' as 'in any degree; in any way; to any extent.'" She met his eyes and smiled—a wicked hot little smile. "That's my *anything*. You—to any degree, in any way, to any extent I want."

Rafe was on fire. He rubbed his hand over his mouth and

found sweat collecting on his brow. "You're not thinking straight."

"In fact, my head is clearer than it's ever been. And since the agreement was anything *I* want, talking isn't included." She lifted one slim shoulder in a careless shrug. "Unless you want to throw in some dirty talk. Bet you're good at it. That might be hot." She slipped one arm around his waist and lifted her chin. "Give it a try. Talk dirty to me, Rafe."

His heart seized. He slapped a hand over his eyes. "Jesus Christ."

Ding.

He grabbed her wrist and pulled her into the elevator, then found himself hoping someone else came on, suddenly rattled at the thought of being trapped in this box alone with her.

She pressed the number for the top floor, and the doors closed without another passenger. Rafe went into offensive mode. "Let's get real, Mia. You're just getting back at me for not talking to you. I'm not stupid enough to think you're serious, so you can drop the act already."

Before he'd finished the last sentence, Mia was pressed up against him, her hands roaming his chest, wrapping around his torso underneath his blazer. Her gorgeous green eyes stayed focused on his.

"You may be smart, but you're epically clueless. So I'm being very serious and very clear for you. This isn't about revenge. This is about reclaiming my life. And part of that is about holding you accountable for your promise. Making sure you follow through on our trade. This is about you being as loyal to me as you've always been to Tate and Joe for a change."

"For a change? What does that mean? I've never been disloyal—"

"Are you going to try to tell me that purposely ignoring me for a year is showing loyalty?"

"Yes," he said with absolute finality. "It was."

"To Tate and Joe, maybe. Not to me."

She had him there. He couldn't think of anything to say.

"Exactly," she said in his silence. "That's why tonight is about you and me and one night together. That's it. Don't make it more complicated than it is. You've given Tate and Joe decades of your loyalty. All I want is one night. One full night of you, naked, in my bed, fucking me until you can't fuck me anymore."

Rafe's breath whooshed out. His knees turned soft again, and for the second time in his life, he had to catch himself with a hand on the rail lining the elevator.

His vision grayed at the edges, probably because every ounce of blood in his body now resided in his cock. He was breathless, like he'd been skating sprints. Sweating like he'd been lifting weights. To keep himself from lunging for a woman he should think of as a sister, even though she was anything but, he gripped the bar on the wall with both hands.

"This is... What are you..." Sweat crept along his forehead. "Fuck, Mia..."

"There you go. Now we're on the same page." Reaching for his tie, she began working the knot open. "And let's ditch these clothes, because I really *am* sick of the starch in my life."

She leaned into him. Her flat belly rubbed his cock and launched a craving that clawed through his lower body.

"Oh yes," she purred, rocking into him until he saw stars. "We are *definitely* on the same page."

He was losing the battle. He felt the last threads of control slipping from his grasp. And Rafe's mind transitioned from denial to damage control. But that tiny shift opened the floodgates on a desire unlike any he'd ever known before. "What... what about your brother?"

She laughed. "He's not my type."

"Mia."

She glanced around the empty elevator. "Do you see my brother? I don't see my brother."

"What if he finds— Holy fuck." He reached up and stilled her hands with one of his. "Kilbourne. Kilbourne is going to tell everyone—"

"You've *got* to be kidding me. Cole is going to be your best friend tomorrow.

If he does what I told him to do, he's going to be taking Ashlee to bed in about half an hour and calling you the dumbass tomorrow for bailing. Just tell him if he talks, he won't be getting any of your leftovers next time."

She unbuttoned the top button of his shirt, and he cut a look at the numbers lighting the strip above the door. This had to be the slowest elevator ride in the history of the twenty-first century.

"You're not talking like you," he said. "You're not acting like you."

"You wouldn't know, would you? You haven't seen or spoken to me in a year. A lot can happen in a year."

Ouch.. "Okay, I totally deserve that. But this isn't—"

"As for Tate, I'm certainly not going to tell him about this. And neither are you. None of us needs the useless stress that would create. Don't even get me started on the topic of how many of *my* friends *he* fucked during visits home after I left for college. Besides, we're grown adults, Rafe. We can fuck whoever we want to fuck. I certainly don't tell him who to—"

"Please stop saying that." He couldn't breathe.

She wrapped her arms behind his neck, leaned into him, and pulled his head down. Her breasts pillowed against his chest, full and soft. Her abdomen rested against his gut, flat and tight. Her hips pressed and rocked against his, rubbing against his cock.

He had never felt anything so heartbreakingly perfect in his entire life.

"What don't you want me to say?" Her lips were a breath from his, her eyes hot, heavy lidded, and direct. "Fuck?" She said the word slowly. Deliberately. Softly. And Rafe couldn't keep himself from watching her mouth move as she said the dirty word he preferred not to hear out of a woman's mouth. A word that—coming from Mia—created flash-fire in his blood. "Does it turn you on to hear me say I want you to fuck me?"

"No." He had to stop and deliberately focus on drawing his next breath. "No, no, no."

She laughed, the sound soft and naughty. "Oh yes. Yes, yes, yes it does."

She moved against him, and pressure pulsed in his cock. Spread through his pelvis. Gathered at the base of his spine.

"Jesus." Nothing had ever felt as good as Mia's body against his. He'd dreamed, fantasized, but never, *never* believed he would ever know the reality of it—so much sweeter, so much stronger, so much deeper than his imagination had been able to conceive.

But part of him, that deeply loyal part she'd talked about, knew he *shouldn't* know the reality.

Rafe squeezed his eyes closed to cut off the sight of one of his longest-standing fantasies: Mia's beautiful face drenched with the raw desire of wanting him.

He needed to push her back and walk away.

He needed to pull her closer and hold on.

"I want you to fuck me, Rafe." Her voice was husky and dripping lust. "And I want you to fuck me like you mean it. Like you want it. Like you love it. I want you to fuck me like you're hungry for it. Like you can't get enough. I want you to fuck me so perfectly, I'll never need you to fuck me again. I want us to fuck and forget."

Ding.

Rafe heard the doors slide open. Felt Mia ease away. But he didn't move.

"... fuck me so perfectly, I'll never need you to fuck me again..."

Something stirred inside him. Something vague, deep, and unpleasant.

"...fuck and forget..."

His heart, so full and aching just seconds ago, deflated until it felt like it was crumbling. He shook his head and opened his eyes. Mia stood between the doors, holding them open, her gaze expectant.

"No, Mia." Hurt darkened his voice, and hearing it made him realize just how quickly she'd fileted him open. Just how stupidly hopeful he'd been. How completely unrealistic. "I'm not a *rebound* guy."

"Rebound?" Her voice held a note of incredulity. Turning, she hit the Door Hold button and approached him. Winding her arms around his neck again, she slid that delicious body along his and held his gaze with a look that was pure Mia—open, kind, warm, and affectionate. "You're right, Rafe, you're not a rebound guy. You could *never* be a rebound guy. And you sure as shit are not, and will never be, *my* rebound guy."

The heat of anger thrumming through his belly transitioned into need. He released the bar and gripped her waist. "Then what is this?"

With one hand combing into his hair, the other cupping his jaw, her beautiful green eyes softened and her lips turned in a little smile. "It can be absolutely anything you want it to be. But only for tonight." Her thumb slid over his cheek, and her gaze lowered to his mouth. "Only one night. And it stays between you and me."

Again, a conflicting sense of disappointment stabbed his bubble of hope. But before he could ask any more questions, the hand in his hair tightened, and Mia pulled his head down. She rose on her toes to meet him, pressing her lips to his for the very first time since they'd met two decades ago. The way he'd dreamed she would for at least ten of those years.

Her lashes didn't dip until after their lips touched, and in that split second, before he let his eyes close, Rafe witnessed the most beautiful wash of emotion drift over her face. Emotion that eased her features into an expression of such desire and bliss, it turned him inside out.

When her lips moved against his, suckling and sliding, Rafe's breath eased out on a moan. He curved his arms around her until they'd doubled at her waist and her delicious little body was as close as he could get it while they were clothed. Mia answered with her own sound of satisfaction and hunger, parting her lips and demanding more from Rafe.

After the sheer number of women he'd kissed over the years, he didn't know how it could even affect him anymore. But the feel of Mia's supple lips under his didn't just affect him, it moved him. A mountain of emotion shifted inside him, absolutely none of which he understood, but all of which overwhelmed him in a way that made it instantly clear he couldn't let her go now. There was no turning away. No heading home. No pretending this didn't happen. At least not to himself.

He didn't give a shit why she'd chosen to bring this up tonight. He didn't care that she'd come here to screw Kilbourne and ended up with Rafe. Nothing mattered to him now but getting his chance with Mia.

The elevator buzzer sounded, signaling they'd held the door open too long. But Mia didn't care. Her tongue slid over Rafe's lips, pouring liquid fire into his groin. He groaned, opened to her, and stroked his tongue into her mouth. Her warm, wet, sweet mouth.

At the same time, he lifted her off her feet and carried her out of the elevator, letting the door close behind them. Rafe pushed his hand into her hair, cupped her head, and held her as he took the kiss deeper. She softened and swayed into him. And she tasted so damn good, like abandon and bliss and forever. She felt so right, like that missing piece, his other half, his soul mate.

He loved the slide and roll of her tongue. The way she varied the pressure of her lips. The scrape of her teeth over his bottom lip with a little whimper, like she needed more. Like she wanted to eat him.

"What room?" he said, barely clearing his lips from hers to ask before tasting her again.

She tapped the keycard against his shoulder, and he took it from her, all without breaking their kiss. Rafe took one more, long, deep taste of her before he pulled back and fought to focus on the sleeve holding the card for the room number. But Mia's mouth moved to his neck, then his throat. One hand worked on the buttons of his shirt. The other slid down his belly, past his belt, and cupped his cock through his slacks.

Pleasure ripped through Rafe's groin, and his entire body jerked. "Ah God..."

He grabbed Mia's shoulder to steady himself, but that left him defenseless against her assault, and she took great pleasure in exploring every hard inch of him.

"Mia," he begged, breathless. "Let me read this so we can get out of the hallway."

"Want to taste you," she murmured against his throat, but eased the pressure on his cock and lifted her hand to his face. "Want to lick you...and suck you..."

He blinked the white flashes from his vision, read the number, and glanced for room directions. Then stepped away from Mia, took her hand in his, and hurried her down the hall toward the room.

"I can't believe I'm doing this," he muttered, his gaze blurring over the richly patterned gold-and-green carpet. But what he really meant was he couldn't believe he was *finally* doing this. He couldn't believe he was *getting the chance* to do this.

He forced his mind off Tate and Joe, men whose trust and

respect he would lose if they discovered this fling with Mia. This was just one-and-done. Something Mia instigated. Something Mia wanted.

Justifying it helped him get the keycard into the door. He turned the handle, then pushed the door open and held it for her to go first. The door closed behind him as she flipped on a light, and Rafe paused when he got a look at the room. Correction: the mini suite.

One dim lamp burned on a side table, casting the room in an intimate glow. Everything was done in gold and white. The bed was a four-poster with a matching footstool and nightstands. There were two upholstered chairs with ottomans and a table in one corner, a working desk in another, a curved settee in another.

This was the epitome of Mia's life now, filled with fashion shows, cocktail parties, and meals at fancy restaurants. She dated suits that took her to the symphony and Broadway.

Rafe had plenty of money, but money didn't buy sophistication or experience. And as Mia tossed her purse on the stool at the foot of the bed, Rafe was more than a little uneasy to realize he wasn't sure exactly how to handle a woman who deserved more than a hard fuck and a slap on the ass on the way out.

"This room had to cost a mint," he said, trying to ease the new nerves with small talk. "That job of yours in New York must be paying better this year if—"

His words cut out as his gaze returned to Mia, her hand tugging on the single tie at the back of her neck.

The dress's neckline softened, and the fabric fell off her like molasses over vanilla ice cream. Slowly, smoothly, sensually, inch by slow inch, Mia's gorgeous body came into view until her dress pooled at those sexy heels.

Rafe's body temperature spiked. His brain short-circuited. He couldn't breathe. He could only sweep his gaze over her again and again, taking in the black lace bra, panties and naughty garter holding up sheer black thigh-high stockings. All finished off with those flashy heels that screamed *do me now and do me hard.*

He didn't know how many women he'd slept with. Didn't remember names or places or specific encounters. But he knew he'd never met a woman as beautiful or as brave as the one standing in front of him right now.

"Jesus Christ." The words reached the room as barely more than a whisper. And he couldn't utter another when she came toward him. This time, he did step back. And he put his hands up. "I... You're... This is...just so much to take in all at once."

She smiled and continued toward him, until her abdomen pressed against his hands, until his back hit the wall. She lifted her hands to his shoulders, slipped off his jacket, and tossed it on a side chair. "No rush. We have about eight hours until morning."

Only eight? Only eight hours to do everything he'd always wanted to do with her? Suddenly, it wasn't near enough. But when she reached for the buttons of his shirt, Rafe grabbed her wrists. Her eyes darted up to his.

"I'm not a suit, Mia," he said in warning. "I wear one to and from the games, but you know me. And you know I'm nothing like the men you date in New York."

"I thought I knew you. This last year has proven me wrong."

That was the second time she'd stung him in the last half hour. Deserved, but... "Then why do you want me?"

"Why does it matter? Do you give all your one-night-stands the third degree over their motives?"

"It matters because you're not all women."

It also mattered because this wouldn't be like any run-of-the-mill one-night-stand.

He walked her backward, holding her wrists. He pushed her to a seat on the edge of the bed, set his stance wide, strad-dled her knees, and pressed her hands to her thighs.

She tilted her face up to his.

"And because," he said, looking down at her, "you're probably used to certain behavior in the bedroom. Things that I don't do. Or that I do differently. Things you may not like."

"Like what?" she asked in a husky almost-whisper, her eyes sparkling with lust.

Rafe felt the snap of his restraint as a rush of adrenaline spurted through his body. "I'll have to show you."

He pressed one knee to the bed and pulled her arms over her head as he laid her back on the gold embroidered coverlet. Transferring both her hands into one of his, he traced his fingers slowly down the side of her face and across her lips. He pulled her mouth open and leaned down to kiss her. When he barely touched his lips to hers, she arched and pulled against his hand, mouth open and reaching for his.

Damn, that was a rush.

He rewarded her with a long, deep, slow kiss, stroking and swirling his tongue against hers until she moaned into his mouth. Until her fingers curled around his hand.

Rafe was dizzy when he pulled back and let his free hand slide over the swell of her breast, her ribs, her flat belly, her thigh.

"You're even more gorgeous than I imagined." He cupped the knee closest to him, and as he pulled her leg wide, he draped his over it as an anchor.

Then he moved his open hand up her inner thigh. Smooth. Warm. Supple. Her warmth and arousal floated on the air and added another burst of flame to his blood. He would taste every inch of her body over the next eight hours. But by the way she panted and squirmed, Rafe had to take care of first things first.

He slipped his fingers under the edge of her panties and moved them to the side. Her pussy was pink and glistening with wetness. Rafe groaned and stroked one finger through the soft folds.

Mia gasped. Her fingers tightened on his hand. "Rafe..." She breathed his name, filled with urgency and need, just like she did in his fantasies. "Let me undress you. Let me touch you."

He stroked two fingers back the other direction. Mia's body tightened, and her head fell back on a moan.

"Normally, I don't do foreplay. But for you..."

He spread her wetness through her folds, gently searching for the bud of her clit. His finger slipped over the tiny bubble at the same instant Mia sucked a sharp breath.

He smiled, propped himself up on his elbow, and leveled his eyes with hers. A little confusion floated. Then he positioned his thumb and used her slickness to rub the slightest, gentlest circles directly on the raw tip of her clit.

"Ah..." Her mouth dropped open. Surprise flared in her eyes. But after a few more strokes, her expression relaxed into bliss. Her eyes rolled back, and her spine arched on a moan. "*God...*"

"For you," he said, watching pleasure flash over her face, "foreplay will include a number of quick, intense orgasms before the real fun begins."

She made a sound deep in her throat. Her hands clenched and released around Rafe's where they were still trapped. And her body writhed against the bed. This was so much better than any fantasy he'd ever created in his own mind. Hearing Mia's pleasure, smelling her skin, feeling her warmth, her body... This was absolute ecstasy.

"Rafe," she choked out. "God."

That was the only downside to these orgasms—they came fast and sharp. Of course, that wasn't a downside when you needed to get a woman off so you could get rid of her, but in this case...

He lightened his touch even more and lowered his head to press his lips against hers. Her lids closed, and her lips pursed against his. But only for a moment before the pleasure became too intense. Her breaths came fast and hot. Her eyes hazed with ecstasy.

Having this kind of power over her was so good, it was a little scary. He didn't have an addictive personality, but Mia could be his one exception.

"Rafe," she breathed against his lips. "Please."

Lust spurted through him in a hot gush. He growled and pulled back to focus on her face. He added a little pressure, a little speed. A pained look of extreme pleasure flooded her face. "Ah God..."

"I'm going to watch you come."

"Yes, yes, yes."

"God, you're beautiful."

"Rafe," she choked. "God...yes, ah, *ye*—"

Her orgasm broke the way they always did, like a firecracker. With a hard crack through the body, a scream, then gone, leaving Mia dazed, limp, and glowing.

The sweetest emotion crowded Rafe's chest. He had an overwhelming urge to wrap her in his arms and just hold her. But she wasn't a child. This wasn't her first orgasm—even if it was her first with him. And tonight was just one night.

So he pressed his face to her neck and whispered, "So beautiful."

He released her wrists and smiled against her skin when she just left her arms there, stretched above her head.

Wrapping an arm at her waist, Rafe slid her farther up on the bed, then started his exploration of her body while she recovered. He unfastened her bra and eased it off her arms. Her breasts were little more than handfuls of perky, supple flesh he'd spent more time dreaming about than he should have. And now they filled his hands, softer, bouncier than he'd imagined. Her nipples were deep pink and hardened instantly at his touch.

"I never believed I'd ever get to touch you," he said before opening his mouth over one breast.

"Mmm." She hummed with pleasure as all ten of her fingers combed through his hair. Her nails scraped his scalp, and tingles spread down his neck. She fisted his collar and tugged. "Let me get you naked."

Oh no. If he were naked, he'd be inside her. And it was way too soon for that. He stroked his tongue over her nipple again and again until she arched beneath him. Then he moved his mouth to the other breast, licked, scraped, and sucked.

"Rafe," she complained, pulling at his shirt again. "Come here."

Obviously, she was ready for more distraction.

He moved lower, kissing her ribs, her belly, her navel. He still couldn't believe this was Mia. That his hands and mouth were on *Mia.* He hooked his fingers into her panties at the hips and dragged them down her thighs, standing to pull them all the way off.

Then he stared down at Mia Leighton lying in the middle of a king-size bed of gold, her hair a tousled mess, in nothing but black garter, stockings, and heels, waiting for Rafe.

"You are a serious fantasy come true." His voice was dark and rough. He met her eyes, which were a little shy now, her knees bent and turned to the side. "Tell me how you want me to fuck you again, Mia."

He reached for her knees, slid his hands behind them, and pulled her to the edge of the bed.

She squeaked in surprise, then laughed a little and covered his hands with hers. Rafe took a long, slow, sweeping look at the curves of her body, at the small strip of hair over her pussy, and met her eyes again.

"Tell me, Mia," he repeated, "how do you want it?"

He pulled her thighs wide and dropped to one knee. And with his gaze at eye level with her pussy, he slid one finger into her heat, slow and deep. Mia sucked a breath, and her belly hollowed out.

"Fuck me like you want it." Her words drew his gaze up, and he found her watching him, lust etching her expression. "like you need it."

He stroked her walls, searching for ridges. "You are going to feel so damned good around me." Pulling out, he added a second finger and pushed deep until Mia's eyes closed and she arched with a moan. "You're going to be a tight, tight fit. I'm going to stretch you all around me."

"Yes. Now."

"Mmm, no." He slid his wet fingers over her pussy, parting her folds and exposing that juicy clit again. "We're still in Savage foreplay."

Rafe lowered his mouth to her pussy with so much antici-pation, his chest felt like it would crack. And when she was in his mouth, flooding every taste bud, he was sure he could have climaxed with little more than a brush of his cock. She was so soft. So warm. So delicious. And the way she rocked against his mouth and pulled at his hair made him want to tongue fuck her all night.

"Oh my God." She rolled into a half crunch and held his head with both hands. He hummed and turned his head side to side, licking and sucking. Her mouth dropped open, eyes rolled back, fingers curled into fists. "*Oh my God.*"

Jesus, her pussy trembled beneath his mouth in a pre-orgasm shiver. She was so easy to get off, it was almost too easy. Almost. But in Mia's case, the more pleasure he could give her in this short time they had, the better. He put his tongue to work, stroking her with wide, solid swaths. She broke after the second. And continued to tremble as Rafe continue to eat. He wasn't ready to stop. He'd been starved for her for years.

"Rafe, Rafe, *Rafe...*" Each call of his name increased in pitch until she screamed and bucked and broke again in a shivering hot mess.

Rafe still wasn't done. He was starting to wonder if he'd ever be done. The more he got, the more he needed. The harder she came, the harder he wanted her next climax. And he pushed two fingers deep into her hot, wet pussy. "Mmm, so good. Can't get enough."

She had one hand fisted in her own hair and one in his. Her body started to move, and she whimpered.

This climax he teased out of her, getting a wicked high out of torturing her with pleasure. While he rubbed the growing bubble deep in her pussy, he barely flicked her clit with the tip of his tongue.

"Rafe." She slammed both hands into the bed and fisted the comforter, then lifted her hips, rocking them toward his mouth. And damn, that was just so goddamned hot.

He covered her, growled, then took her clit between his lips and sucked and sucked and sucked.

Mia climaxed so hard, her scream was cut short. She bucked and twisted and moaned and whimpered. Then shivered and trembled and panted, while she kept a heavy hand on Rafe's jaw.

"No more..." She said between breaths. "Need...a break."

He pushed up, licked his lips, and leaned over her. "Don't get used to it." He pressed a kiss to her belly. "We've still got a lot of night left ahead."

6

M ia was fucked.

Well, not yet. At least not in the literal sense, but she already knew this night wasn't going to be what she'd planned, expected, or needed.

In fact, as she caught her breath, sprawled on the bed in next to nothing with the man who'd owned her heart since she'd been a teenager kissing his way up her body, Mia knew tonight might just turn out to be the worst mistake of her life.

Rafe pressed his face to her neck, kissing her with a hum of pleasure. Mia closed her eyes on emotions so strong and so wildly unexpected that tears stung. She wrapped her hand around the back of his neck, and as soon as he lifted his head, she pulled him in and kissed him, pouring all those emotions into the connection.

He tasted musky and male. So alive. So primal. Mia used what little strength she'd recovered to push him onto his back and roll on top of him. And when she lifted her head, she found him smiling up at her. A big, authentic, quintessential Rafe grin, complete with that deep crescent in his right cheek.

He reached up and pushed her hair off her face, then cupped her cheek and stroked her skin with his thumb.

Mia closed her eyes and leaned her head into his hand, and when she looked at him again, his smile had faded.

"Where have you been all my life?" he asked, semiserious.

She laughed softly and started working on the buttons of his shirt to break the intensity of their eye contact. "Right behind my brother."

Rafe sighed and stroked her arms up to her shoulders, then cupped her breasts. They tingled and tightened, her nipples hardening instantly. He brushed them beneath his thumbs, and a tug teased her pussy.

"Mmm." She pushed his shirt open and stroked her hands over his cut abs, across his wide, muscular chest. Skin she'd seen countless times in the past during summer swims and gym workouts, but only imagined touching. Then trailed her hands down to his pants and worked his belt open, his button, his zipper. Leaning forward, she pressed one hand to the bed at his shoulder, and with her eyes on his, she pushed her hand into his pants, beneath the edge of his boxers. Her fingers slid over his length, followed by her palm and by the time she curled her hand around his cock, his gorgeous gray eyes were hazed with lust.

His lids closed, his brow furrowed, and a sound, part sigh, part groan, rolled from his chest.

He was long and thick. Hot and hard. Hunger gnawed low in Mia's gut. Her pussy clenched for the feel of him filling her. Fucking her.

She pressed her lips to the center of his chest and stroked his cock as her mouth moved her way down to his navel. Tucking her fingers into his pants, she dragged them down his hips, carefully lifted them over his erection, and pulled them lower.

His cock bounced free, and Mia's desire tripled. He looked

even better than he felt. She'd never thought the male sex anatomy particularly attractive...until now. Maybe her feelings for Rafe or her depth of wanting him skewed her view, but scanning his cock made her mouth water. And she didn't wait to get his pants off to dive in for a taste.

She gently stroked him, then opened and took as much of him as she could.

Rafe choked out a sound of shock and pleasure. His back arched and his hand fisted in the covers. Déjà vu. Only in reverse. Mia liked that idea. And she put all her focus into bringing him as much pleasure as he'd just brought her, which was certainly no chore. He felt like silky steel in her mouth. He tasted salty and musky and supremely male. The sounds and sights of his pleasure turned Mia on in a way she'd never experienced before. And made Mia want to spend the night driving him crazy.

But she felt like she'd barely gotten to know all the intimate spots that made him moan and shiver when he took her face in his hands and drew her mouth from his cock.

When she met his eyes, his were dark with an intensity of desire she couldn't ever remember seeing in a man's expression before. "I'm not like you, baby. I can't have orgasm after orgasm and be ready for another in minutes. And I really need to fuck you like I mean it. Like I want it. Like I love it. Because I'm hungry for you, Mia. And I can't imagine getting enough of you in one night."

Mia's lips parted, but nothing came out. Her heart squeezed too hard to get her brain to work, leaving her speechless.

He reached for his pants, pulling his wallet from his back pocket. The thud-thud of his shoes on the floor behind her startled Mia out of her momentary stupor. She slid off the bed, and stripped off his pants and socks. Then stood there a moment, staring at the stunning male beauty of him.

She'd dated great-looking guys. Active guys who went to the

gym every day or participated in athletics of one kind or another. Rafe's body wasn't the first fantastic body she'd seen, touched, or experienced. But it was obvious that the man behind the body made all the difference, something she'd never known before this moment. Something she only just realized was exactly what her exes had complained was missing in their relationships. And something she wished she hadn't discovered. Not here, not now, and not with Rafe.

But here she was. With several hours left of her one night with a man she'd loved for so long, she almost couldn't remember when it started. And feared it would never end.

He sat up, slipped his arms around her and pulled her between his thighs, where he pressed his face to her abdomen and kissed her. Then he tilted his head back and met her eyes. "We can stop anytime. If you're having second thoughts—"

"Only regrets that it took us so long to get here." Her voice shook. She cradled his face in both hands while the words "I love you" filled her mouth, pushing to get out. If she wanted to lose what ground they'd gained, that would be a surefire way to do it. So she swallowed them back and smiled. "But we're here now."

She reached for the wallet he'd left on the bed, leaning into him at the same time. "I assume you've got condoms in here."

Rafe closed his arms around her and kissed her chest. One of his hands slid down and gripped her ass; the other moved up and pressed against the middle of her back. "Mmm-hmm."

When she straightened, arms stretched behind him as she went through his wallet, Rafe kissed her neck, scraping his teeth along her skin and licking sensitive areas that made her tingle everywhere.

She found a condom, dropped the wallet with a relieved sigh, and ripped open the package.

"Mmm," he hummed against her skin. "I love that sound."

That statement hit Mia square in the stomach, and not in a

good way. It reminded her of how often he did this. How insignificant the act of sex was in his life. That she was just another random drive-by for him, the only difference being that he'd known her longer than a week or a day. Or an hour. Rafe was a man whore. That wasn't a secret. And there was nothing wrong with it. He was single; he made no promises. Just like he'd made none tonight.

Mia had to take a second to remind herself that this was about letting go, not grabbing hold.

"Give it to me." He leaned away and reached for her arm.

But Mia pulled it back and smiled. "I got it."

She took the erotic moments of rolling on the condom to reinforce her goals. To remind herself of how quickly and completely he could shut her out and how badly that hurt. How badly it affected her life.

Mia had a refreshed one-and-done frame of mind by the time the condom hit the base of his cock. And when he kissed her with a new ferocity, she let herself get swept up in the passion, while holding the emotion in the distance.

He wrapped one arm tight at her waist, slid back on the bed, and pulled her thighs wide, straddling his lap. He reached between them and rubbed the head of his cock across her opening. The friction felt so good, she moaned and her eyes fell closed.

Rafe slid one hand up her back and clasped her nape. Wrapped the other arm low on her hips and pressed his forehead to hers.

"Look at me, Mia." His demand was soft, shaky. "I want to remember this moment for the rest of my life."

Mia's eyes opened, and her breath caught. Just when she thought she'd gotten her emotions under control, her chest expanded with a flurry of complex feelings. Her mind and heart spiraled with questions and confusion.

But before she could say anything, Rafe tightened the arm

at her hips and drew her down. His cock impaled her in one swift thrust. Mia's muscles tightened, and a cry of surprise, pain, and pleasure rolled from her chest. She fisted her hands in Rafe's hair.

Almost instantly, the pain disappeared, leaving Mia with a decadent pressure where Rafe filled her.

Rafe. Filled. Her.

"God," Rafe whispered. "So perfect, Mia. *So perfect.*"

He lifted his head and looked deep into her eyes. His expression was so soft, so affectionate, so filled with the same emotions filling her, and her heart broke a little. But she wasn't sure why.

Then he rolled his knees under him while he held her in position. Once they were upright, face-to-face, he started to move. Using those muscled thighs that made him one of the fastest hockey players in the world, he drove his cock deep, leaving no room for anything but rush after rush after rush of intense, mind-bending pleasure.

Mia clung to his shoulders as he pummeled her, driving toward his own release. His features hardened and sharpened. His eyes hazed over with a level of lust that reached deep inside Mia and twisted.

And when he finally let his eyes fall closed, turned his face into her neck, and whispered, "Mia, Mia, Mia..." with a tortured kind of bliss, tears rose to her eyes.

She dropped her forehead to his shoulder and held tight, riding wave after wave of penetration with his name whispering past her own lips.

The way he held her, so tightly, so lovingly, the way he controlled his thrusts in long, deep strokes, as if he wanted to feel every inch of her, as if he wanted to draw out the moments he was inside her, made something elemental shift in her chest.

She'd never been loved like this. If this was a hookup, if this was purely sexual, then she'd been missing the boat all her life.

Because no one had ever made her feel so wanted, so loved, or so cherished as Rafe did now.

And even when his thrusts quickened and his body vibrated with his impending release, when other men could think about nothing but sating their own overwhelming need, she was at the front of his thoughts.

He took hold of her chin, pulled her gaze to his, and demanded, "Come with me, Mia."

Then he kissed her, mirroring the hunger of his body in his kiss. The combination of physical and emotional assault coalesced, and Mia broke with a scream. She buried her face in Rafe's neck, her body still quaking with aftershocks when his own climax hit. His strong body twisted and bowed and shuddered in the fiercest, most stunning display of male sexuality Mia had ever witnessed.

They stayed wrapped in each other's arms while their bodies settled and they caught their breath. And as Rafe pressed sweet kisses to Mia's neck, she knew this exercise in letting go of her girlish fantasies of the boy from her past had not only backfired, it had created an even deeper need for the man he'd grown into. A need that would stretch long into her future.

7

R afe shut off his car and jogged to the player's entrance of
the Verizon arena in downtown DC. Showing up late for
the scheduled routine on a game day would set him back five
grand, the Rough Riders' standard fine.

But as he pulled the door open and started down the
corridor toward the locker room, Rafe smiled. He'd overslept
because Mia had held him to their agreement and they'd gotten
lost in each other until they couldn't keep their eyes open
anymore.

The familiar sound of his teammates' voices and the use of
equipment echoed off the cement, but Rafe's mind was still
piling up memories from last night, making his grin grow even
bigger.

If he did get hit with a fine, it would be worth every penny.
Because today, despite his lack of sleep, Rafe felt like he was on
top of the fucking world. His body sang with energy and
strength. His mind was clearer and more focused than it had
been in months.

He could breathe deeper, think faster, and settle quicker.

He turned the corner into the main locker room, found it

empty and dropped his duffel on the bench. The guys were scattered, some with the physical therapists, some in the gym, some with the coach.

But as he changed into workout clothes, his mind drifted to waking in an empty bed and a *Kick-ass in the game tonight* note on the dresser. That was the only part of his night with Mia that didn't sit quite right with him. He tried to smooth down the edge of nerves by remembering that quiet moment, deep in the early morning hours, while they'd lain tangled together, sweaty and sated, she'd mentioned meeting a couple of girlfriends for breakfast. And despite staying awake and active until nearly five a.m., she'd still been gone when he'd awoken at seven o'clock.

Damn, he wished he could have made love to her one more time. He'd been more than ready when he'd stirred. The memory of rolling to reach for her and finding her gone still pinched his gut. He'd so badly wanted to love her slowly and sweetly, then lie with her in his arms until he absolutely had to get up for practice.

And that was only one of the things he'd never wanted before but now craved with Mia. The woman was phenomenal in bed. She was spontaneous and sensual and erotic. She didn't shy away from anything—no position too weird, no play too rough, no fears over letting him have control. Or taking control, for that matter. They'd been equals in bed, and he'd never known what a turn-on that could be. She also had a sexual appetite that matched Rafe's.

Put it all together and Mia had blown away every last fantasy-induced expectation. Add in their friendship and their affection for each other, and Rafe realized...

He realized one night wasn't enough.

"I want us to fuck and forget..."

He'd understood that going in. Now he couldn't help but

wonder if that was the way she'd felt this morning, walking away. God, he hoped not.

Pulling on an old T-shirt, Rafe smiled at the memories of her cuddled up to him after sex. The way she never stopped touching him and kissing him. The way they'd laughed and played. They'd found the old Mia and Rafe again. Before all the complications of life and careers and boyfriends and brothers had pushed them apart.

Yeah, Rafe could get used to the idea of having Mia loving up on him every night. They'd connected the way he'd secretly been dreaming of connecting with her for years. And after last night, it was clear there was no way they could stay away from each other. At least not while she was in town. Rafe was going to have a sit down with her at his first opportunity—probably tonight— to talk about this. New York was only an hour's flight away.

He sat, pushed his feet into tennis shoes, and tied the laces, knowing the distance was the least of the walls between them. Tate was a major problem. Tate and this team. And then there was Joe.

Rafe just needed to tackle them one at a time. When Tate and Joe knew Mia was on board with this, that she wanted to be with Rafe as much as Rafe wanted to be with her...

But, they hadn't discussed that. In fact, he and Mia hadn't discussed anything. They'd been too busy seeking out and delivering pleasure all night.

A few of the guys wandered into the locker room, chatting.

"There you are." Beckett Cross, the team's captain, stopped at his bench in a sweat-stained T-shirt, shorts, and running shoes. "Everyone's been looking for you. Tremblay's going to fine your ass."

"It's only ten minutes." Rafe looked up, finished with his laces, and pushed to his feet just as Tate came up behind Beckett and sidestepped their teammate. "I just oversle—"

Rafe only had a split second to register the fury on Tate's face before his friend threw a right cross. Tate's knuckles cracked against Rafe's eye socket, and the force behind the punch whipped Rafe's head right. Shock dulled the initial pain for a couple of seconds, but by the time he stumbled backward, fire exploded all through Rafe's face.

"What the *hell*?" Beckett yelled. "We've got a game tonight."

But Rafe wasn't thinking about the game. He'd just come to the painful realization that Tate knew. Somehow, *Tate knew*. Which meant his best friend had just punched him based on— as far as Tate knew—a rumor.

Tate shoved Beckett back and came at Rafe again. Still bent at the waist, Rafe rammed his shoulder into Tate's chest and slammed him into a wall.

"Knock it the fuck off," Beckett bellowed before hauling Rafe back by the arm and stepping between them. "Put your petty shit aside. We're in the fucking *playoffs*, you jackasses. We need both of you at your best."

Rafe straightened and scowled at Tate. "What's wrong with you?"

Tate stabbed the air between them with his finger. "Kilbourne told me. You bailed on the date chick and went home with Mia."

The depth of Tate's anger blew away every hope that his friend would ever understand Rafe and Mia being together.

"I did *not* go home with Mia." That was technically true, but judging by the hurt and rage burning across Tate's face, it wasn't enough. "And why the hell are you taking Kilbourne's word instead of asking me first?"

"Because Mia didn't come home last night, and Kilbourne told me she was all over you at Bellissimo. He told me you two talked about hitting the sheets."

"Mia pretended to be my girl so I could get away from that

mouthy contest chick before my head exploded. I don't know where Mia went after she left me."

It was all true. Yet all a lie. And after all Tate had done for Rafe, all Tate's father had done for Rafe, he felt an inch big right now.

"You're so full of shit." Kilbourne sauntered into the locker room and joined the rest of the team going about their business with one ear and one eye on Tate and Rafe's fight.

Beckett pointed at Kilbourne. "You've caused enough trouble."

"You and Mia were so hot, you couldn't keep your hands off each other," Kilbourne said to Rafe. "Why else would you have handed that smokin' hot chick off to me?"

"Because she talked about minutia until my ears were bleeding, you idiot," Rafe yelled so loud it echoed off the walls. The pressure shot pain through his head, and Rafe swore and pressed the back of his hand to his eye. It came away bloody. "For fuck's sake."

Kilbourne's superior smirk faded. His gaze went distant. "She did talk a lot. Even while I was banging her, she never shut up."

Rafe lifted his hand toward Kilbourne and told Tate, "See."

Then Kilbourne lifted a shoulder and continued to his locker. "Whatever. You bailed on one hot fuck. Bet I'm playing way better than you tonight."

Rafe lunged for Kilbourne but never made contact—Beckett grabbed him by the shirt.

"It's over," Beckett said. "Get your head back in the game." He released his shirt and gave Rafe a shove toward the gym. "Get in a light workout."

Beckett continued to his locker, and Rafe shot a scowl at Kilbourne, but his anger faded when he looked at Tate again. His hands rested on his hips, his shoulders sagged, and his expression had gone from furious to sullen.

"I'm sorry," Tate said, his tone frustrated. "I've been worried about Mia, then you came late this morning, and Kilbourne's story started making sense— Never mind. I'm just... I'm sorry, man."

Instead of relief, anger sparked. Tate was confirming what Rafe already knew—his best friend would never see Rafe as good enough for Mia. And seeing her without Tate's blessing would drive a wedge between all of them. Which also meant damaging Rafe's relationship with Joe and screwing up the balance on the team.

"Forget about it." Rafe grabbed a towel from a pile on the bench and turned for the gym.

Tate sidestepped and held a hand up, his expression wholly apologetic. "It's just... Mia's going through a rough transition right now. I'm worried she's, I don't know, not exactly using her best judgment at the moment."

"And your first thought was that she was sleeping with me? Good to know you consider your best friend a poor judgment call. I'm good enough for you but not your sister, is that what you're saying?"

"You know how hard relationships have been on Mia. She needs stability. Someone who will stick. You fuck someone different every other night. So, no, that's not the kind of guy I'd want for my sister, and if you thought about it for a second, you'd know it's not the kind of guy you'd want for her either. I don't even know why we're talking about this since nothing happened."

"Get to work, ladies," Beckett yelled across the locker room.

Tate looked back at Rafe and lifted his hand in a fist for a bump. "We're good?"

A hot rock bottomed out in the pit of Rafe's stomach, but he met Tate's knuckles with his own. And as Tate passed toward the physical therapist's office, Rafe continued into the gym with all thoughts of hooking up with Mia again fading to black.

8

Mia's hands curled into fists against her thighs as she watched Rafe scrap with a Flyer to unlock a puck from between his skate blades and the boards. Finally, Rafe worked the puck loose and followed it in a circle back toward the goal, but with three Flyers on his ass, he passed to Tate.

Mia cut a look at the clock. There was only a little over two minutes left in the game and the Rough Riders were up two to one. They were going to win, Mia had no doubt. What she really wanted was for Rafe to get a hat trick tonight. Wanted it so bad, she could taste it. He'd been the only player to score all game, and one more goal would earn him a hat trick in the Cup playoffs—a memory he would cherish forever.

As the Rough Riders continued to hash out a shot on the ice, Mia's mind flashed to the night before. To that moment of anticipation when Rafe's cock had pressed against her entrance. To the passion in his eyes, his barely controlled lust, and his deliberate pause to make sure she was looking into his eyes when he took her for the first time.

"Look at me, Mia. I want to remember this moment for the rest of my life."

Her chest squeezed, but she didn't have time to savor the moment.

Eden, Beckett's girlfriend, grabbed Mia's arm. "Rafe's got it!"

Mia refocused on the ice and found Rafe breaking away from the Flyers, approaching the opposing team's goal all alone. She shot to her feet and cheered at the top of her lungs along with Eden. As he neared the goal, Mia stopped clapping, clasped her hands at her chest, and held her breath.

Approaching the goal, he faked left. Faked right. Then flipped the puck past the goalie's arm. It cleared the pipes and hit the net.

Score.

Mia and Eden threw their hands overhead and screamed along with the other fifteen thousand fans filling the stadium. Lights flashed, buzzers and alarms sounded, smoke poured from the ceiling.

Excitement surged through Mia. She couldn't stop grinning as she watched Rafe shake his stick with triumph. Or as he slid into a circle with his other four teammates to congratulate each other on a job well done. Or as he turned and skated along the wall and bumped gloves with all his other teammates lined up at their bench.

Baseball hats of every color fell from the stands like confetti. And while the ice girls gathered the hats from the ice so the teams could finish out the last thirty seconds of the game, Rafe skated past Mia's seat section. His head turned toward the stands, and his smile was electric. His gaze locked on Mia, and he tilted his hockey stick toward her with the slightest nod of acknowledgment.

That's all you, baby.

Mia could read the thoughts behind his eyes as well as if he'd whispered them in her ear. The way he'd murmured the night before after their last round of sex before he'd fallen asleep. *"I'm gonna play like a motherfucker on fire tonight."*

Mia's breath caught. Emotion swelled in her heart.

"Did he start the game with a black eye?" Eden's question drew Mia's gaze as the game started again. "I swear I didn't notice it earlier, and he didn't fight tonight."

Mia refocused on the ice and searched for Rafe, but he was moving way too fast to see his face. He certainly hadn't had one last night. And they might have gotten playful and even a little rough in bed—something that shot sparks through her every time she remembered—but she hadn't given him a black eye. "I didn't notice."

"Must be fresh," Eden said with the confidence of someone in the medical field. She'd recently completed her paramedic training and had met Beckett on this very ice because of an injury. "Sometimes a hematoma can take a few hours to show through the skin as a bruise."

The end-of-game buzzer sounded with another round of playoff wins for the Rough Riders, winning them the division title and pushing them closer to the Cup

"Come on." Eden pulled on Mia's arm. "Let's go stake our claim at Top Shelf."

Mia started from the stadium with Eden, but she had mixed feelings about seeing Rafe tonight for a dozen different reasons. Last night had not been what she'd expected. Or even what she'd wanted. In fact, last night had done absolutely nothing to relieve her desire for Rafe. Nor had it put sex with him into the ordinary, I-can-get-that-anywhere category. And now, after what was, hands down, the most intense, most loving, most all-around amazing night of her life, she had to admit that sex with the man she loved was very, very different from sex with someone she cared for.

And that was a huge problem when she was headed across the country in a little over a week.

One thing was sure, she'd stuck to her pattern of screwing things up with the men in her life.

But she should go. If for no other reason than to put even footing beneath them now that their night was over. He'd been sleeping so hard when she'd left for breakfast, she hadn't wanted to wake him. She'd also known waking him would have made her late. And watching him sleep, knowing it would probably be the last time in her life she'd ever have that level of intimacy with him, had torn her up inside.

So she should go to Top Shelf, say hello, talk a little, and show him that she was holding to her agreement. That there was no reason for them to feel awkward around each other. Maybe, with time and distance, her feelings for him would dim. Maybe, someday, she could look back on these years of unrequited love with fond memories. She'd learned from her childhood that time might not eradicate pains from the past, but it did dull them.

As she and Eden moved through the crowd toward the exit doors and spilled onto the blocked streets of downtown DC, Mia wondered about Rafe's black eye. He'd never had issues with any of his teammates. Even as much as Kilbourne irritated Rafe, he'd always been respectful and loyal. While he fought on the ice, he'd never fought off it. Not even in high school. Tate, on the other hand...

But Rafe would never have told Tate about him and Mia. Rafe cared too much about Tate's friendship and Joe's respect. Rafe cared too much about his teammates and their relationship and getting his team to the Cup.

Rafe cared about everyone and everything before himself. So that black eye hadn't come from Tate, because that would have meant he'd wanted Mia enough to risk Tate's fury, Joe's disappointment, and his team's position in the standings.

And one thing Mia had learned for sure over the last year was that while she knew Rafe cared about her, she also knew with equal certainty Rafe would never put her first.

Yeah, she should go to the bar. Stay until Rafe got there. Let him see her unfazed by the puck bunnies hanging all over him. Unbothered by the way he turned back into the playboy he'd been since he hit puberty.

Once she and Eden hit the street and cleared the crowd, Mia's gaze landed on Top Shelf's front door. The sight of the familiar postgame hot spot pounded Mia with a sense of loss so unexpected, all her ideas changed on a dime. She wasn't ready to let go of their night or of Rafe. She wasn't ready to let go of her friends or the family she'd developed within the Rough Riders. She wasn't ready to let go of any of it. And her stomach flipped and rattled with nerves.

"Isn't this weather gorgeous?" Eden said, referencing the perfect night. "God, I love spring in DC."

"Eden," she said, "I think I'm going to head back to Tate's and finish cutting out the pattern for Faith's dress."

"Oh," Eden complained and linked arms with Mia. "Just come for one drink. And about that dress... What would I have to do to get one?"

Mia pushed out a laugh, trying to pretend her heart hadn't turned into one big knot.

"Really," Eden said, squeezing Mia's arm. "I need one way more than Faith. She's got all kinds of cute dresses to wear to these dinners and parties. I, on the other hand, have worn a uniform every day for years. I only have a few cute things from several years ago, and I *am* the one hooking you up with Beckett's mom and her sewing machine." She gave Mia her sweetest smile. "*Please?*"

Mia smiled, but a piece of her heart broke off as they stepped into Top Shelf and the magnitude of all that she'd be losing in a week crashed down on her. "I'll see what I can do."

The Rough Riders' favorite postgame haunt was crowded. And as soon as the guys got here, this place would go from crowded to crazy.

Mia took a deep breath and sucked up her reality. She'd

made a choice to better her life by taking this job. When she didn't think about what she was losing, Mia was excited about her future. Well, at least her professional future. And with the hours this new job would demand, that was really all her life would be about for the foreseeable future. Given what had happened with Rafe, that setup would work out best—because she couldn't fathom wanting another man.

Mia and Eden found seats at the bar, and by the time she was sipping her wine, Mia had assured herself she could pretend for an hour. If it would settle her relationship with Rafe into a comfortable groove so she could leave on solid footing with him. Yeah, she could pretend.

Mia let her worries slip away while she enjoyed Eden's tales of her new job with a local fire department. And by the time the team flooded in, Mia had convinced herself she could handle this.

The Rough Riders were greeted to applause and cheers and twittering DC urbanites. Young, beautiful women flocked to the guys for autographs and photos, most hoping to land one of the sexy hockey studs for a few hours, if not the night.

This was how Rafe was treated after every game. Eighty-two games a year. Not to mention the accolades they received during team, sponsor and charity events. Mia knew firsthand how hard these guys worked, so she knew they all deserved every bit of attention. But seeing those perfect, young puck bunnies dancing around the guys, all but offering themselves to whichever one would have them, instantly deflated the self-confidence Mia had drummed up to face Rafe.

She laughed softly at herself with a shake of her head. God, she'd been so stupid to think she could handle any of this on a level other than sister and friend.

"I know," Eden said, misreading Mia's humor. "If they only realized how desperate they looked."

That was when Rafe walked through the door—in a charcoal suit, a crisp white shirt, and deep blue tie, loose at his neck. His hair was still wet, his jaw unshaven. While the door closed behind him, Rafe's gaze scanned the bar, and when he found Mia, his gaze locked. But he didn't smile.

Mia's stomach surged and twisted. Her head filled with his murmurs from the night before.

"How did it take us so long to figure this out?"

"You feel better than every fantasy I've ever had about you."

"Can't get enough, baby. God, can't get enough."

He broke their gazes when someone called to him, and Mia got a better look at his eye. That bruise and the cut just beneath had come from a right cross. She'd seen the results of enough hockey fights to know.

"Ouch," Eden said, her gaze also on Rafe. "That looks worse than it did under the stadium lights."

"That's because his helmet was hiding it."

She searched the crowd for Tate, and she found her brother merrily chatting with a mixed group of fans and players. No bruises or cuts on his handsome face. Just as she was about to look away, Tate caught her eye and lifted his chin in greeting. Then his gaze flicked toward the door—toward Rafe—before returning to her, his smile gone. With an expression Mia couldn't quite read, Tate returned to his conversation.

A burn radiated through her torso. She cut a look back to Rafe. He'd been greeted with rousing applause by the entire bar. Friends and fans and teammates said everything from "What got into you tonight?" to "Whatever you did to play like that, just keep doing it until we're playin' for the Cup." And now he was busy with fans and puck bunnies, leaving Mia to wonder and worry. But worse—hope.

Even the slightest possibility that Rafe might have confessed to Tate gave Mia goose bumps. Not just because the thought of continuing this thing with Rafe thrilled her—heart and soul—but because that meant he'd finally put her first.

He's stood up to Tate for her. She'd meant enough to him to fight to be with her.

Her stomach fluttered, and emotion rushed in. No other man had ever done that. Not the father who'd abandoned her, not any college professor who'd supposedly mentored her, not any of her boyfriends, some who'd professed to love her.

Tate took care of her, but it wasn't the same. From the time Joe had discovered Tate's existence and taken on his role of father with 200 percent enthusiasm, her brother had constantly been compensating Mia for getting stuck with pond scum as a sperm donor. But he'd never given anything up for her. He'd never fought for her—unless that black eye was his doing.

Beckett came toward them, paused at the bar, and wrapped an arm around Eden's waist. She congratulated him on his win, and they talked a little about the game.

"Mia and I can't figure out how Rafe got the black eye," Eden said. "Is he okay? Did the team doc look at it?"

Beckett's expression shifted into concern and annoyance. "I don't know what got into those two today."

"What two?" Mia asked.

"Your brother and Rafe. Rafe came in late this morning— no big deal. One minute I'm telling him his ass is going to get fined, the next Tate's whaling at him over my shoulder. Dumb shits."

Eden was both amused and puzzled. "Why?"

"Fuckin' Kilbourne."

Mia's stomach chilled.

"Oh God," Eden said. "It will be a miracle if that guy makes it through the end of the season without a major injury. What did he do now?"

Beckett shot Mia an apologetic glance. "Started a stupid rumor about Mia and Rafe. I don't think it would have both-ered Tate coming from anyone else. He would have just told them to shut their mouths. But Kilbourne gets under everyone's skin. I think Tate just took out his frustration on Rafe."

Mia's heart sank to the pit of her stomach. It had been Cole who'd told Tate, not Rafe.

"That man's stupidity is why I have job security," Eden said, shooting a that's-unbelievable look at Eden, then asked Beckett. "What did Rafe say?"

"Say about what?"

Rafe's voice startled Mia's heart. He came up behind Beckett and glanced at Mia, then Eden.

"Your eye," Eden said. "About Tate hitting you."

Rafe's gaze returned to Mia. "I think the stress is getting to him."

Eden took a minute to look at the cut and probe the area. When Rafe winced, Beckett pulled Eden away. "Enough, Miss Nightingale. It's just a black eye. He'll live. I promise."

He stole Eden away to a quiet corner, and Mia was left facing Rafe. But he remained a good five feet away and didn't make any move to close the distance.

Mia didn't know what to say or where to start. And now she wasn't sure where her footing lay either. "Congratulations on your trick and your win. You killed it tonight."

"Thanks." But he was uncharacteristically subdued, his gaze guarded, and his eyes immediately dropped away in a look Mia could only identify as guilt. The idea that he regretted their night together hammered her heart.

He drifted to the bar, leaning his elbow there, and ordered a beer from the bartender. A couple of puck bunnies tried to start conversations, but he brushed them off after he gave them an autograph.

Once she and Rafe were in another tiny bubble of privacy, she worked up the courage to ask him what was wrong—beyond the obvious black eye—but Tate pushed through the crowd and stepped up to the bar. He looked at Rafe, then Mia, and she felt the whole atmosphere shift. A new tension weighted the air.

"Can we talk?" Tate asked in a way that made her stomach fold. She suddenly wished she hadn't come after all. Slipping off the stool, she said, "Let's talk tonight when you get home. I'm tired, I'm going to—"

"It's important." His tone alone told her it wasn't something good either. When she chanced a glance at Rafe, he was facing the bar, leaning on the shiny wood with his forearms, both hands clasped around his beer like it was a life preserver. His expression was tight, and his jaw jumped.

"I'm sure it's something that can wait—" she started.

"I know you're a grown woman," he spoke over her, and Mia braced for combat. "And I know you've lived on your own in a big city. But when you're staying with me and you're not going to come home, could you at least call so I don't worry?"

An absurd laugh stuttered out of her mouth. "I'm not sure if that's sweet or insulting. Do you want to apply the same rules to *your* schedule?"

"I heard you were with Kilbourne, of all people," he went on, growing more forceful. "Then I heard you went home with Rafe, and look how that turned out."

He leaned back and gestured toward Rafe, who cut an angry look at Tate. "Shut up. This wasn't her fault."

Oh, but it was. At least partially. And that both hurt and infuriated her. "Let me get this straight." She turned narrowed eyes on her brother. "You *punched* your *best friend* based on something Kilbourne said? *Kilbourne?*"

"You didn't come home last night, which you never do," Tate said, growing even more aggravated. "Rafe came in late, which he never does. Kilbourne was in bed with the woman Rafe had been talking about banging for a week, but then dumps her after you come on to him."

That felt like another knife in her stomach. Beyond Tate,

Rafe closed his eyes and dropped his head in shame. Which meant it was true. And that meant Mia had been a convenient second choice to Baywatch when she'd turned into a talking head.

Mia had gotten exactly what she'd come for. She had no right to be upset, yet she'd never felt so hurt. She had no right to be angry, yet fury roiled in her gut. So while her brain was telling her "congratulations, your plan worked," her heart was telling her "congratulations, you've not only damaged two of the best relationships you've ever had, you've screwed yourself over in the process".

Tate threw his arms out to the side. "What did you expect me to think?"

Mia snapped. She leaned toward Tate, looking him directly in the eye. Because even if she'd made a mistake with Rafe, she didn't deserve to have Tate treating her like an ass.

"I expect you to think Kilbourne's an *idiot*," she shot back. "I expect you to *ask* before you *attack*. I expect you to treat both Rafe and me with more *respect*. You don't get to play that double standard, Tate, and I'm sick of it."

"Guys." Rafe cut in, his gaze darting between them, then around the bar. "Let's not do this here."

The look on his face told Mia he didn't want to do it at all. He wanted Mia to drop it. And she realized she was standing here, fighting for *them*. She was laying the groundwork for Tate to realize he doesn't get to dictate her life or Rafe's life or whether or not they choose to sleep together. But Rafe didn't want to have anything to do with it. He wanted what he always wanted, to make Tate happy. To hell with Mia's feelings.

"It pisses me off that I have to do this at all," she told Rafe. "But I've let it go on too long already. Did you even stand up for yourself or did you just let him walk all over you?"

"He told me it was all fake." Tate's words snapped Mia's head back toward her brother. "But that's not the point. You *know* you can't mess with team members. We've talked about this. You're my *sister*. You *know* if you mess around with team members, it screws with the dynamic. You *know* how fragile that is and how important it is. Especially now. We're almost to the Cup, Mia. The fucking Cup. Of all the times to start screwing with my team—"

"I'm not *screwing* with your precious team." She yelled the words even though they weren't completely true. Several of the guys and a few people at the bar looked their way. "And don't give me that fragile bullshit. You love to talk about how professional you are, so act like it. Professionals work together even when they don't agree, even when they don't like each other. Professionals put their personal feelings about each other aside to get the job done. Did you not notice how well you all played tonight? Like you were on *motherfucking fire*? Don't tell me I'm screwing with your team."

"Tate," Rafe muttered beside him without meeting her eyes. "Drop it, for God's sake. I told you you're making something out of nothing."

Nothing.

Fake.

The words cut at her. Worse, they opened the door to uncertainty. And Mia wondered for the first time if everything he'd done last night had been an act. The same act he used with all women. If what she'd thought was so special had actually just been Rafe's MO. And that—for him—it *had* all been fake. The fact that he didn't step in to straighten Tate out certainly said everything Rafe wouldn't. It just wasn't what she wanted to hear.

Mia was closer than she'd ever been to completely losing her shit. In public. While they were both with their teammates surrounded by fans. But she pulled on the composure she'd developed under pressure in her industry and drew herself up.

"I guess it's good to know exactly where I stand with both of you." She couldn't do anything about how Rafe felt, but she could change how Tate treated her. "Let me be perfectly clear, Tate. I am a grown woman, and I make my own decisions. They don't have to be perfect, and you don't have to like them. But you do have to respect me. And that means showing it, not just saying it."

She picked up her purse and met both Rafe's and Tate's gaze in turn. "I'm glad you'll be in Boston next week. I could use some time away from you. Both of you."

9

M ia knelt on the family room floor in Tina and Jake
Croft's home, holding pins between her lips and scissors in her hand. But her gaze wasn't on the fabric in front of her. She was watching television, where the Rough Riders' fourth playoff game against the Bruins filled a massive screen above the fireplace hearth.

The room was stuffed with Beckett Croft's family—his parents, his sister, Sarah, Sarah's two daughters, Amy and Rachel, Beckett's own daughter, Lily, and Eden. Since they were all watching the game from home tonight, Faith had also come over to hang out and add inspiration to Mia's work.

So as Rafe sprinted toward the opposition's goal with solid command of the puck, Mia didn't have to yell in hopes of seeing him make it. The entire room was screaming for her.

A Bruin cut in front of Rafe. Rafe turned to protect the puck, skating backward, still pushing toward the goal. But the Bruin reached in, knocked the puck from Rafe's control and right into the stick of a fellow Bruin. Then the puck was spirited back down the ice in the opposite direction.

Everyone in the room deflated.

"Man, poor Rafe." Eden sat on the sofa again and pulled Lily into her lap. "He's had a really rough couple of games. He's going to be beating himself up."

"They're still winning." Mia refocused on the work in front of her, tuning in to the announcer's account of the game while also trying to ignore the empathy that naturally surfaced for Rafe. She had enough problems. But here, ensconced in this little haven among people who had become her temporary family, Eden's disappointment over her fallout with Rafe didn't hurt quite so bad. And she wasn't quite so lonely. Plus, they offered a distraction to keep her mind off her stupidity.

But that wouldn't last long. The team had played in Boston for the last two games and were at their home rink tonight. She hadn't seen or spoken to Rafe in a full week. Very possibly, the worst week of her life, while she'd had all the time in the world to berate herself. Endless silence in Tate's apartment during the day to remember every glorious, sweet, loving moment of their time in bed together. Then every awkward, hurtful moment at Top Shelf. And get confused and angry all over again. Hurt all over again.

There was no way around it, the last week had been hell.

She finished cutting the piece of fabric, then pulled the pattern off. "Okay, Faith, let's test the fit before I put it on the machine again."

Faith jumped up from the sofa and shed the little cardigan she was wearing, bearing her tank top. "Ooooooh, I can't wait."

Eden, Sarah, and Tina all lost interest in the game, their gazes glued to Mia as she draped the new Rough Riders jersey over Faith's body, really just a bunch of other jerseys cut and re-sewn into a new design, one that didn't just fit a woman's figure, but showcased it..

She used her hands to tug and pull the fabric where she wanted it.

"I'll give it a tuck here and here," Mia said, "finish off all the edges in a contrasting thread color." She shrugged and smiled. "Cute, no? Nothing fancy, but quick and easy." She added in a whisper, "And if you wear a little pushup bra, you'll have some seriously lickable cleavage going." In a normal tone she added, "I can have one for all of you by the time I leave."

"I love it!" Eden said.

"It's perfect," Sarah added.

"So cute." Tina crossed her arms and tilted her head. "You know, we should all wear them to the family skate next week."

"Us too?" Lily wanted to know, crawling into the circle at Eden's feet. "With my daddy's name on it?"

"We could all match," Rachel added with her infectious smile.

"Well, let's see how much time Mia has," Tina said, laughing. "I spoke before I thought."

Jake's groan pulled everyone's gaze to the screen, where they replayed another one of Rafe's poor moves. "Man," Jake said, his hand to his jaw, "what's wrong with him tonight? He's playing for—"

"Dad," Sarah cut in, grinning. "Little ears."

Jake glanced at Sarah, then at his granddaughters, and grinned. "Right."

The commentators on television continued their conjecture over what could have turned Rafe's game sour, and Mia winced. "Since I'd rather not spend any more time around them than I have to while they're playing like this, I have a feeling I'll find plenty of time to sew." She pulled the fabric off Faith and smiled hopefully, then darted the same look toward Eden. "Maybe we could make a trade—dresses and jerseys for one of you taking my place at the family dinner tonight?"

Faith winced. "I totally would, but it's my anniversary with Grant. Dating a year and a half today. We've got dinner reservations."

Mia frowned. "Who celebrates their year *and a half* anniversary?"

"Um...we do," she answered, hardly convincing.

"Aaaaand, um, I've got Lily," Eden worked up quickly, pointing at the little girl she'd all but adopted as her own since she and Beckett had gotten engaged. "I have to get her home and tucked in."

"Oh, honey," Tina told Eden with a mischievous smile, "I'd be happy to—"

"No, no, Tina," Eden said, waving her off over-politely. "You know it's my favorite time of the day."

Mia laughed a moan. "Why am I sure this is going to be the longest dinner of my life?"

Faith, the only person in the room who knew about Mia's future move and her plans to break the news to Rafe and Tate at this family dinner, patted her back and murmured, "Because it is, honey. It is."

10

The Bruins' goalie was acting like a fucking brick wall tonight.

The Bruins' goalie was acting like a fucking brick wall tonight. And he goalie wasn't the only thing working against Rafe. Nothing had been right since he'd pushed Mia away. His blades weren't responding the way they should. His stick felt like lead in his hand. And, man, his timing *sucked*.

Beckett slammed the Bruins' right wing into the boards, freeing up the puck. Rafe swooped and sprinted down the ice. Two Bruins flanked him down the ice. The one on his right shoved his stick against Rafe's. Rafe shouldered the guy off and swung behind the net. He took a tight turn at the pipe, hoping to sneak in at the corner in the goalie's blind spot.

He shot. The goalie dropped his knee. The puck hit. Bounced off. And a Bruin grabbed the rebound.

Fucking A. He couldn't make a goal to save his ever-loving life.

Somewhere on the ice, a penalty stopped play, and Rafe straightened, letting his muscles relax and breathe. He glanced toward the stands and the empty seat next to Joe where Mia should be. Where Mia always sat during home games when she came to town. Whether Joe came into town or not. Whether Rafe was talking to her or not. She'd never missed a game. In fact, she'd never missed texting him after a game.

Over the last year, because Rafe didn't text her back, her comments had become shorter and less enthusiastic, but she'd always texted him. *Great moves* or *tough game, you'll get 'em next time. That ref was a hard-ass,* or *congrats, you killed it.* Something. Last night was the first time in his entire hockey career that she hadn't texted him. And Rafe had fallen asleep alone in his hotel room with his phone clutched in his hand, just *waiting* for some sliver of connection with her.

She wasn't even returning *his* texts. He'd texted her the night after their argument at the bar with Tate, apologizing. He'd texted her twice yesterday, checking in to see how she was, and once earlier today asking why she was ignoring him—even though he already knew why. He didn't deserve the effort of a text. He didn't deserve *her.* Which was exactly why he needed to leave her the hell alone.

The ref called them into the face-off, and Rafe glanced at the stands as he slid into position. The fact that she'd missed a home game was bad enough. But missing one when she should have been sitting beside a man she considered a father was even worse.

Rafe bent at the waist and positioned his stick, but the ache cutting a path from his chest to his gut distracted him. For the first time in his life, he wasn't 200 percent invested in the game.

The puck dropped, and Isaac smacked it toward Rafe, but a Bruin intercepted. Muscle memory had Rafe stealing it back. He skated backward, protecting the puck while he searched for an opening to pass. One of the Bruins' defensemen came out of nowhere and slammed Rafe into the boards. Another Bruin stole the puck and headed toward the opposite goal.

God dammit!

Before Rafe could even sprint down the ice after the other player, Andre Kristoff, their first line center, cut across the Bruin's path, stole the puck, set up, and slammed the damn thing right past the goalie and into the net, putting the Rough Riders on the board for the first time tonight.

Lights and sirens joined applause from the crowd, but Rafe still heard Tremblay's order to return to the bench. He'd spent more time on the bench tonight than he had in any other game since he'd joined the NHL.

He dropped beside Tierney, and before Rafe could pick up his water bottle, Tremblay's hand settled on his shoulder from behind.

"You hurt?" he asked. "Sick?"

Rafe's stomach dropped. As if playing shitty wasn't bad enough, now his coach thought he had a physical impediment. Which meant Rafe was playing worse than shit. "No, Coach. Just having a bad game."

"Professionals don't just have bad games," he said. "Figure it out. Whatever you did to play like you played last week is what I want you doing before every fucking game from now until we win the Stanley fucking Cup. Got it?"

Rafe nodded and shot water into his mouth. But he doubted Mia would be amenable to "doing" him senseless before every game. Though he was starting to think that was exactly what he needed to get back on track.

"What's wrong with you, man?" Tierney wanted to know. "You went from white to black in twenty-four hours, and now you're stuck there.

"You think I haven't noticed?"

One of the Bruins' defensemen tripped Tate and took a penalty. While the Bruin skated to the penalty box and the others set up for a face-off, Rafe's gaze drifted to the stands again. That empty seat made his gut squeeze. He wondered if she'd show up to the dinner they had planned with Joe tonight after the game. Rafe wouldn't blame her if she didn't. Who needed this bullshit? Tate on her back, Rafe acting like she didn't matter. Hell, maybe she'd hopped a plane back to New York like she'd threatened a week ago.

That thought stabbed him so deep, he closed his eyes and rubbed them.

The puck dropped, and Rafe refocused on the game. Watching the movement on the ice, he asked Tierney, "You're not a suspicious guy, right? You don't believe in habits and good luck charms, right?"

"Not like those disgusting socks Belanger wears, or that stupid rabbit's foot Jaeger sticks down his shorts before every game. But I believe there are things you can do to get you into the zone. The way Lawless goes into the rink before anyone arrives and piles those stupid pucks into two R's on the ledge of the bench box when it's quiet. That's like meditation. It gets your head and your heart in the right place, you know? It focuses you. Centers you. That I believe in."

Centered.

Rafe's chest warmed and chilled at the same time.

That was what he'd been missing since he'd pushed Mia away. He was fragmented. Distracted. He felt like all his pieces were jumbled and mixed up. Some of them missing.

Mia centered him.

But a lot of good figuring that out did. It took a lot to keep Mia away from a game. She'd clearly had enough of his and Tate's bullshit.

The second period ended with the Rough Riders two points behind. And as they filed into the locker room for the break, frustration permeated the air around the team. Rafe shouldered his share of the blame, and even though his teammates never said a word about Rafe's shitty play, he knew they were all thinking about it.

The coach didn't lecture. He highlighted the good, gave

direction to improve the bad, and let the guys have a few quiet minutes to rest.

Rafe set his helmet on the bench beside him, wiped the sweat from his hair and face with a towel, then kept the terry there as he rested his head in his hands. He needed to get his groove back. Needed to find a way out of this funk.

"What's going on?" Tate's voice interrupted Rafe's thoughts, and he mentally rolled his eyes before dragging the towel away and picking up a water bottle.

"I'm playing for shit, that's what's going on."

"*Why?* You were on fire two nights ago."

Because Mia sets me on fire.

For a split second, Rafe thought of voicing that fact. In the next second, he realized that would turn this mess into a catastrophe.

He took a long drink of water, rested his elbows on his knees, and stared at the concrete. "I don't know why. When I figure it out, I'll make sure to notify you, okay?"

"Don't bother. Just get rid of this asshole attitude before we meet Dad for dinner."

Tate walked away, and Rafe closed his eyes on a sigh of dread, dropping his head back to his hands. Dinner with Joe.

And Mia.

After he'd played like shit for two days.

God, he hoped Mia's pattern of no-showing held true through the night.

NOT ONLY COULDN'T Rafe get lucky enough to have Mia pass on dinner, he couldn't be lucky enough for her to come in something casual and ordinary. He could have done a decent job of ignoring her curves in jeans and a blouse. A dress would have made it a little harder to focus on dinner, with his mind constantly veering toward sliding his hands up her legs, beneath the skirt, and over her tight ass.

But there was no ignoring all her luscious sexuality in the burgundy number she had on now. From the front door, she set confident strides toward their table. Rafe loved the way she moved—with a little of that model swagger she'd been exposed to on fashion runways and all the confidence of the woman she'd become.

Her dress sheered up one side, pulling the soft fabric at angles across her body and accentuating every delicious curve. The sleeveless tank's neckline and hem were modest, but the way the design showed off her body was sinful. And Rafe couldn't help but wonder what she had on underneath.

He fisted his hands and clenched his teeth. This dinner was going to last for-fucking-ever.

Mia sauntered to their table, and all three of them stood, something Joe had taught them young. Mia ignored Tate and Rafe and walked straight to Joe with a genuine smile. She gave him a big hug and kissed his cheek.

"Hey, you," she said, pulling back and sweeping a glance over his casual khakis and button-down. "Someone's losing weight."

Joe chuckled and slid a hand over his moderately sized belly. "Down ten pounds."

"I can tell. And in just, what? Didn't I see you a month ago?"

Joe traveled for his work as a corporate attorney and often visited Mia in New York. "Five weeks."

"Congratulations."

"Thank you, sweetheart. It's a start." He kissed her cheek and pulled out her chair. As she sat, he said, "You look beautiful. Is this dress one of yours?"

Rafe glanced at Tate for explanation, but Tate was listening to the conversation.

"It is," she said. "You like it?"

"One of your what?" Rafe asked.

"Her designs," Tate answered, equally subdued tonight after losing the game.

"Designs?" Rafe looked back at Mia and Joe. "You designed that dress? Like, from scratch?"

Joe laughed, but Mia didn't think Rafe's ignorance was funny. Neither did Rafe. He was annoyed that he was the only one at the table who didn't know Mia had risen to the level of designing her own clothes under the guidance of a well-known New York designer. But there was no one to blame for that but himself. That's what he got for avoiding her all year. For not asking about her work since she'd arrived.

"I did," she told Joe. "I also designed the dress I was wearing the night I got here." Her gaze turned on Rafe, and he felt the heat of her stare straight through his body. "Remember, the one I was wearing when I saved you from that date from hell?"

Her *get laid* dress.

Rafe didn't answer. All he could remember about that dress was the way it looked sliding off her body. And how goddamned beautiful she'd looked. Like now, with her dark hair falling in loose curls to her shoulders. Her makeup was soft, enhancing her eyes, cheeks, and lips just enough to pop. Just enough to send his mind into fantasy mode.

Joe covered Mia's hand with his and squeezed, smiling at her. "Sweetheart, you are one talented woman."

"Thank you."

"I ordered you a wonderful Syrah," Joe told her.

"I can't wait. I've found all my favorite wines with you."

Rafe stared at the table and turned his fork over and over and over.

"So," Mia said, "how was the game?"

Rafe's hand froze. But it was Tate who voiced what Rafe was thinking.

"What do you mean how was the game?" Tate's voice was filled with attitude. "Didn't you watch it?"

"No. But judging by your faces, I'm going to guess it was bad, so we can just move on to other subjects if you'd like."

"Other subjects?" Rafe said, lifting his gaze to hers. She never wanted to talk about anything else after a game. "Who are you, and what have you done with the real Mia?"

She gave him a cursory smile. "Sorry it's a sore subject. I'm sure it's just a blip. You'll hammer them in the next game."

Tate's gaze darted to Rafe. "Not if Rafe doesn't get his head out of his—"

"Don't," Rafe warned. "If you want this to be a nice dinner, just don't."

Mia hung the strap of her purse on the back of her chair and turned her gaze on Joe, totally ignoring Rafe and Tate. "How'd your merger go in Milwaukee? Did the trophy wife cause as much trouble as you thought she would?"

"Hold on," Tate interrupted, leaning into the table and giving Mia a pointed stare. "I think a more important question would be, where have you been sleeping the past two nights?"

Rafe's mind hit a brick wall. He glanced between Mia and Tate several times before the information that Mia had not gone back to Tate's apartment that night she'd left the bar or the night they'd been out of town sank in.

"Wait," Rafe said before he could stop himself. "*What?*"

Mia drilled them both with very deliberate stares. "I suggest you both heed Rafe's earlier advice. If you want this to be a nice dinner, *don't.*"

"Whoa, whoa, whoa," Joe cut in. All three of them stopped talking but didn't stop glaring as Joe's mediating voice soothed the ruffled feathers around the table. "Hey, now, what's going on here? This isn't how my kids act. Especially not to each other."

No one bothered to point out that only one of his children

sat at the table. From the time Joe had discovered Tate existed, he'd treated Tate's half sister and Tate's best friend as his own kids. All because Tate loved them. Joe had provided for both Rafe and Mia financially and emotionally where their parents couldn't or wouldn't.

"I know the playoffs have you boys stressed," Joe said. "I can only imagine the pressure you're under. But don't take it out on Mia. She's got a lot of stress in her own life, and it's no less important than yours."

He glanced at Mia and seemed to choose his words carefully. "When you have your own kids, you'll understand that you never stop worrying about them, no matter how old they get. Is there anything you need to tell me about where you've been sleeping, young lady?"

Mia cast an apologetic look at Joe. "I've been making some things for the girls. You know, Eden, Faith, Sara, and Tina. And for the kids too. I'm using Tina's machine at her house, and it was so nice to feel welcome and appreciated that it made me realize I didn't feel like getting lectured by Saint Tate every time he got home. So I stayed at Tina's one night and with Faith and Grant another. I got so good at couch hopping in New York, it was like second nature."

"Couch hopping?" Rafe asked, confused.

"What's this Saint Tate bullshit?" Tate asked.

"Tate." Joe reprimanded his son for swearing.

"You do everything right." Rafe knew exactly what the Saint Tate bullshit was. "That's what it means. You always do everything you're supposed to do. Follow all the rules and social mores. You have all the manners and morals. Sometimes your standards are a little hard for us mere mortals to live up to."

"Mores? Since when do you even know what asocial mores are?" Tate sat back in his chair. "And, why am I getting hammered for doing the right thing?"

"Sounds to me," Joe said, "like you're getting hammered for

being harsh on the people you love when they don't do every-thing perfectly by your standards."

Tate opened his mouth to argue just as a waiter came by and set drinks on the table. By the time he was gone, Tate's ire had faded. "I'm sorry I've been rough on you," he told Mia. "I worry, that's all."

Mia sighed and rolled her eyes with a little shake of her head. "It's not an apology when you lie, Tate."

"See, you're wrong," Tate told Rafe. "I obviously can't even apologize right."

A different waiter stopped by to take their orders, which seemed to hit reset on the mood at the table. When he left, Joe tried to turn that somber mood around by reaching for Mia's hand and giving it a squeeze with an upbeat "Maybe this is a good time to share your news, honey."

Rafe's gaze snapped up from his glass, wondering what else he didn't know about her life. "News" when said like that meant big news. Like she was getting a promotion. Or buying a house. Or getting married. Dread pinched his gut.

"Sure, why not?" Mia said with a stiff smile. "I...took a new job."

Rafe released a breath he hadn't known he was holding. "I thought you loved your job."

"I do. I mean, I did. But it was an apprenticeship that was coming to an end and I got a really amazing offer I couldn't turn down." She picked up her glass and sipped. "It's time for me to move on."

Somehow, Rafe got the impression she was talking about more than her job. "You already quit your old job?"

"Yep. Thought I'd come see you guys between jobs, though that hasn't turned out to be as pleasant as I'd expected."

"Is it for the same designer? The same company?" Tate asked.

"No." The way she paused to take a deep drink of her wine gave Rafe a bad feeling. "New company."

Rafe glanced at Joe, who was grinning like an idiot, then asked Mia, "Why are we having to pull this out of you?"

She pressed her forearms to the table and cradled the bowl of her wineglass in her palms, her long slim fingers spreading out over the globe. Hands that had touched every inch of his body in unforgettable ways. Hands he hadn't stopped craving since that night.

"Because she's making a big move," Joe said for her. "And I'm guessing by the way you two have been acting the last few days, she's not particularly eager to tell you about it."

"Why wouldn't we be excited about a big move for her?" Tate asked. "Is it more money?"

"No," Rafe said, drawing Mia's eyes. His gut went cold. "It's not for the money. At least that's not why she's holding back, is it, Mia?"

She held Rafe's gaze for a long moment, confirming he was right. Then she looked at Tate and said, "The job's in California."

California? Shock pierced Rafe's gut.

"*What?*" Tate said. "What the hell is in California?"

"Los Angeles," she said, a little defensiveness entering her tone. "And my job. A really cool job, actually, thanks for asking."

Reality leaked in little by little, turning Rafe's shock into a fiery mix of hurt, anger, and resignation. Everything she'd done with him, she'd done knowing she was leaving.

Anything he'd believed was special between them had either been his imagination or her fabrication. She really had meant that she wanted to fuck him and forget him.

Rafe was still reeling with that revelation when Tate's anger hit.

"Is this about Sam?" Tate demanded.

Sam must have been the ex-boyfriend's name Rafe couldn't remember. The one Tate had told Rafe she'd broken up with recently.

"Why would this have anything to do with Sam?" she asked with a scowl.

Tate sat forward again. "Because you were living with him, and it was *his* apartment. I *told you* not to move in with him. I *told you* to keep your own place. You know how hard it is to find apartments in New York."

"Yes, Tate, I do. *I* lived there, *not you*, remember? And I told you I couldn't *afford* to keep my own place."

"Okay, now—" Joe started.

"And I told you I'd give you the money," Tate spoke over him.

"And *I* told *you* I didn't want your money."

"Mia, honey—" Joe tried.

"You and Sam broke up," Tate said with that *I know everything* tone, "and you didn't have anywhere to live. That's why you've been couch-hopping. That's why you're moving. I *knew* this would happen."

The angry hurt on Mia's face indicated an explosion was imminent. And even though Rafe wanted the answers to a hell of a lot of uncomfortable questions too, he sat forward and put force behind his next words. "Tate, *knock it off.*"

But Mia wasn't helping the situation. She crossed her arms and cocked her head with attitude. "Really?" she asked Tate. "And how did you *know* this would happen? Do you have a crystal ball?"

"Because it *always* happens. It happens with *every* damn boyfriend. They all break up with you for the same reason—"

"Tate—" she warned.

"You hold back. You're emotionally unavailable. When it comes down to it, you can't commit. And you just keep screwing up your life—"

"*Tate.*" Joe's bark shut down everyone within a ten-foot radius. All eyes turned to their table. "*Enough.*"

When others refocused on their own dinners, Mia reached over and covered Joe's hand with hers, then spoke to Tate in a quiet, controlled voice. "You are *not* a psychiatrist. And you do *not* know what's best for me. This job is a once-in-a-lifetime opportunity. It came from a contact I made in design school. Just because the timing came on the heels of a breakup with Sam doesn't mean that's why I took it. And I can guarantee you I'm not screwing up my life with this move."

Tate heaved a sigh. "How do you know?"

"Because I'm working on the set of *Wicked Dawn*, you pompous asshole."

Rafe's mouth dropped open. He knew Mia was talented. Knew she had ambition and drive and work ethic. But he'd obviously cut off communication with her at a critical time in her life. And she'd soared. "'The' *Wicked Dawn*? The one on HBO?"

"Yes, Tate, *that* one. The one heading into its seventh season and rivaling *Game of Thrones* for ratings. That *Wicked Dawn*. They've hired a new costume designer for the next season, and I'm working directly with that designer," Mia said.

"It's the kind of job I would only find on Broadway in New York, and considering other designers read the obituaries to leap on a job opening like that, I didn't think homicide was the best option. So while I may not be able to hold on to a guy, at least I won't be screwing up my career. And before you judge my relationship failures, Tate, take a look in the mirror."

That last comment knocked the wind from Rafe's chest. Mia never brought up Tate's ex-wife. She'd always been incredibly sensitive over how that loss had nearly crippled her brother. But she wasn't pulling any punches, and Tate's gaze warred with Mia's.

"I know what happened with Lisa was hard on you," Mia

said, her anger turning to pain in her eyes and bringing tears that welled but never fell. "And I know there has to be a transition period. But honest to God, Tate, I'm tired of waiting for you to turn back into the guy you were before that bitch took over your life."

A waiter passed, and Mia flagged him down. "Cancel my order please. I have to go."

Rafe rubbed a hand down his face, searching for a way to pull this from the fire, but came up with nothing. He could barely tackle his own emotions over this revelation. He sure as shit couldn't take on Mia's hurt over losing Tate or Tate's inability to move on after Lisa.

She gave Joe a sad smile and patted his hand. "Can we have dinner tomorrow night? Before you catch your plane?"

Joe looked miserable. He lifted a hand to her face and wiped at her cheek. The gesture made Rafe realize her tears had spilled over and it wrenched his gut. He couldn't remember ever seeing Mia cry.

"Of course, honey." Joe kissed her forehead. "I'm so proud of you. And your brothers are too. It's just...this Cup."

Mia nodded and stood.

"Mia." Tate planted his elbows on the table and rubbed his face with both hands. "Don't go. I'm sorry, I'm..." He looked up at her. "I'm an ass. I'm stressed, and I'm worried about you and—"

"And we'll talk about it later," she said with finality. The same finality she'd used when she'd told them she was moving across the goddamned country. "After we've both had time to cool off."

She looked at Rafe, and the glimmer of tears still in her eyes made everything inside him twerk. "And you're wrong too. It *is* for the money. A lot more money." She shot one last look at Tate. "Neither one of you knows me the way you think you do. I'm beginning to think you never did."

11

M ia had finished half a bottle of wine by the time she'd exhausted her Internet apartment search in Los Angeles. She was going to move into her friend's two bedroom until she got settled in the job, but Mia wanted to stand on her own. She'd already let Tate pay for her education, which had been difficult for her independent spirit. Living on her own, especially in light of how Tate viewed her, was more important than ever.

His hurtful words—or more to the point, their accuracy—stabbed at her heart again, and tears pushed into her eyes, blurring the screen. She pulled another Kleenex from the box on the coffee table and pressed it against her face. As soon as she'd gotten home, she'd ditched the high heels, washed her smeared makeup off her face, coiled her hair into a bun on top of her head, and curled into a corner of the sofa with her laptop.

She closed her browser, picked up her phone, and scrolled through Instagram, trying to keep her mind busy until she was too tired to keep her eyes open or Tate got home and they started fighting again—whichever came first.

A knock at the door made her jump, then she rolled her

eyes. "He forgot his key?" she muttered, setting down her phone to start toward the door with her wine, calling, "Would serve you right if I left you in the hall."

She opened the door, but instead of Tate, she found Rafe, and her stomach squeezed. He'd loosened his tie and unbuttoned his shirt. His expression was tight and dark. Turbulence brewed in his eyes. His intensity pounded awareness through her body, but her heart balked. Mia had been hurt enough. Great sex and good looks wouldn't fill the hole there.

She glanced behind him into the hall, suddenly self-conscious about her own miserable state of red swollen eyes and blotchy face. "Where's Tate?"

"He and Joe went to have some father-son time." His voice sounded as rough as the stubble over his jaw. "They're hitting a few of their favorite pubs."

"Well. Good for them." Mia was done with Tate and his misplaced overprotectiveness. Maybe Joe could whip him into shape. Nothing else had worked. "Wish I'd known, because you are *definitely* staying in the hall. Good night."

She shut the door in his face.

But Rafe's hand hit the wood before the latch caught, and pushed it open. "No, I'm not." He stepped in, nudging Mia backward. "We have shit to talk about."

She set her wine down on the kitchen bar, wandered deeper into the condo, and crossed her arms. "Like how I wish I could go back in time and walk away from you at the hotel when you asked for help? Or how I wish I'd never taken you back to my room?"

"No."

He followed her, advancing in a slow, predatory way that unnerved her. She felt brittle and weak. She felt alone and unwanted with a difficult future ahead and no strength to face it.

"Like how you lied about not using me as a rebound fuck,"

he said, voice tight and rising. "Like how you came here with a deliberate plan to fuck me out of your system then move three-*fucking*-thousand miles away."

The rasp of his voice as he tried to keep it down scraped over Mia's skin. The scent of his cologne and the heat of his body teased her with memories. She wanted to cave. She wanted to lean into him and feel his arms around her. Wanted to feel his lips against her skin. So she kept inching away, because that wouldn't solve any problems, and that desire was how she'd gotten here in the first place.

The vortex of emotions she'd spent the last hour calming threatened to slip from her control again. "You'd have to be inside my head to make that call. And you're not. You haven't even talked to me in a damn year, so don't you dare stand there and tell me you know my motives better than I do."

"Then *why*?" he yelled, making Mia flinch. Her heart stuttered and raced ahead. "*Why* did you sleep with me after twenty years and hundreds of other opportunities when you didn't? Why do it right after you broke up with Sam and before you move across the *fucking country*?"

Pain seeped into his voice, and Mia's strength waned, all the hurt rushed back.

"Because Tate was right," she yelled. "And I'm sick of guys walking away from me because my heart is somewhere else. I did it because I wanted a fresh start, okay? I just wanted to finally let go."

His hands closed on her biceps, and he gave her a shake. "Let go of *what*?"

"*You*." She threw her arms out to break his hold. "*You*, you idiot."

He straightened away from her, his expression shifting from confused to hit-with-a-puck-between-the-eyes.

Mia crossed her arms again, pulling them tight across the pain ripping through her heart. What the hell difference did it make if he knew how she felt now? She was going to be across the damn country soon.

"It was stupid, I know that now." The admission swamped her with guilt. She was better than this, and she didn't know how she'd been drawn to such lows. "I'm sorry I dragged you into my mess. I'm sorry it's become a problem between you and Tate. I'm sorry it's created trouble for everyone. But you guys, you all just go about your life, and I'm always an afterthought."

The truth hurt, and she couldn't hold the tears back. "Joe loves his job and deals with important cases. He travels all over, and he's got the perfect son. Tate has an awesome career and the best father a guy could ask for. He could also have any woman he wanted if he'd let go of Lisa's betrayal. You get Joe and Tate and any puck bunny you smirk at."

She wasn't going to go into all the ways her life failed to measure up. "I get the leftovers. I get the occasional visit from Joe, the occasional call from Tate, and then you dropped me completely. Which reminds me," she said, anger renewed, "fuck you, Savage. You have no right to come here and—"

In one step, Rafe closed the distance. She startled, but before she could react, he clasped her face in both hands...and kissed her.

The gears of Mia's brain stalled, and a murmur of surprise escaped her lips. She fisted her hands in his blazer, trapped between shoving him away and sinking in.

Before she'd decided, he broke the kiss abruptly.

"Stop," he said, a little breathless. One hand pushed into her hair. He dropped his forehead against hers, and his eyes closed. "Just stop." He pulled back only far enough to focus. "Go back to the part about why you came. Why you slept with me. Why you're *really* pissed at me right now."

"Why? Just so I can humiliate myself again? Forget it. And don't tell me what to do. I'm sick of you and Tate throwing your weight around. If you didn't hear what I said the first time, too damn bad."

He pulled her in for another kiss. This time, she pushed at his chest. But he wrapped his free arm around her waist and hauled her off her feet.

She turned her head to escape his mouth. "Rafe—"

He dropped to the sofa, pulled her in to straddle across his lap, and held her there.

"I'm not going anywhere," he told her.

"Then you're going to have another black eye soon, because if Tate walks in on us like this, he's going to go ape shit—talk with Joe or no talk with Joe."

"So you *did* come to fuck me out of your system," he said, ignoring her warning. His eyes were narrowed and intense, and she couldn't read him. And those stupid kisses were messing up everything.

"You have a hearing problem...among others."

He huffed a laugh, and his lips quirked on one side, but it wasn't a smile. His eyes were still dark as they lowered to her mouth. "I always did love that smart mouth of yours." He lifted a hand to her face and ran his thumb over her lips. A rough, slow rub that pulled her mouth open. "Such a dirty, sassy, smart mouth."

His thumb moved across her cheek, but he didn't meet her eyes. His cock was right where it should be, riding the heat between her legs. And he was hard. His expression, his voice, his touch, everything about him told her he was hungry. And her body was conducting a mutiny.

She wanted him worse right now, even hurt and pissed off, than she ever had—including their first night. Because now she knew exactly how much pleasure he could deliver. Now she had memories of his passion. And it took every sliver of resistance not to rock her hips against him. Not to bend her head and taste him.

"Did it work?" His question was low and rough.

"What?" She frowned, pushing against his chest to lean away. "What are you—"

His gaze cut to hers, deliberate and hot. "Did it work? Did you fuck me out of your system?" He waited only a heartbeat to continue. "Because you are infused in my blood."

"That's lust, Rafe. You should recognize it by now. And it's not what I want anymore. It's not enough. I may want you, but I don't like you right now. And honestly, anyone who could pull away from me so completely for so long, as if I didn't exist, doesn't even deserve any part of me."

"I did that because I had to," he snapped. "Because talking to you and seeing you got too hard. I knew I'd never be able to have you all to myself with this twisted little family we've created. I couldn't stand seeing you with other guys when you came to town. And I couldn't stand the way you turned away from me and went running to your boyfriends when not one of them was there for you the way I was.

"That night in New York, I realized my expectations were way out of line. And I knew I had to put some distance between us. The fact that you were mad at me over it only helped."

His anger turned sullen, and Mia's mind darted to the last time she'd seen him. To the week from hell in her previous apprenticeship and how she'd called him in a moment of weakness when her boyfriend at the time had been too busy at work to take her call. Then her mind jumped forward, to the way he'd shown up in New York that very night to make sure she was okay, only to have her boyfriend show up fifteen minutes later.

Before she lashed out at him for not telling her how he felt, she caught herself. He couldn't tell her. Not without messing things up in their family. Just another illustration of how Tate and Joe always came first. In this case, he'd also been thinking of Mia. She knew him, and she knew Rafe wouldn't have wanted to mess up her relationship with Tate and Joe either.

His hand slid around the back of her neck and into her hair. It felt so good, Mia's eyes closed. All her anger waned, and desire spiked in its place. She couldn't change him. She didn't even want to. His loyalty was one of the things that made him Rafe. One of the things that made her love him. She only wished...

It was stupid to wish. She felt like she'd been wishing her whole life.

She had to stop wishing and just accept reality.

He shifted beneath her, rubbing against her, reminding her that this was her current reality. And that she could either take what she could get or get nothing.

When his strong hand pulled her head to his, she didn't resist. But he only pressed his forehead to hers and massaged her scalp.

"This past week had been hell on earth."

The distress in his voice pulled her eyes open, and she found his closed in a look of pain.

"I can't stop thinking about you." His jaw clenched. "I feel like shit over this situation with Tate and how much it's hurting you. I don't know what to do to make any of this right. I fucking slept with my phone, hoping you'd call or text me back."

A huff of humor and disbelief passed her lips, and her heart skipped.

But Rafe didn't smile. He opened his eyes and looked deeply into hers with a kind of misery she understood too well. "I can't believe you're leaving."

Her heart wrenched open against her will. She framed his face with her hands, tilted her head, and kissed him. The hand at the back of her head tightened and pulled her deeper into the kiss as he opened to her. The sparks instantly caught fire. Their tongues met, and hunger exploded deep in Mia's body.

A sound of longing and desire rolled in Rafe's throat. A growl that reverberated through her. He released her waist and gripped one of her wrists, but just left his hand there as he kissed her and tasted her and moaned with the pleasure of it. All Mia's worries and hurts fell away. She could only focus on the heat and taste of his mouth. The way he kissed her like he never wanted to stop. Like he couldn't get enough.

When he broke the kiss abruptly, Mia fell into him. She wrapped her arms around his shoulders and kissed his jaw, his neck. Licked the spot behind his ear.

He groaned and lifted into her.

"Oh..." she breathed, swamped in the delicious pleasure he pushed through her lower body.

His fingers flexed and released. "Mia, God," he rasped, his voice low and hungry. He combed his hand through her hair and wrapped his arm around her head, clutching her close. "Need you."

That didn't just snap her restraint, it bulldozed every barrier. She turned her head and kissed him again, open and hot and wet, while she dropped her hands to his waist and worked his belt open.

He broke the kiss again murmuring her name. "Mia, Mia, Mia..."

"Wallet," she managed through her quick breaths.

She flipped his button open, pulled his zipper down, and moved his clothes out of the way to slide her hand over his thick, hot length.

Rafe's hips pulsed. He clenched his teeth around a curse and dropped his head against the sofa, eyes closed, face tight with pleasure. The sight pumped lust and power and need through her body.

"Condom," she reminded him, anxious to get him where he belonged. Anxious to close all the distance between them, to bond with him the way they had the first night.

He lifted his head, his eyes heavy lidded. "Do we need one?"

Her hand froze with his hard length in her palm. "What?"

He combed both hands through her hair and pulled her to him, kissing her, long and slow. When he pulled away again, Mia was light-headed.

"Do we need one?" he repeated. "Are you taking something?"

Birth control. He was talking about birth control. Jesus, her head was not working. "Yes." The thought of feeling him with no barriers hammered her with lust. She met his eyes directly. "*Do* we need one?"

His lips quirked for a millisecond before he went serious again. "No." And with a little shake of his head, he pushed his hands up her thighs, under her skirt, and hooked his fingers in the fabric of her panties at one hip. "Just got a clean bill of health."

One jerk and her panties snapped.

She startled and gasped. He moved his hands to the other side and did it again. Snap.

Mia started laughing. "Rafe."

But then his hand slipped between her legs, and she siphoned a breath at the touch. Then he moved, and damn if Mia didn't forget everything but the decadent glide of his fingers. She moaned and rocked against his touch.

So perfect. Slow and direct and thorough. Pleasure coiled tight between her legs. He was so damn good with his hands. His mouth. His cock...

He sat forward and pressed an openmouthed kiss to her throat. "This is all I could think about for the last two days," he murmured against her skin, then moved to another spot and kissed. "Touching you is like coming home."

She leaned her head into his and begged at his ear. "Please, Rafe..."

"Mmm, baby." He turned his head and kissed the other side

of her neck. "I missed you." His tongue stroked a line to her earlobe, and he took it between his teeth, biting gently, then licking to soothe. "Come get it, Mia. Come take what you want."

Knots of lust lined her spine, filled her stomach, and choked her heart. She fisted her hands in his blazer and used her knees to push his hand deeper and faster and harder. Whimpers and moans and random words spilled out of her. "Rafe, God. Mmm, so good."

"I want you to come for me, Mia. I want you all wet and hot for me when I push inside you." He closed his teeth at the base of her neck. The sting took her pleasure a notch higher. "Gonna feel ever perfect inch of you."

The orgasm gripped her pussy like a fist. Her body shuddered hard, suffusing her with a stream of hot pleasure. Her brain evaporated in bliss, and she pressed her face to his shoulder, muffling her cry against his blazer.

Rafe held her tight with one arm, his face buried in the hollow between her neck and shoulder. It brought back memories of their night together and how he'd always drifted back to that place after sex. Breathing her in, kissing her pulse point as it raced.

When her body finally relaxed and Mia was panting against his shoulder, he slid his hand free of her body and sucked two fingers into his mouth. The sound of pure pleasure rolled through his throat, and his lips smacked. "Damn, you taste good."

Heat rushed to her face, but it also rallied between her legs.

Without warning, Rafe clasped an arm around her waist and stood, carrying her with him. A sound of surprise popped from her mouth, and she automatically wrapped her legs and arms around him to hold on while he headed toward the guest room.

He kicked the door closed, pressed one knee to the bed, and laid her back, following her down. Then the real assault began,

his mouth and hands almost frantic with passion. He pushed
one strap of her dress off her shoulder, dragged the fabric clear
of her breast, and covered her with his mouth, while his hips
pressed between her legs.

He flooded her with desire and need. He loved her like
there was nothing more important in the world. Nowhere he'd
rather be and no one he'd rather be with. Tears pushed at her
eyes again, but she didn't know why. Her chest was so full, it
ached.

She combed her fingers through his hair, loving the feel of
the thick strands in her hands. Loving his weight pushing her
into the mattress. Loving the spicy, male sent of him. The man
made her delirious. She'd never wanted anyone like this. Never
needed anyone like she needed Rafe.

Even knowing what a huge problem this would be in the very
near future, all she could do was hold on tighter, denying reality. At
least for a little while longer. Because right now, all she could focus
on was his hands and mouth all over her body, setting her on fire.

He didn't even bother shedding one thread of fabric before
he slipped one hand between them and rubbed the head of his
cock against her. Skin on skin.

"Oh..." she breathed.

"So sweet," he groaned.

Propping himself up on his elbows, he stroked his fingers
into her hair and cradled her head. Looking into her eyes, he
thrust, pushing inside her. All Rafe. All heat. No barriers. And
so damn good.

God, she still couldn't quite believe she was with Rafe.
Really with Rafe. She couldn't begin to count the times she'd
fantasized about this very moment. Yet the real thing was far
more intense than she'd ever imagined. So much deeper than
anything she'd had with any other man.

His eyes closed. Jaw clenched. And he echoed her thoughts.

"So *sweet.*" He opened his eyes, and the fire there sparked in Mia's gut. "Mia. God, Mia."

He pulled out and thrust again—long, slow, and deep. The decadent stretch of him filling her made her mouth drop open, made her fingers curl into his shirt. She wanted him naked. Wanted to do this all night.

"Baby," he said, breathless, pressing his forehead to hers, "I can't believe...*how fucking...good* you feel."

Mia reached lower, slid her hands beneath his clothes, and gripped his ass, pulling him into her while she tilted her pelvis to take him deeper.

He growled, eyes falling closed. The heat of his cock burned inside her. His hands tightened in her hair, and he kissed her—deeply, hungrily. And just kept kissing her. Like he'd never get enough. Like he could kiss her for hours.

And as much as she wished they had hours, they didn't.

"More," she told him, rocking her pelvis back to draw him out, loving the drag against her walls. "Give me more, Rafe."

He exhaled, opened his eyes, and they burned into hers. "Baby, I'm not gonna last..."

"You don't have time to last." Every minute that passed ticked down to the moment when Tate would return. "And I need more."

He growled, but delivered with long, deep, steady thrusts that pushed Mia toward climax with shocking speed. All while keeping his eyes focused on hers. His expression so primal, so intense he burrowed into her heart and drove her body toward ecstasy.

"Yes, yes, yes..." Her nails dug into the muscle of his ass. A tight, muscled ass that flexed and released on every thrust. His hair fell out of that hastily gelled, negligent bad-boy style and fell into his eyes. Sweat glistened on his forehead. God, she wished she could memorize him. Right this second. Memorize him and save that memory as clearly as if she were in the moment.

"Baby," he murmured. "I never want to stop. Want to stay inside you forever."

His passion rose and his thrusts came harder and faster, but he never broke eye contact. That one simple act made the sex even more intense. More intimate. So consuming, she felt like he crawled into her soul.

"God," he growled through clenched teeth. "The way you squeeze me is *heaven*. Want to feel you gush all over me, Mia. Come for me, baby. Want to feel you come, Mia."

She responded as if his words had control over her body. Two more thrusts and her climax burst deep in her pelvis. She clenched as the vise of pressure exploded. One burst of pleasure after another. Arching her back. Forcing sounds of ecstasy from her mouth.

Before the last shudder rocked her body, Rafe curved his arms around her, and, holding himself deep inside her, he straightened, pulling her back to straddle across his lap. Her body weight and lax muscles allowed him to push so deep, the sensation closed her throat. The way his pelvis pressed against her in this position pushed her toward another orgasm before the last had even left her body.

His other hand slid into her hair and cradled her head, holding her gaze to his. "That is so hot," he said between heavy breaths. "I can't even tell you. Need it again. Come for me again, Mia."

Even though she was sure she couldn't climax again, Rafe proved her wrong. With one strong arm wrapped at her hips, he held her steady as he pulled out. Then dragged her body to meet his as he lifted. Every thrust forced a cry of pleasure from Mia's throat. And every thrust was punctuated by Rafe's rough words from behind clenched teeth.

"*So.*"

Thrust.

"*Fucking.*"

Thrust.

"*Good.*"

Hard and fast and deep, he hammered and hammered. "Come on, baby. Give it to me again. Can't get enough. Can't fucking get enough."

Rafe didn't just thrust with his ass. Rafe angled back on his thighs and leveraged the entire powerhouse that was his posterior chain of muscles to lift into the drive. His cock plunged until their bodies slammed, acting like a hammer on a nail, driving the head of his cock against that spot she'd discovered for the first time in bed with him.

"Oh *God.*" The pleasure was so intense, it was almost too big to grasp.

"*Yes.* Bring it, Mia. Look at me." His hand tightened on her face. "Look at me, Mia. I want it all. Give it to me, baby."

He thrust harder. Faster. Lifting her body with the forward momentum, then letting her fall back on his cock in a mind-bending rhythm.

The first orgasm blasted through her like lightning, so sharp it bordered on painful. "*Ah...*"

It ripped through her body, leaving her shaking. And on the heels, another surged like waves on the shore. She held tight as another orgasm crashed. "Oh my God."

"Yes, yes, yes," Rafe rasped, his voice wickedly pleased. "Don't stop, Mia. So wet. So hot. Never been this good. Come, Mia. Come again."

But she no longer had a choice. Her body wasn't her own anymore. It belonged to Rafe. She let her head fall against his shoulder and wrapped an arm around his neck to hold on while his hips lunged, his cock plunged, and thrill after thrill hammered her. And instead of hearing her own voice begging for more, Rafe's lips murmured at her ear, "Don't stop, baby.

Goddamn, Mia. So good. So fucking good. Give me more. *Give. Me. More.*"

Layer upon layer upon layer of ecstasy swamped Mia. Her vision blurred. Her body shook and shivered and broke. Each orgasm different from the last. And Rafe whispering, "Don't stop. Don't stop. Don't ever stop." in her ear.

By the time Rafe's climax broke, Mia's body was coiled tight. He drove deep on a guttural growl, and his hips pulsed through the orgasm. His warmth exploded inside her, spilling through her pelvis, and tipped her over the last ledge.

Shaking with fatigue, Mia floated slowly back to reality. Basking in the experience of finally completely giving herself over to a man she loved with everything she had. Everything she was.

As the present seeped back into her brain, Rafe stroked rough fingertips along her spine. His heavy, quick breaths sounded in her ear. His heart pounded hard against hers.

Then his breathless voice, thick with residual desire, murmured, "Fuck. I never knew…it could be like this…"

His revelation choked a sound from her—part laugh, part sob.

She'd never known she could love like this. This was what all her exes had been looking for. Waiting for. This was what she'd never been able to give.

Only to finally find *The One*, knowing that keeping him meant alienating everyone truly important in her life. In Rafe's life. In their life, together.

12

S weat drenched Rafe's body. His thighs ached. Lungs burned. But his goal was within sight. So close he could taste it. Taste the salty, coppery tang on his tongue.

Score. Score. Score.

Rafe swung into the turn at the corner of the rink with a Bruin headed on a trajectory to intercept. But as the other player rushed to meet Rafe, Rafe leaned back, slowing at the last second and collecting the puck to protect it. The Bruin's skates cut across Rafe's path, just inches from his blades. Inches that gave Rafe the space he needed to pass to Andre.

Andre swooshed a circle around another Bruin and passed to Tate.

And Tate hammered the puck deep into the net.

Score.

Adrenaline surged through Rafe, the game now three-two with the Rough Riders in the lead at the beginning of the third period.

All five players punched a triumphant fist in the air and skated to each other for congratulatory hugs. After tapping gloves with their teammates on the bench and getting kudos

from their coach, Tremblay traded Rafe, Tate, and Isaac out of
the line.

This was game four in the battle for the East Coast conference title. They had to win to play for The Cup.

"You are killin' it tonight," Tate told him, following Rafe to
the bench. "You've touched every fucking goal."

Two goals and one assist out of the three total. Yes, Rafe was
on motherfucking fire. Again. Thanks to Mia.

He couldn't have killed the grin on his face even if he'd
gotten jammed into the boards headfirst—like he had in the
first period, which had earned Rafe eight stitches underneath
one eye.

Even with sweat stinging the cut, he turned his smile on
Mia where she sat in the stands nearby. She was sitting with
Joe, just three rows up from the ice tonight. Rafe loved knowing
she was watching him kill it. Loved having her eyes on him.

He picked up a bottle, squirted water into his mouth, and
glanced at Tate. When Rafe found him talking to Hendrix, he
cut another look toward Mia.

She was already looking at him, and the second their gazes
collided, all sorts of tugs and twists tortured his guts. Sitting
on the edge of her seat, leaning forward, she had her elbows
on her knees and her chin in her palm. And she was smiling.
Right at him. The kind of smile that made his insides tighten
and sing. And while her smile grew to show perfectly straight,
white teeth—courtesy of Joe—Rafe was already wondering
how and where he could maneuver a situation to get her
alone tonight. He'd sure love to expend all his adrenaline
on Mia.

But if they won, everyone would be headed to owner's
home after the game to celebrate their victory.

Cheers from the stands pulled Mia's gaze back to the ice.
Rafe glanced that direction and found Kilbourne fighting to get
the puck around the goalie. When the puck started down the

ice again, he returned his gaze to Mia, but she was talking to Joe.

Her move to California snuck into his thoughts. Something he'd been trying to ward off because it messed with his head and his heart. He couldn't ask her not to go. But if she moved to California, he knew the gains they'd made in their relationship would be lost.

Then he thought of all the other things keeping them from giving this thing between them their all. Remembered Tate's fury when he'd thought Rafe had slept with Mia. Heard Joe calling the three of them "his kids." Then the past filtered in— all the tutoring Joe had gotten Rafe in school, the equipment he'd bought for Rafe, Tate's special coaching Joe had paid to let Rafe join, the hockey camps he'd paid for Rafe to attend. Tate would know Rafe had lied to his face about it. Joe would hear about it. All the trust Tate had in him, all the pride Joe felt... It would all disintegrate when they found out he'd slept with Mia.

Rafe took another drink of water and pushed all that from his mind. He had to focus through this third period. He'd talk with Mia about this later.

He turned to Tate and asked, "Are Mia and Joe coming to the party tonight?"

"You know Dad, never turn down a chance to bullshit with—"

A Bruin slammed Andre into the half wall separating the bench from the rink. Sticks and limbs went flying. Rafe leaned back and covered his face with his forearm to protect his stitched eye, so he didn't see whose punch missed Andre and hit Rafe in the shoulder.

Anger roared through Rafe, and he pushed to his feet. "What the fuck?"

Play had all but stopped while the Bruins' defenseman had Andre bent backward over the half wall, Andre's jersey fisted in one hand, the other curled into a fist and hauled back.

"Do it," Rafe yelled in the Bruin's face, "and you'd better watch your back."

The Bruin's punch in his palm, inches from Andre's belligerent expression.

Rafe twisted the guy's wrist. Not enough to damage him, just enough to make a point.

"Watch your back, fucker," Rafe said, glaring the other guy down. "'Cause I'm bigger than him, I'm meaner than you, and I'm back on the ice in ninety seconds."

He released the Bruin's wrist with a shove, and the defenseman wobbled a little before he found balance and slid backward. The interference had given the refs time to glide in and lay down the law.

"Thanks," Andre said with his thick Russian accent and that dorky smirk of his. "Now I not look like you when I go home."

Play continued, and Rafe relaxed again, a little rattled by his show of aggression. That wasn't who he was. He handled his own fights on the ice, but he didn't get involved in others'.

"You are in fine form tonight, man." Tate grinned from his seat beside Rafe on the bench, and the sight of his friend's familiar ease loosened some of Rafe's stress. But in the next moment, guilt wiped the ease away. A little distress leaked in too. Claiming Mia meant losing his lifelong friendship with Tate.

"Did you clear the air with Mia last night?" he asked. He and Tate had both been busy with workouts and training since they'd arrived at the rink, and Rafe hadn't gotten a chance to ask.

"She was asleep when I got home," Tate said. "I'll talk to her tonight."

Rafe wasn't surprised. He was pretty sure she'd been asleep by the time he'd pulled the covers over her before he'd left her last night.

"What'd you do after Dad and I dropped you off?" Tate

asked, that suspicious you-got-lucky-didn't-you grin lifting his mouth. "Or should I ask *who* did you do?"

Alarm stung Rafe's gut. Luckily—or not, depending on how he looked at it—the refs called a penalty on the Rough Riders, which meant he and Tate were going back in for the penalty kill. While the four stripes talked over the punishment, Rafe stuck one end of his mouth guard between his teeth as he stood and adjusted a glove, ignoring Tate's question. His assumption wasn't out of left field. Before Mia, Rafe had a pattern of ending a game night by picking up a hot puck bunny and expending his adrenaline horizontally.

"Whoever she is, she really does it for you, man," Tate said, standing next to him, shoulder to shoulder. "You ought to think about holding on to her through the playoffs and into the Cup if we get there, because she sure as shit does you like nobody's done you in a while."

Rafe frowned at Tate. "What are you talking about?"

"You. This." Tate gestured the length of Rafe. "You saw her again, didn't you? The same chick you saw the night before you shot your hat trick?"

Rafe's mouth dropped open to deny it, but he hesitated, wondering if he should just play it off as if he were seeing someone, just someone *else*.

Tate took his silence as affirmation and laughed. "I knew it. You haven't had this much *Savage* in you in months. She really clears your head. You were a mess in the last few games. And we're going to need all the Savage you can pull together to get to the Cup."

Tate refocused on the ice and adjusted his helmet, and Rafe realized Tate knew him even better than he'd thought.

"You've got her, use her. That is your gift," Tate said, his cynical side coming out. His view of women had changed one hundred and eighty degrees since Lisa had screwed him over.

"And hell, it's only for another couple weeks. Even you could stick with a woman that long. Only a couple of weeks."

Rafe had no idea what to say to that.

They slid onto the ice and set up for a face-off with Tate muttering, "Shit, bro, *pay* her if you need to. The way you play after you do her is totally worth it." He grinned at Rafe. "Look at it as an investment."

"Shut up, Donovan."

Tate swung in an arc, bent his knees, and readied for the play, grinning at Rafe. "Just sayin'. Anything for the Cup, right?"

For the Cup.

Rafe really didn't care about the Cup. He wasn't like the other guys who'd coveted the Cup since they first stepped onto the ice as kids. But he sure didn't like the way Tate was referring to Mia. And if Tate knew he was talking about his own sister, Rafe would be bleeding out on the ice right now.

Tate's perspective only clarified just how impossible it would be for him to accept Rafe and Mia together. But it also made him wonder if that was how Mia saw their relationship. Did she think that was the way Rafe saw her? Nothing more than another one of his hookups? Surely, she couldn't really believe she was just another puck bunny to him.

Could she?

A fist of dread squeezed his gut.

"Play desperate, boys." Tremblay's order from the bench pulled Rafe's thoughts back to the moment, and he threw all his frustrated anger into the last minutes of the game.

13

M ia knew both Rafe and Tate were vying for their chance to talk to her alone, so she made sure to keep someone close by at all times. She wasn't ready to have a conversation with either of them. So she smiled and nodded as Nika, Andre's adorable young wife, talked about her two-year-old, Dmitri, while her hand lay on her pregnant belly.

"You won't have to count me in the pool of people bothering you for jerseys," she said, her Russian accent milder than her husband's. "I'll have baby weight to lose before I buy anything new."

"You look gorgeous," Mia told her. "I'll just add panels to the sides of the jersey to fit your belly, then take them out when you're back to your normal size."

Andre came up beside his wife and slipped a hand around her waist. "Are you ready to go, *kisa*? I promise Dmitri I read to him before bed."

They said good-bye to Mia, and she hastily pivoted to join Eden as she ended a conversation with a couple of puck bunny dates accompanying other team members tonight.

Eden sighed and met Mia's gaze. "Oh, yay. Someone I can

have an intelligent, meaningful conversation with. Faith told me about your move. I'm so excited for you, but I'm sad for us. We'll miss you. Will you be able to get back here for some of the games and the holidays?"

Another weight piled on the mountain of weights already on her heart. "Thank you. I'm not really sure. I don't know what to expect at this job, but I hope so."

"Well, tell me all about it. I haven't been a *Wicked Dawn* fan, but that's going to change now that I know you're working on the costumes."

Mia let her tension ebb as she told Eden about the job. And her own excitement for the future rose in tandem with the people she told, all of whom were overjoyed for the next step in her career. All except Tate and Rafe.

The thought of Rafe tied her stomach right back into a knot. She cast a quick look at him where he sat lazily on the arm of a sofa, two young women chatting with him. Two beautiful women. Beautiful, young women whose body language expressed keen interest in Rafe.

She forced her gaze and her mind back to Eden. "Tell me about the wedding plans. Have you and Beckett set a date? I'll definitely put in for vacation so I won't miss it."

"No date yet. We're letting Lily settle into the idea of all of us living together for a while."

"I bet that was your idea, not Beckett's. I hear he can't tie the knot soon enough."

Eden grinned, and when she spoke again, she lowered her voice. "Let's talk about what's going on with you and this rumor about Rafe."

Her stomach chilled. "What rumor?"

"What do you mean what rumor? The one that gave him that black eye. I'm glad his stitches ended up on the other side of his face tonight, but it does sort of make him look like an MMA master."

Mia laughed and glanced at him again. He was smiling at something the women were saying. "Probably one of the reasons he gets so many women."

"He does have quite the reputation of a playboy," Eden said, following Mia's gaze. "But in my experience, that doesn't mean they aren't looking for the one woman who can make them want to throw in that towel." She turned her gaze back to Mia, wearing a big smile. "It also makes them pretty damned incredible in bed."

That made Mia laugh. And blush like she had a fever of one hundred and two. But she lied with "I wouldn't know."

"Mia, it's just me. I'm not going to say anything. And when you and Rafe are within sight of each other, the sexual tension is palpable."

That wasn't good. Mia would have to make a concerted effort to shut that down. "I think you're mistaking supreme frustration for sexual tension. Both Tate and Rafe have been testing my patience since I arrived. And I haven't been a stellar example of someone taking the high road."

"Sweetie, I'm on the streets, dealing with all kinds of people all day. I know the difference. If you want to deny it, that's fine, but you aren't swaying me."

Mia looked down at her wine and sighed. "Doesn't really matter either way. Neither California nor my new job will facilitate anything lasting. And I've had enough breakups for a lifetime."

Tate finally started toward her, and Mia groaned. "Here comes one of the problematic men in my life."

Eden glanced over her shoulder as Tate stopped beside her and grinned. "How's motherhood treating you?"

"Amazingly. Who wouldn't love being a mother to Lily?"

Mia knew for a fact Lily's own mother didn't want to have anything to do with the angelic little girl, something she'd never been able to understand.

Tate laughed and wrapped an arm around Eden's shoulders. "No one in their right mind, that's for sure." He lifted his gaze to Mia. "Can we talk a minute?"

Eden reached out and gave Mia's arm a squeeze and smiled sympathetically. "I'll catch you later."

When Eden was out of earshot, Mia said, "I'm not in the mood to argue, Tate."

"Good. I'm not either."

But his tone told Mia it would be inevitable.

"I'm really sorry I upset you at dinner," he said. "And I hate this rift between us. I don't want you leaving until we clear the air."

"That would require you to accept my choices and turn off that judgmental attitude. Can you do that?"

He rolled his eyes and huffed a breath.

"That's what I thought," she said. "Look, Tate, I'm twenty-eight years old. It's my life, and I'm done taking direction from my brother. You're going to have to accept it. With that stubborn streak of yours, I realize that may take some time—that's up to you. But I won't live with your thumb on top of me anymore. When you can deal with that, let me know."

She turned toward a terrace she'd been eying all night as an escape.

"Mia..." he said, his voice filled with exasperation.

Ignoring him, she passed onto the terrace and into the cool spring night. Mia needed the chill on her skin to ease her frustration.

The home of the Rough Riders' owner was in the hills of Washington, DC, and in the distance, the mall and all the national monuments lit up the night. This view always took her breath away and softened her rough edges.

She took a few more sips of wine. When she finished this glass, she was going to head back to Tina's for the night. The team's family skate was tomorrow, and she had a few jerseys to finish sewing for the players' wives and girlfriends.

"Hey."

Rafe's low voice sent a shiver down her spine. Excitement and affection collected at the center of her body, but also pain. The pain of knowing she would leave him soon.

Mia fortified herself with another deep drink of her wine, then glanced over her shoulder. "Hey."

He darted a glance back into the house before stepping out onto the terrace with her. It sucked that they had to always be looking over their shoulders for Tate or Joe or someone else who might start a rumor. Or, in this case, deepen the rumor that already existed.

At the railing, he faced her.

"You played an awesome game tonight, Mr. Savage," she told him. "How's your eye?"

His lips tipped up in a grin. "Which one?"

She laughed and looked back out over Washington's monuments.

"Everything okay with Tate?" he asked.

She lifted a shoulder. "Growing pains. He's having a rough transition with my independence."

"I think a lot of that is because you're going to be so far away. I'm having a hard time adjusting too."

She turned her head, surprised he'd admitted it so openly. So directly. And the thought of leaving him now after they'd just broken through a huge barrier upset her stomach again. "The transition will be difficult, no doubt."

Rafe dropped his gaze, nodded, then looked out at the view with a heavy exhale. Long, turbulent moments passed while both remained quiet. His next question verified they were thinking about the same thing.

"What are we going to do, Mia?"

She shook her head and shrugged. "I think we both know there aren't many options."

His jaw jumped with stress. "I don't want to lose this."

Another surprising admission. He was pensive and restless, frowning out at the view. She'd never intended for this to happen. Her plan had backfired. Big-time. She'd opened a door only to tell him he couldn't step through. But this situation wasn't completely her fault. He was equally responsible for this dilemma. And she'd worked too hard to give up the ground she'd gained for a guy who wouldn't even admit they were seeing each other.

He turned his gaze on her, and the look of turmoil in his eyes mirrored the confusion in her gut. "Will you come to California for our Cup games?"

She frowned. Their first two games in the battle for the Cup were in LA. "I'd love to but I don't have the money to fly across the country to watch a couple of games, only to do it again a few days later." He opened his mouth, and she held up a hand. "Please don't offer to pay for it, Rafe."

He exhaled heavily, and his pensive expression turned frustrated. "Why not? I really want you there."

She had the urge to tell him he didn't get everything he wanted. But, judging by his mood, she doubted that would help the situation. "Because we're going to be living across the country from each other in less than a week."

"I know. And I want to spend as much time together as possible while we can."

Mia inhaled deeply, torn. "Rafe, you may be good at messing around and moving on, but I'm not."

His expression tightened, and he took a step toward her, but stopped himself and glanced inside again before returning his gaze. "What we have is more than messing around. You know that."

"That doesn't solve the problems between us." All the more

reason to back off now to give her time to transition into letting him go and living without him. God, that idea hurt more now than ever.

She turned toward him and reached out to touch his shirt, tracing the edge of a button. Rafe caught her hand, leaned away, and glanced toward the house again.

Hurt stabbed at her heart, making her realize that maybe she needed distance even sooner than she'd thought.

Stepping back, she tried to keep the hurt from her voice when she said, "I think I've said hello to everyone. I'm going to head home. Good night."

But when she turned, Rafe put a hand on her arm, dropping it as soon as she met his gaze again. "I was hoping you could come home with me. Maybe tell Tate you're staying with Tina or something?"

Disappointment joined hurt. Disappointment in Rafe, in the situation, and partially in herself. These men just kept putting themselves first. It was clear that if Mia wanted her feelings, her life, and her needs to matter, she was the only one she could control. "Rafe, as I just pointed out to Tate, I'm a grown woman. And I'm done lying about where I'm spending the night to benefit you or Tate or Joe. I'll see you tomorrow at the family skate."

Mia moved into the house, but walking away from him tonight had to be one of the hardest things she'd ever done, and tears prickled her eyes. She'd waited most of her life for Rafe to want her. But wanting her only under certain circumstances, when there was no chance of anyone else finding out, had never entered into her fantasies. And she knew without a doubt, she deserved more than that.

14

Rafe stepped into the house and watched Mia wander toward the front door, saying her good-byes. The sight created an uncomfortable flutter low in his gut. The kind Rafe got when the third period was winding down and he and his team couldn't do anything to make the goal to put them in the lead. That feeling he got when he knew his team was going to lose.

Only with Mia, it was worse. There was an added element of panic trickling through him. And urgency. He was losing her already, and they'd barely just found each other. He knew what she wanted, what she needed—stability, security, assurance that another man wouldn't tell her she was inadequate. Tate was right. She needed things that Rafe couldn't give her. Not in his current situation.

Knowing that not only left a hot coal burning in his gut but made him feel like the biggest loser on the planet.

"Hey, son." Joe came up behind Rafe and clasped him on the shoulder, but his gaze was on Mia as she left. "Mia's headed home?"

"Yeah." Rafe pulled himself as far out of the muck as he could and smiled for Joe. "Having a good time?"

"Always. Great group of people. I'm so glad you and Tate found a family like this." He glanced the direction Mia had gone. "I hope Mia can find the same in Los Angeles."

Rafe should want the same thing, but his heart believed she belonged here. "She's certainly special. If they can't see that in LA, then they're blind."

"I'm really proud of you, Rafe."

He turned his gaze back to Joe. "For what?"

"Patching things up with Mia. I know you two were on the outs for a while." He lifted a shoulder. "I think that happens in any family, especially when things change. Tate's not dealing with Mia's move well, and it's causing a lot of friction between them. But they'll get past it, the same way you and Mia got past your rough spot."

"I'm sure they will," Rafe said, but knew his own rough spots with Mia weren't over. In fact, they just seemed to get rougher and rougher.

"It's so reassuring to me, as a father, to know you'll always take care of her. Do what's best for her. Sometimes kids need guidance from friends their own age to head the right direction. She listens to me, but..." He shrugged and slapped Rafe's arm again. "I'm just...so proud of how you've turned out, Rafe. I couldn't love you more if you were my own flesh and blood. You know that, right?"

Rafe's heart knotted in his throat. He took a second to swallow past it and returned a rough "Of course. I feel the same about you, Joe."

Joe smiled and nodded. "Well, I'm going to head back to the hotel." He reached out to hug Rafe, then pulled back and gently tapped his face. "Be good, son. I'll see you tomorrow."

"Okay." He watched Joe's path toward the door, much the same path Mia had just taken, with his heart aching just as

much. He loved that man. Rafe wasn't ashamed about loving
Joe even more than Rafe loved his own father. Because Joe had
been a hundred times the father to him than his own had been.

"I know you'll always take care of her. Do what's best for her."

Guilt seeped in. He hadn't always done what was right for
Mia. Breaking off communication with her last year had been
right for Rafe, but it had hurt Mia. It could have been a very big
part of Mia taking a job across the country.

If he was going to do what was best for Mia now, it would be
supporting Mia in her move to California. Helping her find her
own success. Without him hovering in the background, holding
her back.

15

Mia paced the lobby of the Rough Riders' practice rink with her phone at her ear, pulled away from the family skate for a conference call with her design team.

She watched the Riders members and their families out on the ice, laughing and chatting. The women all looked adorable in the jerseys Mia had made for them. The fact that every single woman and female child was wearing them warmed her heart, and she was annoyed about missing this short time on the ice.

But this call was her new reality. This call was her future. Missing out on the skate was just another one of the many things she loved that she'd be letting go to claim that future.

The call connected her to a conference room in Los Angeles where the team of designers for *Wicked Dawn*, including the Emmy award–winning costume designer, Marla Cisneros. The fact that Mia would be working beside the woman and these other experienced, talented designers every day still seemed surreal.

Ty Hendrix slid past the window, making a ridiculous face at Mia through the glass. Laughter bubbled up in Mia's chest, but she shooed him away, and Hendrix lowered his head, rounded his shoulders, and glided away like an unwanted puppy.

She grinned, rolled her eyes to the ceiling, and sighed as the lead team designer continued discussing changes for an upcoming season Mia knew nothing about. By the way her boss was warning everyone to clear their calendars, Mia's hopes of coming back to DC soon to visit dwindled. But, judging by how much sleep she'd lost the night before over Rafe and this stupid makeshift familial situation, maybe that was a good thing. But it sure as shit didn't feel good.

Mia had no problem sitting Joe and Tate down and telling them she wanted to pursue a relationship with Rafe. Or that if they truly loved her, they'd support her and be happy for her whether or not things between her and Rafe worked out. Or that if they were going to give her shit about it, despite how much she loved them, she would distance herself. But Rafe had given her every indication he would never do the same, so she doubted she'd have to have the difficult discussion with the other men in her life.

Movement on the rink drew her gaze, and Hendrix drifted by the glass again, the opposite way this time, joined by Tierney, now both of them distorting their handsome faces like idiots. This time, Mia couldn't hold the laughter back. She pulled the phone from her ear and held it against her shoulder while she covered her laugh with the other hand. Inside the rink, the guys high-fived each other.

Get out, she mouthed to them, stabbing her finger toward the ice.

The guys skated off laughing, and Mia smiled with a shake of her head. She brought the phone to her ear again, but her gaze roamed the rink. And while her new boss's voice spilled into her ear, explaining character changes and episode rewrites in the upcoming season and how those would be reflected in the costumes, Mia's gaze held on all the people who'd become more than friends over the years. The wives and girlfriends of the other players who felt like sisters. The players' parents who had become like aunts and uncles. The team members' kids who felt like nieces and nephews.

Her gaze pulled to Rafe like a magnet and held. He was down on the ice, sitting back on his heels, hands held up, acting like a goalie for Andre's two-year-old, Dmitri. The boy was being held up by his father but was holding the stick on his own, swinging awkwardly at the puck and missing. Mia had no idea what was being said between the men, but Rafe and Andre were laughing so hard, they were fighting to stay upright.

The sight infused Mia with a conflicting mix of joy and loss, and tears rushed her eyes.

"That includes you, Mia." Aaron's voice pulled her back to the conversation, which was coming to a close. "Enjoy your family while you have them close. We won't be doling out vacation anytime in the foreseeable future."

That hit her in the gut, but she tapped the Mute button to confirm she'd heard him.

"I know this probably sounds intense," Aaron told Mia, "but I did an apprenticeship for Shay Lawrence when I was just out of school, and if yours has been anything like mine, this is going to feel like a vacation once you settle in."

That brought a round of laughter from the others but didn't quite bring a smile to Mia. Shay Lawrence had been impossible to please, but she'd always been an hour's flight away from people who could make her feel better.

"We're excited to have you," Aaron said. "And if you happen to get into town a few days early, shoot me an email or text. We're having an end-of-episode party this week. It would be a great time for you to meet the crew in a casual setting. We work hard, but we play hard too."

She said her thank-yous and good-byes, but a knot sat in the middle of her chest.

"Enjoy your family while you have them close."

Laughter touched her ears through the glass, and a heavy sadness filled her. She found Rafe again just as Dmitri skated into him. Rafe grabbed the boy and fell backward, lying on the ice and holding Dmitri over him, tickling the boy into fits of giggles.

A wave of emotion overwhelmed her. She turned her back to the rink and covered her face with both hands. Tears leaked from beneath her lashes. "Shit." She took a breath. Another. "Shit, shit, *shit.*"

Mia grabbed hold of her emotions before they completely unraveled, and focused on the big picture. Sliding her hands down to clear her eyes, she stared blankly out the front glass doors to the parking lot.

"I can do this," she whispered to herself.

Her mind darted to other options, but there were no other options. DC was the antithesis of fashion friendly. Her only choice for a decent career was to go back to the fashion industry in New York. Where she couldn't afford to live. Where there was snow and humidity and wall-to-wall people. Where she would work for yet another elitist designer, stifled by being forced to design in their mold. Even in LA, Mia could afford a decent place to live on her own. She already had a friend there. And her job would be exciting and challenging. The things she'd learn would make her stand out among the competition.

This *was* the right choice. It might not feel like it emotionally, but logically, she'd weighed out the pros and the cons dozens of times before she'd made the jump. Now she needed to trust herself.

She nodded, closed her eyes, and wiped the tears that fell. "I can do this. I'll be fine."

Mia shook off the gloom and reentered the arena. Cold hit her face, and laughter touched her ears. The knowledge that she wouldn't be back to participate in another skate like this anytime soon created an ache beneath her ribs. But she'd been through enough transitions in life to know these feelings were normal and that eventually she'd adjust.

She took off her blade guards, and as soon as she glided onto the ice, Lily Croft skated over to show Mia how much the one-foot spin she'd taught the girl had improved. By the time Lily had executed the move, Amy and Rachel were there, demanding to show Mia what they'd learned. Soon, Sarah was standing beside Mia. And Rafe glided into the group as well. He hung back, letting the girls have the spotlight while Sarah and Mia talked, but his presence felt like a tight wire all through her body.

"Fair warning," Sarah told Mia as they all cheered the girls. "Every woman here is jealous of every *other* woman's jersey. You're going to get hit with a dozen requests by the time you leave."

Mia pulled her gaze off Rachel trying to perfect her waltz jump, deliberately kept her eyes off Rafe, and told Sarah, "By the sound of the conference call I just had, I'm not going to have time for anything but breathing in this new job. Everyone's going to have to find another source for their cute jerseys."

Rachel, Amy, and Lily had joined hands and were doing front crossover steps in a circle. Until one of them misstepped, and all of them ended up in a heap on the ice. Sarah moved in to untangle the laughing bundle, and Rafe came up beside Mia.

"Hey, beautiful." His low voice sizzled over her skin. He skated a slow circle around her, those gray eyes smoldering with too many emotions for her to figure out.

"Hey, yourself."

On the next pass, his hand closed gently on her bicep and pulled her along the ice away from the kids. "Skate with me? I'm pretty sure you've already skated with everyone else here."

Which, evidently, somehow made it safe for him to skate with her now.

She let another pang of disappointment ebb, and when he slid his hand down her arm, Mia closed her fingers around his. She fought the curl of pleasure in her belly, the softening of her heart, but that was futile. He'd been able to turn her inside out since she'd been a teenager.

He sped up, turned, and skated backward in front of her, holding out his other hand for hers. When she laid it in his and met his eyes, his smile rewarded her.

"How was your call?" he asked.

"Fine." When she heard her own melancholy, she added, "Good. Exciting. Terrifying. They sound great, even invited me to a work party they're having this week to celebrate the completion of an episode. I thought that was nice, considering I don't even work there yet. But I like the idea that they celebrate every episode, not waiting for an entire line to be produced to have a party, you know? I wish I could have gone to meet them in person for the interview, but..." She shrugged. "I'm sure it will work out fine."

"I think that's a good idea."

Mia pulled herself into an easy forward skate. Rafe's backward skate remained a fluid, graceful glide. God, she'd missed this. Missed just *being* with him. No pressure. No problems. At least none in the moment. "You think what's a good idea?"

"Meeting them before you start working. I also think Sarah's right about the jerseys. I'd like to see you pursue that."

She laughed. "Then you must not have heard me say my job is going to be—"

"Demanding. I heard. Which makes me wonder when you're going to stop working and start living. Your last three jobs were just as all-consuming."

"Says the man drowning in hockey eight months out of the year," she told him.

"We train hard, play hard, but it doesn't take over our lives. We get breaks because the coaches know that working us too hard consistently leads to fatigue and burnout and injuries. There's a difference between hard work and unhealthy work."

"There's also this thing called paying your dues. And I'm not a superstar like some people who get to call their own shots."

"Maybe not, but you've come a hell of a long way. And I think you have the opportunity to do something special with your jersey designs. It couldn't hurt to have a little extra money coming in, either. We both know LA will burn to the ground before you take a dime from Tate or me or even Joe."

"You make that sound like a bad thing."

"Only because it means you'll be on the other side of the country without being able to come see us."

That was a strange thing to hear coming from the man who'd ignored her for a year. But it was also a trap she didn't want to step in here or now, so she changed the subject. "You always were better at figure skating than Tate. Don't tell him I said that. He's always thought he was better."

Rafe's laugh made Mia smile. "What else is new?"

He released one of her hands, and as he pulled her forward, he turned, sliding her beneath his arm until she was wedged beside him, holding her close. All her thoughts evaporated in the feel of Rafe next to her, their steps syncing in a smooth front crossover glide. He was warm and solid and strong. He felt so right. She didn't know how she could have missed him so much in one day, but having him close again now felt so good, it was almost painful.

He tipped his head down and murmured in her ear, "I still think about my diligent teacher every time I step on the ice."

"Bullshit." Mia laughed. "When you're shooting onto the ice from that bench, the only thing on your mind is *score, score, score.*"

"In games, maybe," he said, "but the rest of the time, it's you."

With a mother who worked all the time, an absent father, and a brother whose life revolved around hockey, Mia had a lot of time on her hands as a kid in rural Colorado. She'd taught herself to figure skate, then taught both Tate and Rafe. It had started off as a dare and continued as a challenge. But when they'd realized how much the figure skating drills helped fine-tune their footwork for hockey, they'd both continued the practice, and both continued to skate with Mia over the years.

And Rafe's confession felt like knuckles rapping on her heart. But she was beginning to wonder which parts of what he said were truth and which were created to get the response he wanted. She didn't think he purposely lied to her, but she did believe the seduction aspect of his psyche responded automatically to a woman he wanted much the way his body responded to muscle memory on the ice.

"I did a lot of thinking while I lay awake, wishing you were beside me." Rafe's low voice at her temple created a shiver over her neck and shoulders. "And I think it would be good for you to come to Los Angeles with us."

She huffed a laugh. "Oh, you do, do you?"

"Yeah, I do. You'll be here alone while we're gone and when we get back, we'll only have a couple of days left until you leave again. I want to spend as much time with you as I can before you're gone."

"Enjoy your family while you have them close." Her new boss's words mixed with Rafe's and threw her emotions into another tailspin.

Before she could say anything, Rafe murmured, "Incoming" and released her in a graceful turn. When she focused forward again, she saw Tate and Joe approaching.

Joe's face beamed with a grin. "You two look amazing together."

Tate didn't seem near as pleased, judging by the annoyed look he shot between them.

"I'm pretty rusty," Rafe said, easing away from her.

"Hey," Tate said to Rafe, "Dad's going to be in California to watch the Cup."

Rafe grinned at Joe. "Awesome."

"You should come, Mia," Joe said. "Then the whole family can be together."

Before she could decline, Rafe said, "I was just telling her the same thing. And I think she should bring her jersey designs. Don't you think John Silver would be interested?"

"What?" She frowned at Rafe, confused.

"The Ducks' owner," Joe said with a tug to his brow before his face brightened. "Hey, good thinking."

"What about him?" Tate asked.

Mia wanted to ask the same question. Rafe had played for the Ducks before he became a free agent and signed with the Rough Riders, but he still had a good relationship with the Ducks owner, Silver.

"He's a really innovative guy," Joe told Mia and Tate. "Makes more off merchandising than any other team in the NHL. What a fantastic idea, Rafe."

She was—still—about to decline when Rafe turned one of those looks on her, one with a whole lot of heat simmering in the background. "Then you could watch the first two games of the playoffs, and in between we'd have time to drive around LA, check out your apartment, the hood where you're going to be living. You could even go to that company party you were just telling me about and meet some of your coworkers."

Whoa. Who was this man? Could a true change of heart come so fast?

He must have done *a lot* of thinking last night to develop this plan, because he wasn't just arranging things so he and Mia could be together, he was really thinking about Mia's wants and needs.

Everything inside her softened, emotions whipped up, and her eyes stung. "You know, this whole jersey idea really isn't mine. Sarah started it—"

"Because there is a demand," Rafe said.

"I really don't know anything about the business end of this. I just design—"

"I can help you with all the business, sweetie," Joe offered. "You should at least show the designs to Silver. We can just take it from there. Make it casual. All you need are your sketches and a few photos. I'm sure the girls would love to pose for you."

"Pictures are already all over the Internet," Tate said. "You should take a look. There are all kinds of comments from people asking where they got the tops, wanting them for themselves. You should do this, Mia."

Holy shit. She couldn't remember the last time all three of these men were focused on her. On her life. On advancing her career. Mia was overwhelmed. Aside from that, selling her jersey designs was so out of her current realm of possibility, the thought added more stress. She was having a hard enough time getting her brain around the move to California and working in freaking Hollywood. Taking this leap into selling her designs was another world she knew nothing about and wouldn't have time for with her new job. Then there was Rafe and this crazy revelation that he wanted time with her.

A girl could only take so many learning curves at once.

"It's settled." Joe clapped and swung an arm around Mia's shoulders. "You and I will fly out together. We'll talk business on the flight and catch up with the boys at the hotel."

She should probably be more excited about the business opportunity, but her mind was on Rafe.

Rafe and a hotel.

Rafe and a hotel, and what an absolutely delicious thought that was.

Only... Yeah. Reality.

"Thanks for thinking of me, guys. I'd love to watch you play and check out LA, but I can't. My budget's already stretched tight with the move. I can't do another plane ticket and hotel right now—"

"I'll take care of it." All three men said it at the same time. When they looked at each other, Mia laughed. Her face heated, and she pressed her hands to her cheeks. Rafe might be right about Mia being fiercely independent, but she was also grateful for all their generosity.

Rafe was the first to look back at her. "We all obviously want you there. Let LA burn to the ground for a change, Mia."

Tate gave him a look. "Huh?"

Rafe shook his head. "Something we were talking about earlier."

Oh Lord. The thought of three days and two nights with Rafe... Of course it wouldn't be just Rafe. And with Tate and Joe and the Rough Riders so close, there would be a lot of sneaking around, but she couldn't deny the excitement and hope this little revelation had created—for her relationship with Rafe, to smooth things over with Tate...

Nerves whipped up in her belly, and she pressed a hand to her stomach.

Tate laughed. "That's her nervous tell. She's gonna do it."

Rafe smiled and nodded at Mia, and his expression was filled with a sort of intimate pride. "I'll make the call."

16

Rafe stopped at Mia's hotel room door, blew out a breath, pulled at the cuffs of his shirtsleeves, and knocked. He let his eyes drift to the ceiling, set his feet, clasped one hand over the other. Then took another breath. And let it out slowly.

I'm going to be good.

This is about her business.

This is an important meeting.

The fun stuff can come later.

His teeth clenched, and his eyes closed. God, he wanted the fun stuff now. He hadn't felt Mia in days, and he swore he was going to go insane.

The door handle clicked, and as it opened, Rafe solidified his vow to stick to business for Mia tonight. To win her some confidence with Silver. Maybe even a little business gig on the side. Nothing major. Just a step in the right direction.

"Hey." Her voice dragged his gaze down. "You look as handsome as always."

He saw the flash of a red dress before she opened the door wider and stepped aside to let him in.

"Nice," he said, looking around at the mini suite.

"Joe says they automatically upgrade him because of his frequent-traveler status."

Rafe turned toward Mia at the same time she stepped toward him. Her fingers slipped under the lapels of his blazer, and her body pressed against his. His surprise melted in the warm, curvy, soft feel of her against him. And she smelled like sex on cloud nine. Like wildflowers and passion and heat and desire and... God, he wanted her.

"Wow," he said, stroking his hands over the silky fabric covering her shoulders. "This is a nice surprise."

She let the door close, then slid her hands up to his shoulders. Rafe walked backward, trying like hell to remember the fun stuff was supposed to come later. But his back hit the door, Mia eased against him, and all his blood rushed south. While he was fighting to pull some back to his brain, her hand wound around the back of his neck and pulled his head down.

And as soon as her mouth opened under his, all those great intentions of Rafe's went straight to hell. He groaned, cupped her head, and kissed her back. Licked into her mouth, ate at her lips. God, it felt like he hadn't kissed her in forever. And he didn't realize how hungry he was until he'd tasted her again.

Before he knew how it happened, he had her pinned against the opposite wall, her legs wrapped at his hips, his erection rubbing between her legs. He broke the kiss and pressed his mouth to her shoulder. "Mia," he said, breathless. "Jesus Christ. You make me...*insane*."

She ran her fingers through his hair. Kissed his neck. "We don't have to go. No one will know. Let's stay in—"

"Silver will know." He eased back and released his hold so she slid back to the floor. "Joe and Tate will know."

Pulling away from a beautiful, willing woman had *never* been this painful.

Her big eyes gazed up at him, flooded with heat and

emotion and desire that twisted him inside out. "Let's cancel," she said, her voice husky. "Just tell them I'm not feeling well."

Yes. *Yes, yes, yes.* There was nothing he wanted more. But he said, "No, Mia. This is important."

She sighed, released him, and stepped back. "It's more important to you than it is to me, but I still can't quite figure out why."

"What do you mean, why?" He already missed the feel of her. "It's a great opportunity for you, that's why." He reached up and lifted her hair off her forehead. "And there's a car downstairs waiting. Grab your things."

She moved to the table, picking up a portfolio and clutch purse, and Rafe glanced around the hotel room while he pulled himself together.

"Ready," she said.

Rafe turned toward the door and took his first full look at her. Hundreds of thousands of brain cells instantly imploded. Her dress was indeed red. Fucking fire-engine red. It hugged every perfect curvy line of her beautiful body and made Rafe ache everywhere. It was also that soft see-through material with a solid layer of color beneath. The straps were all sparkles, the bodice barely more than a bikini top. The material was gathered in a crisscross across the top, supporting her breasts in a way that created cleavage Rafe wanted to lose himself in. The knee-length skirt gathered on the side beneath another shiny jewel, giving the dress an uneven hem and Rafe a mouthwatering view of one toned thigh.

"That's, that's..." Yeah, he couldn't find words.

"A mini empire chiffon," she said, looking down.

"No, that's not what I meant. It's..." He shook his head and took her in again, head to toe, then met her gaze. Her hair was in a bun just above her nape, her long bangs loose on one side. It was like seeing her for the first time. Seeing her without all the filters he'd used for years.

"Gorgeous doesn't even begin do it justice. Or *you* justice."
He was blown away by this whole amazing, stunningly strong
woman. "You have never looked more beautiful."

Her expression softened, and her gaze dropped away.
"Thank you."

On the way to the elevator, Mia asked, "Are Joe and Tate
meeting us downstairs?"

Rafe hit the button for the first floor. "No. I got them their
own car." When Mia just lifted one brow, Rafe said, "I wanted
to give you some time to relax before the meeting. And I didn't
think Tate and Joe would let you do that."

Outside, Rafe opened the door to the Lincoln Town Car for
Mia and slid in after her. Champagne was already waiting in
chilled glasses. Rafe gave the driver their destination, the time
they needed to arrive, and asked him to take the long way. Then
he lifted the smoked glass between the compartments,
stretched out his legs, and sighed.

Now, if he could just keep a couple of feet between him and
Mia for the next half hour...

He picked up the champagne glasses, offered one to Mia,
then raised his own. "To new business ventures."

Mia tapped his glass, then tipped her champagne back,
drinking until it was gone.

Now it was Rafe's turn to lift a brow. "Are you okay?"

She sighed, set the glass back, then shifted on the seat,
curling up real close until her breasts and belly pressed against
his arm. Her flat hand slid across his abdomen, and heat
flooded south.

Rafe put his own champagne away before he spilled it, and
stroked a hand over her arm. Screw distance. This was way
better. He circled an arm around her shoulders and pulled her
closer. And when he looked down at her, she was staring back
with these big green eyes.

"What is this really about for you, Rafe? Wanting me on this trip. Setting up this meeting..."

He changed the subject. "Are you still planning on going to your work party tomorrow night?"

She nodded and set the glass back in the holder.

When she didn't go on, Rafe said, "I'd be happy to go with you if you don't want to go alone. You don't have to claim me as anything other than a friend, and I won't cling and cramp your style. Just an offer in case you, you know, would like a familiar face in the crowd."

She sighed and glanced around the car's interior with a distracted "That would be nice."

Rafe reached over and put his hand on her knee. The warmth and softness of her skin registered immediately. "Mia, what's wrong?"

Her gaze came around. "This is all incredibly extravagant, but..." She shook her head and angled to face him. "I don't understand this push. I don't want this, Rafe. Honestly, I'm here because it was so important to all of you for me to do this. I'm barely keeping my calm with everything I've already got going.

"This new, demanding job in this new, demanding field, working with new people, across the country from the people I love most. Living in a new apartment with a new roommate, in a new town with a new culture. Even the weather is all different. I think that's enough to adjust to. This probably isn't the best time to take on the freelance design market. We can't all be stellar shots on the spur of the moment in any situation."

"Mia," he said, his voice filled with apology, "that's not why—"

"And to be honest," she cut him off, "if I'm going to use what little energy I have toward something, it's going to be toward figuring out what's going on with us. Then figuring out how I'm going to leave it behind in a very short time. I came on this trip *hoping* I'd get more of you than a quickie before the games.

Hoping we could talk about what you said yesterday on the ice."

His stomach and heart squeezed at the same time. "You're always so clearheaded. So straightforward. I wish I was half as sharp."

"Says the man leading his team into the Stanley Cup playoffs." She shifted on the seat, curling up real close until her breasts and belly pressed against his arm. Her hand slid across his abdomen and heat flooded south. "What is this really about for you, Rafe?"

"This is about something special, just for you, Mia." He covered her hand with his own. "All your life, everything has been about me and Tate. We've gotten all the attention, all the breaks, all the opportunities, all Joe's time. You said it yourself; you get the leftovers. You've always lived in our shadows, and it's a crime. You're so talented, so smart, and you work so damn hard for everything you have. Success is about three things— talent or knowledge, taking or making opportunities, and who you know. You've mined the hell out of two of those assets. I think if you take that last step, you're going to find that you're ready to stop working for other people. And I'd really like to see the fruits of all your talent, smarts, and hard work come back to you for a change. *That's* what this is about."

She searched his eyes, clearly skeptical. "Why now?"

"Because you're different. I don't know if it was your last apprenticeship or your last relationship or our time apart over the last year, or all of it, but you've grown. You're..." He exhaled. "I don't want you to take this wrong, which is probably impossible, but you're just more...mature. You've always been sensible and responsible and compassionate. But now you're just, I don't know, now you're savvy. Clever. Charming in a different, more worldly way." While still being the girl next door, which made him absolutely crazy. "And your designs..."

He glanced down—something he'd been trying not to do.

Her breasts swelled into the sheered fabric crisscrossing the bodice, her skin smooth and glowing. Swells and skin he wanted in his hands, his mouth. He wanted her so bad, every cell of his body ached with the need.

Swallowing against a dry throat, he asked, "Is this another one of yours?"

"Yes." Her answer was smooth and soft and leading. "Do you like it?"

He wasn't going there. "You've really broken out, baby. Your designs are sophisticated and bold and beautiful." He pried his gaze from the length of her smooth thigh stretching from beneath the short hem. "Yet you can whip out fun, stylish jersey designs on the spur of the moment and produce them in a matter of days. I don't have to be fluent in design to know that's an incredibly valuable asset. The fact that Hollywood snapped you up is confirmation."

He lifted his hand to her face and tilted it up to his. Her lips were parted and just inches away. He needed to taste her. *Needed it.*

"Just talk to him. If it's not for you, fine. If the opportunity presents itself and you want to explore it, great. But don't close the door before you even check it out. You're so ready to take this step."

Her eyes searched his, and a soft smile turned her mouth, one that pulled him back in time. "Sometimes I still see that kid you used to be. A smile, a look, and you drag me back to those Colorado summers."

Rafe might not have noticed her when he'd been sixteen and she'd been fourteen, but when she'd turned sixteen and he'd been eighteen, that changed—in a big way. She hadn't just blossomed into a woman, she'd exploded. Rafe remembered it as an overnight transformation from the skinny, leggy fifteen-year-old tomboy challenging him and Tate to springtime figure skating competitions on the local pond, into the curvy, eye-popping, sixteen-year-old lifeguarding at the local pool.

"It was a good thing I got swept away by the Eagles," he said, mentioning the farm team he'd joined that summer. "Otherwise, my hormones would have overridden my brain and there would have been hell to pay with Tate."

Which would have ended his relationship with Joe. And those two men were the reason Rafe was where he was today. The main reason Rafe had all he had.

She smiled. "I miss those days." She pulled her hand from under Rafe's and stroked it across his belly, stirring heat. "And I still prefer that old truck of yours to this ride. Those greasy burgers at the café on the corner to whatever five-star restaurant we're going to tonight. If you lost everything now..." She lifted a shoulder, and her lips curved in the slightest smile. "I'd still hang with you."

Rafe laughed. His heart softened. And yearned. She was everything he couldn't find in any other woman. All she'd been to him in the past. All she'd stayed to him over the years. All she'd become to him as he'd risen to the top of his profession. She knew him. Understood him. And loved him anyway.

"I know you probably prefer those silly puck bunnies I see you with in the media." She kept stroking her hand back and forth over his dress shirt, but her fingers got lower with every pass. "So I guess I can pretend to be one of those for now, go meet this important person, play the superficial socialite."

With her eyes holding his, she lowered her hand to his belt and hooked one leg over his thigh. Then her fingers went to work on his buckle. Excitement fired through Rafe's veins. He circled her wrists and darted a look at the driver. But the glass was in place, and the man behind the wheel was singing along to whatever was on the radio.

Rafe looked back at her and found her eyes heavy and hungry. She pulled his belt open.

"You wanted to get away from me a couple days ago," he told her. "What changed?"

She twisted her arm from his hand, draped her leg all the way across both his thighs, and slid right onto his lap. Rafe's heart rate spiked. His lungs shrank. And his cock throbbed.

"Someone suggested I enjoy the people in my life while I have them close." Both her hands worked his button open and his zipper down. Her biceps crowded her breasts, deepening the cleavage there and making Rafe moan. "The way I feel about you hasn't changed for fifteen years. It's not going to change now. Leaving you will be the hardest thing I've ever done, no matter what happens between us."

Rafe's heart skipped, opened, and ached. He laid his head back against the seat and cupped her face. "Mia."

Then her hand slipped beneath his boxers and stroked down his shaft.

Pleasure rolled through his lower body. Excitement sparked all along his spine. Rafe gritted his teeth around "*God,* Mia."

And while she continued to stroke him, she used her other hand to cover his, now clutching her jaw, and pulled it under her dress and between her legs.

She was naked. No panties. Just perfectly soft, perfectly sweet, perfectly Mia.

"And I really," she said softly, leaning in to tease his lips with a kiss, "want to enjoy you, Rafe."

The sensual tone of her voice tightened his gut. She covered his mouth with hers, tugging his lips between her own one at a time, sinking her teeth in just to the edge of pain, then licking and sucking and stroking her tongue into his mouth. Twirling it with his until her pussy wet Rafe's fingers. The she pulled back and looked into his eyes as she lowered onto his cock.

Slow, slow, slowly, until Rafe was grinding his teeth. Until her knees stretched wide. Until she took all of him.

Her eyes slid closed, her brow tightened, her lips parted, and she moaned, "So... good."

Rafe's control slipped. Her body was so...fucking...perfectly wrapped around him, sweat broke out on his forehead. "Mia." Her name came out of him like a guttural growl. "Mia, Mia, Mia..."

He pushed her skirt out of the way, dug his fingers into her hips, and rocked her on his cock.

"Oh my God," she moaned.

He loved knowing what she liked. Loved knowing exactly how to please her. He lifted her, just as slowly, watching his cock slide from her pussy, engorged and glistening. Bare. Skin on skin. The pleasure of it—both physically and emotionally—was blistering hot.

Before he was ready, she lowered her hips and plunged him deep. Pleasure ripped through his pelvis and teased his spine. Stars lit off behind his eyes.

Mia braced her hands on his shoulders, and with her eyes half-closed, her teeth scraping over her bottom lip, she held his gaze as she set a rhythm. A hypnotic, mind-bending rhythm.

"Mmmm," she moaned, her voice tight. "Missed this."

Then she kissed him, her mouth just as hot and hungry as her pussy. Her hips quickened, and she lifted her lips to whisper, "God...I love the way you feel...inside me."

The statement thrilled him. Lust surged. Emotions tangled. "You're so sexy." He pulled her mouth back to his tasting her, connecting with her, loving her. "Mia, baby, Mia..."

He loved saying her name. It reminded him this was reality, not a dream. Not a fantasy. He was loving Mia—*his Mia*—the way he'd always dreamed of loving her. She was a fantasy come true. Knowing she was slipping away like sand through his fingers made his need even more urgent. More intense. And when she climaxed, it was way too soon for Rafe.

He pulled her mouth against his shoulder to muffle her

cries, but the triumph, the satisfaction, the love that swelled inside him made him even more ravenous. He rested a moment while Mia shivered in his arms. She turned her head, and her hot breaths bathed his neck. He ran a hand through her hair and realized her clip had fallen out. The silky strands between his fingers brought back memories of their first night. Of the way he'd skimmed his fingers through her hair while she slept. Tears burned his eyes out of nowhere.

"We can make this work." His rasp came as barely more than a whisper. He hadn't even fully thought the words before they touched his own ears. And he immediately knew they were a wish, not a fact. "I want to make this work, Mia."

"Shhh." She took his face in both hands and brought her lips to his again. "Don't. Just enjoy what we have while we have it." And when she kissed him again, Rafe released the restraint on his passion. He gripped the back of her neck and held her head to his own, lifting his hips to drive into her.

Mia turned her head, pressed her mouth to his hair, and murmured a frantic stream of "Rafe, oh God Rafe. Yes, yes, yes..."

Until she broke again. Until her pussy squeezed his cock and spilled her juice and Rafe let go. His orgasm surged through him like liquid fire, searing pleasure through his body from his pelvis out. He tipped his head and pressed his mouth to Mia's neck to smother his groan.

But when the pleasure receded to a low, pleasant burn, his throat thickened with emotion. As if the orgasm had cleared his brain, he could see all too clearly that he was going to lose her. And not just to California. He was going to lose her entirely. She was going to move on with her life, grow and change and experience things, and Rafe would be too far away and too busy with his own demanding career to share them with her. Then she'd find someone else, someone closer who appreciated her like he did.

God, he felt like she was already gone, and he was still inside her.

Mia melted against him, boneless, her cheek on his shoulder. Rafe went lax into the seat beneath him, closed his eyes, and tried like hell to absorb the absolute perfection of the moment. He would give up everything in his bank accounts right now to be able to hold on to this, hold on to Mia, and still keep his best friend and Joe.

"So," Mia said, voice languid and soft, "when I act like a zombie in this meeting, I can blame it on you, right?"

He smiled. "Uh, no. Who climbed on top of who?"

She exhaled. "Ah, right." Mia pushed back, gave him a tired, lazy smile, and stroked his face. Her gaze lowered to his mouth and went distant, her expression a little melancholy. "And here I always thought those divas were clamoring to hang on your arm for your looks and your heart. Little did I know..." She laughed softly and shook her head, more *stupid me* than humor. She sighed and brightened her smile. "I guess I'd better get myself back together."

Rafe cupped her face in both hands and pulled her in for another kiss. He wanted to tell her she was wrong, but she wasn't. Women did come to him for a good time, which included sex. All kinds of sex. All but the real kind. The kind that involved emotion. The kind he had with Mia.

He leaned back with the wild urge to tell her that she was different. That she'd always been different. That he wanted so much more than they had. Having Mia within reach suddenly made picking up a different woman every other night a chore. He was tired of wondering where Mia was, what she was doing, and who she was doing it with. Tired of worrying about her and wondering whether she was happy or hurting. Damn sick and tired of missing her. But most of all, he was tired of hiding his feelings from everyone—including himself. It was exhausting.

He reached for the strap of her dress that had fallen off her shoulder and put it back into place, searching for the words to open that subject, while knowing there was no point.

She lifted herself off him just as the car slowed. Rafe glanced out the window for the first time, where a row of upscale shops and restaurants lined the street. Her gaze strayed the same direction as she grabbed some napkins from the bar and tossed him a few.

"Someone lined up a very haute couture sort of evening," she said with a sassy little smile. But Rafe wasn't feeling sassy or happy. "And with Tate and Joe on the other side of the table, I'd better put myself back into that pretty little box they expect."

As they cleaned up, disappointment knotted in the pit of Rafe's stomach. Once he had himself put back together, he said, "Mia..."

She pulled skimpy red lace panties from her purse and slipped them over her heels and under her skirt. That did make him smile. It also made him forget what he was going to say. Probably something they'd already talked about. Probably something their situation rendered moot.

She grinned in return and lifted her hands to her hair, shaking her the dark strands. Rafe unknotted his tie, rolled it around his hand, then slid it into his pocket while Mia collect her shiny clip again and expertly refasten her hair into a pretty bun. After a quick look in a small mirror and a dab of lip gloss, she leaned in to straighten Rafe's collar and tame his hair.

The driver rounded the back of the car and stood at the rear door.

Rafe cupped her face. "Hey, don't be nervous. Silver's a really nice guy."

Mia grinned with a flash of white teeth and a sparkle in her eyes. "I'm not nervous." She patted his chest pocket, his side pockets, then opened her purse and dug around. "I've been to hundreds of these meetings over the last few years." She clipped her purse closed and slid a pen into his front breast pocket. "I can't believe you and Tate still leave the house without a pen when you know at least a dozen people will want autographs." With one more look over him, she exhaled and smiled. "Okay, you're set."

Then she pushed the door open, and the driver took her hand, helping her to the curb.

Rafe hesitated a moment, trying to figure out the uncomfortable buzz in his gut. He felt vaguely...serviced.

Screwed. Straightened. Handed a pen for signatures.

Just as he grabbed the doorframe to step out, someone bent to look inside. Rafe leaned back and focused on the face and found Tate. Grinning.

"What the hell are you doing in here, dude?"

Rafe lifted a brow at him. "Dude?"

"We're in California."

Rafe laughed, planted a hand on top of Tate's head, and pushed. "Get out."

Damn, he wished he didn't love this idiot so much. Or wished he loved Tate's sister less.

When Rafe stood, he found Mia near the door to the restaurant, talking with Joe. She still took his breath away. And he wasn't the only guy who noticed how gorgeous she looked. A group of three businessmen waiting for a cab were all staring at her. Mia either didn't know or didn't care. She had her arm linked with Joe's, her smiling face turned up to his as he talked about something.

Rafe pulled his wallet from his pocket and drew out cash for the driver's tip. He tuned in to Mia's sweet laugh and Joe telling her some funny story about his Metro ride.

"I just talked to Tierney," Tate said as Rafe handed the money to the driver and thanked him.

"Yeah?" he asked absently, stuffing his wallet away. He took a step toward Mia and Joe, but Tate put a hand on Rafe's arm.

"The Hardys are in town for the playoffs."

Rafe quickly associated the name with the liquor company, a large Rough Riders sponsor. "And?"

"And they're hosting a concierge floor at the Marquis." Tate's voice rang with excitement. The Marquis was Anaheim's version of the Four Seasons. "A *floor*, dude, not a suite."

"Cool. Have fun. I'm not bailing on Mia after setting up this meeting."

Tate stopped Rafe's forward momentum again, and Mia glanced toward them.

"It's not optional. Everyone is somewhere tonight." Tate rattled off a dozen other names of team members doing their part to schmooze sponsors. "We just happened to luck out and scored the best gig. Hendrix and Tierney are already there, and the sponsors are expecting you and me to show up sometime tonight. Tierney's been texting me pictures. The chicks are smokin' hot."

Rafe raised his brows at Tate. His friend had—as far as Rafe knew—been celibate since his shitty wife had bailed. "You talk as if you're actually going to do something with one of them."

Tate smacked Rafe in the chest. "Shut the hell up. We're going. And maybe I will."

"Fine." He took another couple of steps. "When this meeting is over, I'll catch up—"

"No, man." Tate stopped him again. "The party's been going for an hour. You wait until the meeting with Silver's over and everyone who matters is going to be so hammered, they aren't going to even remember you were there."

"Then it's not worth going at all, is it?"

"I told you, this isn't optional—"

"It's okay." Mia's voice pulled Rafe's attention. She wore a cardboard smile and fluttered a hand toward them. "Go do your thing. Have fun. I'll make your excuses."

His stomach dropped to his feet. "Mia—"

"Silver knows all about sponsors," she said. "He'll understand, but you should go before he comes. Otherwise, he'll trap you in conversation and all the hottest girls will be snapped up. I'm going to turn in early, so kick ass tomorrow, guys."

That phrase hammered Rafe in the gut. The same phrase she'd left on the dresser when she'd bailed on him in the hotel their first night.

"And Rafe?" This time her smile was authentic. She tipped her head in that sweet way that made his stomach ache, and gestured toward the restaurant. "Thanks for this."

Then she disappeared inside with Joe.

And all Rafe could do was clench his teeth, stuff his fisted hands into the pockets of his blazer, and rail silently.

Fuck, fuck, fuck.

17

Now that the meeting with Silver was behind her, Mia could focus on her future.

She watched the taxi ease toward her at the hotel's entrance, trying to keep her mind off Rafe by worrying about her attire. She smoothed the fabric of her long, wrap-around skirt, muttering, "God I hoped I'm not underdressed."

Aaron had said California casual. But for someone who'd never even been to the state, California casual meant nothing. Now, standing at the curb, she was worried the halter top with lace from the A-line to her navel was too revealing. And the clingy fabric of her skirt with sandals might be pushing it, even for a California beachside bar. She was going to be meeting her future coworkers, and first impressions were important.

But the cab was here, so she exhaled and tried to release the stress lying heavily in the pit of her stomach. Her mind veered back to Rafe. She was disappointed that he wasn't coming, but after watching him leave the night before with Tate for an impromptu-but-mandatory night surrounded by quality booze and puck bunnies, she knew it was best. She gave the "love him while you can" method a go. But she hadn't slept when she'd returned to the hotel. And she knew Rafe and Tate hadn't returned until the early morning hours because she'd talked to Joe at two a.m. when he'd texted with *Have you heard from the boys?*

She was doing the right thing, easing Rafe back where he belonged—out of her life and into his own. He'd played another great game, the perfect kick-start to the final playoffs. He should be out celebrating with his team, not acting like her security blanket.

But as the taxi slid into place at the curb, Mia had to accept that the nerves strung tight across her shoulders wouldn't be loosening up until she suffered through introductions at the party on her own and got a few drinks in her. Or maybe not until she'd moved into Danielle's apartment. Or until she'd found her local grocery store, gym, gas station, and Starbucks.

A young valet leaned in and smiled as he opened the door. "Here you go, miss. Do you need directions or recommendations tonight?"

Yes, she needed step-by-step directions on how to go back in time and unsleep with a man. She also needed recommendations on how to find and live on a remote island where no one had ever heard of the game of hockey.

"No," she said, returning his smile, "thank you."

She gave the driver the address of the bar in Long Beach where the crew was meeting, then settled back in the seat.

Before the valet had even closed the door, she was struck by how very different this situation was from the night before. Memories of her fairy-tale-like ride just twenty-four hours ago made a melancholy smile turn her lips.

"Mia!" Rafe's voice pulled her attention back just before the door closed on a *click*.

She sat there a long second, unsure whether to respond or ignore him.

Rafe made the decision for her when he opened the door, a

look of complete confusion on his face. "What are you doing? I thought we were going together."

He was wearing what he usually wore into the stadium on game day—a charcoal-gray suit and a crisp white button-down, minus the tie. His freshly showered scent drifted in and teased Mia's nose. And, damn, she hated seeing him so soon after a game. His hair was still wet, his face still flushed, his eyes still sparkling from all that adrenaline. Heat stirred between her legs.

Dammit.

"You must not have gotten my message." She went for cool but not bitchy. "I said—"

"Great game? Celebrate with the guys, I'm going to do the party on my own? Screw that." He slid in beside her and closed the door. The driver peered over his shoulder, his dark eyes darting between them. "Go wherever she told you to go."

The driver cut a look at Mia. She sighed, nodded, and avoided talking to Rafe until they were on the road and the angry aura around him had simmered down a notch.

"Thought you'd be in a pretty good mood tonight," she said. "You kicked ass in the game." She looked at the rasp above his left eye. The one he'd gotten from a header into the boards. A header that had cut off Mia's air for long seconds until he stood up again. "You should probably put ice on that."

"I was going to grab some at your room," he bit out, cutting her an angry look, "but you weren't there."

"If you had read your messages," she said trying to hold her own temper, "you would have known I wouldn't be there."

"I didn't check my messages because I was hustling to get ready so I wouldn't make you late."

"Don't take out your pissy mood on me. Dekker's the one who slammed you into the boards."

"Dekker's not the one who put me in this pissy mood."

"Why are you yelling at me?"

"Because you just tried to ditch me, and you've ignored my texts all day when you're the only thing I can think about."

He hooked a hand around her neck, pulled her in, and covered her mouth with his. An angry murmur vibrated in her throat, and she pushed a hand against his chest. Rafe broke the kiss and curled his fingers into her hair, making her gasp. Then kissed her again. Taking advantage of her parted lips, he plunged his tongue into her mouth, stealing her breath.

Mia's frustration melted in the heat, and she tightened her fingers in his shirt. Rafe hummed into her mouth, the sound hungry and pained as he took the kiss deeper. Then he tipped his head and cradled hers in the crook of his elbow. His other arm slipped around her waist and tightened.

His heart thundered beneath her palm. His tongue warmed her mouth. Mia wanted to drown in him. Wanted to beg him to make her world stop spinning out of control.

He broke the kiss and dropped his forehead against her shoulder while he gasped for air.

When he didn't speak, Mia eased her hold on his neck. "I need to make a good first impression on these people. You know, pretend I'm stable. Someone with a normal life who will be dependable and predictable. Not someone who does rash, risky things that disrupt everyone around me. And as volatile as you and I have been lately, I thought it would be better for us to retreat back into our own lives. We have to do it soon anyway."

"The reason we are so volatile is because we're always worried about Tate finding out." He lifted a hand to her face and cupped it. "This is the perfect opportunity for us to be together without anyone watching. Just be ourselves with each other without worries we'll be seen or word will get back to Tate."

That might or might not be true, she didn't know. It all depended on how closely this group followed hockey. "You make it sound like we haven't already known each other for twenty years."

"What is wrong with you tonight? Why are you so angry?"

Mia's patience snapped. "Because I'm leaving you in a couple of days. Because I have to learn how to live without you in my life all over again." She hadn't meant to yell, but her words reverberated in the cab, and the driver cast frightened looks in the rearview mirror. "I shouldn't have come. I should have known I couldn't keep things casual with you. Why couldn't you have been an asshole after we slept together the first time? Why do you have to be so, so, so damn *you*?"

She looked out the side window, and the streetlights and taillights blurred in the tears filling her eyes. Which, of course made her angry. "Damn you," she said with less force as she wiped at her eyes. "Now you're going to make my mascara smear."

Rafe swallowed her in a hug, pulling her into his body and pressing his face to her hair. "Stop," he murmured, holding her tight. "Stop, Mia. I'm right here."

But he wouldn't be right there for long, and the realization turned her into a freaking faucet. And even though she tried to push Rafe away, he held tight, reassuring her with a patient, warm voice. "Shhh, I know this is hard. I know you're scared. It's going to be okay, baby. It's going to be better than okay. They're going to love you. You're going to love them. Shhh…"

When she quieted, he loosened his hold but didn't let go. Pulling back, he used one hand to wipe at her tears. "Let's just be Mia and Rafe tonight. Put hockey and Tate and Joe in the closet. I want to meet the people you're going to work with, hear about your job, watch you make new friends." He combed his fingers into her hair and let them sift through. "I'm not gonna lie, I *don't* want you across the country from me, Mia, but I know you can't do what you want to do in DC. And I really do want you to be happy and successful."

She sighed and broke eye contact, focusing on the buttons of his shirt.

"What do you say?" he asked, his rough fingers skimming across her cheek. "Just a night out? You and me, being you and me?"

The thought of having him by her side did settle her nerves a little. "Yeah," she breathed. "Okay."

He kissed her forehead and sat back against the seat, pulling her with him. "You look gorgeous."

She huffed a laugh. "Thank you."

"Tell me about your meeting with Silver. Joe told me a little bit. What did you think? How did you feel?"

That was a bit of a double-edged sword considering it brought up the memory of him bailing for a party with Tate. The fact that he couldn't have done anything different without going against his coach's orders and his owner's expectations or raising suspicion about their relationship didn't ease Mia's hurt or disappointment.

"It's moot," she said. "He's got a year left in his contract with the firm designing and manufacturing the team's current retail jerseys. He was excited about mine, loved all the industry data I came with, said he wants to meet again closer to the time his contract expires, but a year is a long time. A lot can happen in a year. Who knows what the market will do, what he'll want, where the team will be, where the industry will be." She shook her head and shrugged. "It may be a good idea, but unless I'm ready to run with it in the moment, there's no point pitching it. And I'm miles away from being able to run with it."

"You wouldn't be if you—" Rafe started.

"Don't, Rafe. Don't throw money at me."

"I'm not throwing it. I'm offering it. I'll invest, we can make it a loan, do it however you need to do it to make you comfortable with taking it. I just want to see you break that damn glass ceiling—"

"And I *want* to do this *myself*." She pulled back to meet his eyes. "Why don't any of you understand why it's important to me to do it on my own? You and Tate and Joe have been there for me my whole life. You've all been constant safety nets. You said you wanted that meeting last night so I could have something of my own. This"—she pointed to the floor of the cab— "this is my own. This job. This career. Whatever I make out of it. This is mine. If I take money from any of you, no matter what you call it, I'm giving you a piece of my success, and I've done that all my life. You and Tate made your success on your talent and your hard work. I just want to do the same."

Rafe exhaled and pressed his lips together.

"It may not happen fast enough for you," she said, "but it will happen."

"Okay, okay," he said, tucking a strand of hair behind her ear.

For the rest of the drive, he kept her close, and they talked about the game. About strategy they planned to try next game. Revisited their plans for the following day.

When a natural lull slipped into their conversation, Mia looked out the window.

"Nothing happened last night," Rafe said softly. "At the party, I mean."

She nodded, and another lull fell.

"Did Tate see anyone he was interested in?" she asked.

"He talked to a lot of women. At least a freaking dozen hit on him. Another half dozen offered to blow him in the parking —" He stopped short, then swore.

A huff of laughter escaped Mia. "Which means two dozen hit on you and a dozen offered to—"

"It doesn't matter how many women do or offer anything. Because just like Tate, I wasn't interested in any of them."

But Mia knew all about Rafe's lifestyle. And she wasn't naïve enough to think it would turn on a dime because of her.

Not when she lived across the country. But the thought of him with another woman would completely snap the last fiber of sanity holding Mia together, so she pushed it out of her mind.

They turned off the freeway to signs signaling Long Beach. Then the taxi slowed in front of a nondescript six-foot-high ivy hedge running over a hundred feet along the road bordering the ocean. Only one door led through the vine wall, and it was closed. No sign marked the property. The area was definitely commercial, with other shops and restaurants lining both sides of Highway One, but...

The taxi driver stopped and tapped the meter. "Cash or credit?"

Rafe pulled his wallet from his pocket. "Credit."

"Are you sure we're at the right place?" she asked the driver.

"Sullivan's," he said, casually tossing a gesture toward the unmarked property. "Right there."

While Rafe paid, Mia stepped out and looked around. The fog was still out over the ocean and a soft, heavenly salty breeze whispered over her skin. Rafe came around the car to her side, and the taxi started down the quiet road. The two of them stood there in the night bathed by the sound of ocean waves in the distance and laughter drifting from behind the ivy privacy barrier.

Mia took a deep breath and let it out, but nerves still buzzed in her belly. Then Rafe's hand encircled hers, warm and gentle. She looked up at him and found him smiling.

"Welcome to your future, beautiful. Seems pretty damn nice so far."

Mia filled with so much love, the words almost spilled out. Giddiness replaced her unease. Gripping his lapels, she pushed to her toes, leaned into him, and kissed him. "That's for chasing me down and being here with me."

His fingers skimmed her face, his eyes warm and serious. "I could say the same."

They kissed, and Mia felt that familiar shift inside her again. One that was happening far too often. She lowered and stepped toward the mysterious door. The handle turned easily enough in Rafe's hand, and he stepped aside, letting Mia go ahead.

Passing through the door felt a little like stepping into another world. White lights were strung between trees and poles. Lanterns lit each patio table. A large outdoor fireplace roared with crackling wood. Waves washed the moonlit beach beyond the restaurant, which sat on a cliff.

Mia felt like she'd walked into a fairy tale.

"There she is." The excited female voice drew Mia's attention. Cynthia rushed over to her, arms outstretched, her dark face glowing with a gorgeous smile. "*Mia.*"

She wrapped Mia in her arms, and they hugged tight, rocking back and forth.

"Oh my God," Mia said, "you got rid of your dreads." She pulled back and looked at her friend again. Her black hair, once held in carefully tended dreadlocks to her shoulders, was now a frisky, cropped headful of tiny coils. "God, I *love* it. You look *beautiful.*"

She laughed. "So do you. It's so good to see you. I'm so excited you're here." Releasing her, Cynthia slid her hand down Mia's arm and tugged her forward. "Let me introduce you— Aaron," she yelled across the patio filled with people. "Mia's here."

Mia swore every head turned. She experienced a millisecond of *oh shit*, until everyone smiled, raised whatever they were drinking, and shouted boisterous rounds of "*Mia!*"

She was laughing when she reached for Rafe. He was standing back, hands in his pants pockets. And when she hooked her hand through his elbow and met his eyes, she found him smiling. His expression filled with a sweet, raw, real joy. Joy that she was the center of attention.

"Come on. Let me introduce you," she said. "Cynthia, this is one of my best friends in the world, Rafe."

Rafe offered his hand and a genuine greeting.

"Rafe," Cynthia said, "you have good taste in friends."

"And I have good taste in designers." The man who came to Cynthia's side was white, in his midthirties, good-looking, and gregariously friendly. He offered his hand to Mia first, then Rafe. "Aaron. So glad you could make it."

The gate behind them opened, drawing Aaron's and Cynthia's gazes. Mia turned to a well-dressed older couple arriving to a cheering crowd.

"Wouldn't you know it?" Aaron said to Cynthia, grinning. "Just like Tony and Martha to steal the limelight." Without waiting for an answer, he turned to Mia and Rafe. "It's the producer and his wife. Let me just give Tony the costume costs of this episode, and I'll be right back with you."

"Of course," Mia said.

Aaron gripped her shoulders, gave her a little shake, and said, "So glad to have you, Mia."

A laugh of surprise popped out of her, making Aaron smile. He released her, told them to help themselves to anything, mingle, and he'd find them again, then moved on.

Cynthia took over, sliding her arm through Mia's and staying close by her side as she walked her through the patio, all while Rafe hung back. But every time she turned to look for him, he was right there with a reassuring smile.

Mia had lost count of how many people Cynthia introduced her to when she finally stopped and tugged on her friend's arm. "Uncle. I'm never going to remember everyone's name, let alone their faces and their positions. I've hit my threshold."

Cynthia laughed. "Yeah, you're right. I'm just so excited. You're going to *love* it here, Mia."

She smiled and nodded, sure Cynthia would have been right if it hadn't been for the man standing behind her. The man she reached back for now. The man who easily wrapped her hand in his like he'd done it a million times, threaded their fingers and gave her a squeeze of reassurance. If it weren't for Rafe, Mia might have been able to be very happy here. And maybe, in time, she still would be.

"Well, it just so happens this is the perfect place to end our tour," Cynthia said, wandering toward one of the most bois-terous tables on the patio. There were four men sitting in chairs and four women either in chairs or on the men's laps. One of the men and a couple of the women looked familiar, but the only one she could pin down was the golden-haired beauty closest to Mia. A woman who was either Giselle Diamond, the newest breakout country music mogul, or her twin. Cynthia put her hand on one of the men's shoulders and grinned at Mia. "I call this the Los Angeles-is-for-beautiful-people table."

While Mia agreed wholeheartedly, the group at the table erupted in guffaws and snark. Various items were thrown in Cynthia's direction, making her squeal, and laughter erupted from everyone in a thirty-foot radius.

Rafe slipped his arms around Mia's waist from behind, and his laugh vibrated into her back.

"This is our stunt team, the Renegades," Cynthia said, still laughing. "They're based here in LA, and they helped us finish up our episode today. Jax, Wes, Keaton, and Troy. And these are their beautiful ladies, Lexi, Rubi, Brooke, and Ellie. Renegades, this is Mia, a new addition to our costume team, and her boy Rafe."

"Oh my God." This came from the stunning—as in gorgeous beyond words—woman draped over Wes's Lap. Fighting through the catalogue of names, Mia decided that would make the woman Rubi. "You're in the costume depart-ment? Don't you dare tell me you made that." One long, red-tipped finger moved up and down Mia's body. "But you'd better tell me where you bought it, because I have *got* to have it."

Without taking her eyes off Mia, she tipped her head and spoke to Wes. "Don't you think that would look good on me, baby?"

Wes's grin was pure kid-in-a-candy-store joy. "You look good in anything, and you look good in nothing. I will take you any way you come and any way I can get you."

Rubi's own smile beamed, and her attention veered from Mia's outfit back to her boyfriend. "I sort of ask those things just to hear you say that."

"I sort of already know that," he said, "and I sort of never get sick of saying it."

"Get a roooooooo—" Troy's bitch was cut off by his girl-friend's mouth as she kissed him, making the group laugh.

Then Rubi's gaze returned to Mia, sharp and intent. "I'm totally serious. I'll pay you a thousand dollars to make me what you're wearing." Mia didn't even get a chance to inhale before Rubi said, "Okay, two thousand."

"Um, I—" Mia started.

"Damn, you drive one hell of a hard bargain, girl. But if you're workin' for Aaron, I know you're worth it. Five thousand, not a penny more."

Lexi, the stunning blonde woman sitting on Jax's lap, leaned over and wrapped her hand over Rubi's mouth from behind. "Shut up, already. You're outbidding yourself."

Rubi slapped Lexi's hand away, and Mia was laughing so hard, she leaned back against Rafe for support.

"We're meeting you on our way out," Jax said. "Our job on the episode just finished up."

"You'll be back," Cynthia said.

"True."

"What do you do, Rafe?" Wes asked.

"I play hockey."

Mia fought the urge to say more, to pass the spotlight back over to Rafe as the NHL star. But there was so much more to him that got overlooked, so she stayed quiet.

"Professional hockey?" Jax asked. When Rafe nodded, Jax asked, "What team?"

"Rough Riders. We're out of—"

"DC," Rubi finished, then told Jax. "They're here playing the Ducks for the Cup."

For the first time, Keaton, spoke. "How do you know that?"

Rubi shot Keaton a superior grin, but didn't have to say anything. The woman on his lap, Brooke, offered a teasing "Because Rubi knows everything. You should know that by now."

"Plus it's all over the news," Rubi added with a smirk. "If you got your head out of your girl's panties once in a while you'd know what's going on in the world."

That brought more laughter and another wave of snark between the Renegades. This group was obviously tight enough to finish each other's thoughts. The way Mia had once been with Rafe and Tate and the rest of the team and their families. She would be losing all that when she moved here.

Mia glanced around at the others who worked on the *Wicked Dawn* set. They would be her new family. They were nice enough. And California was certainly as beautiful as everyone said. Yet she still couldn't work up any enthusiasm for the move or the job or this new phase of her life. Not after experiencing this connection with Rafe.

"Sure," Rafe was saying, pulling Mia back to the conversation too late to understand what they were talking about. "My schedule can get pretty hectic during the season. But we come out here to play several different teams, and I could just stay an extra day or two depending on my games."

"Great," Jax said. "It's always good to have experts of every kind we can call on for a quick lesson. The movie industry is crazy, and we never know what we'll get asked to do next."

"You're forgetting I know how to skate," Troy told Jax.

"You call that sliding around the ice on your ass skating?"

Jax shot back. "I remember it was a good thing that guy teaching you was in the off-season, because you needed a lot more than a few lessons. You sucked."

"I got the hang of it eventually." He turned heavy-lidded eyes on the woman sitting in his lap and tapped a gentle kiss to her lips. "And I didn't suck when I was out on the ice with you."

"No," she admitted, scraping her fingers along his neck. "You were definitely two hundred percent Prince Charming when you asked me to marry you. I won't ever forget that performance."

Performance. That was enough to seal the woman's identity for Mia. Hadn't everyone told her Los Angeles glittered with stars? It really wasn't all that different from New York, except in New York, Mia often saw "stars" like Robert Downey Jr. riding the subway or Katie Holmes grabbing Starbucks.

Troy tilted his head and kissed his smiling fiancée.

And from across the table, his buddy Wes treated him to a little payback with, "Get a rooooooooo—" only to be cut off by a kiss from his girlfriend, Rubi.

And once again, laughter filled the air.

Mia laughed too. Rafe gave her a squeeze and murmured at her ear, "I think you'll be really happy here."

On impulse, she turned her head and kissed him. Just a press of lips against lips—their first public kiss. The act held more power than she realized. It pumped a thrill through her veins. She felt stronger. More powerful.

And when she pulled away, she looked him directly in the eye and said, "I just wish it was closer to you."

When Aaron finished up with the producer, he and Mia drifted away from Rafe for longer conversations with several key people in costume. Over the course of the next two hours, she got a better idea of the industry, how television episodes were taped, and the impact of that schedule on costume.

She also clearly recognized how completely her world

would revolve around this job. Not a clock, not sleep, not meals, certainly not friendships, relationships, or relaxation. Cynthia had, in essence, said the same thing. And Mia had lived the life in several different jobs. But something about the stoic intensity with which Aaron delivered that news now sat on Mia's shoulders like lead, exhausting her before she'd even begun working.

Standing near the bar, she accepted her third glass of wine from the bartender and refocused on Aaron, who'd been explaining the company's benefits package. She scanned the patio and found Rafe with yet another group of people, engaged in yet another conversation. He'd definitely gotten the better end of this deal tonight. Had been meeting and enjoying almost everyone here.

His gaze drifted through the crowd and halted on her. He seemed to assess her in seconds. Until now, she'd smiled, he'd smiled, and the night went on. Now, he tipped his head toward the exit. *Oh yes. Thank God.* Mia inclined her head.

Rafe spoke to the group, shook a few hands, and started her way.

"I know this may sound overwhelming at first," Aaron was saying, "but we have a lot of fun at work, and we don't put you on salary, so you're compensated for every hour you work with overtime. Holidays are double-time. And there are all kinds of unexpected bonuses that vary season to season depending on the actors and directors and producers. They're always throwing special parties and doling out great quarterly and yearly bonus checks."

All great perks. If Mia wasn't so seasoned, she'd see those for the glittery carrots they were meant to be. But she'd learned about two jobs back that no amount of money or parties or gifts could replace freedom or serenity or peace or love.

But she told Aaron, "That sounds fantastic."

"Excuse me." Rafe stopped next to Mia and offered Aaron a

smile. "I hate to break in, but I should get back. Early practice tomorrow."

"Of course," Mia told Rafe.

While Rafe ordered an Uber driver, Mia gushed over Aaron's hospitality and his time. Told him how excited she was to start the job. Then she found Cynthia, gave her a hug, and promised to call her in the morning so they could meet to see the apartment and get a tour around town.

When they finally stepped outside the ivy-covered wall and back into reality, an SUV was waiting. They climbed in, and Rafe told the driver where to go. Then he collected Mia in his arms, pulled her close, and murmured, "Put your head down and close your eyes, baby. I know you need to decompress from all that."

Mia exhaled. Tears welled in her eyes. With no outlet, she did as he suggested, and with her cheek on his shoulder, his strong arms wrapped around her, his warmth and scent grounding her, the turbulence that party had whipped up inside her calmed for a moment. She couldn't voice her fears. Couldn't lament about wishing she could go back and change her mind over this job. She was afraid Rafe would validate her fears, and it was too late now.

Way too late.

18

"Maybe tomorrow," Rafe told Mia, "we can rent a car and drive along the coast. Stop in those little towns you love and walk around. Shop at the little stores. Pick up some new things for your apartment." Remembering her budget, he added, "It'll be my housewarming gift."

Her lips curved, and she snuggled closer in the backseat of the car. The vise gripping his heart tightened a little more.

"We can have an early lunch at a beachside café, just hang out there, sipping sangria and soaking up the sun while we listen to the waves. When our butts go numb, we can take a long walk on the beach."

She sighed, and her warm breath penetrated his shirt. He bent his head to kiss her temple and closed his eyes, pulling in a deep lungful of her scent. Damn, she smelled like heaven and heartbreak all rolled into one.

"What about practice?" she asked.

"Doesn't start till three. That will give us time to stop at your apartment on the way back and see Cynthia. And after I spend an appropriate amount of time with the guys at dinner, I'll sneak back to your room and spend the night with you."

Tangled up in the sheets, naked, making love to her every way he could think of to show her how passionately he felt about her.

"God," Mia closed her eyes on a soft moan. "That sounds like heaven."

They fell silent for the rest of the drive, but Rafe's brain spun for a solution to the distance that would soon face them. He didn't want to accept that there was no reasonable way for them to be together.

He could wait until June and the end of hockey season to talk to Tate and Joe about his feelings for Mia. But her new job was a real problem. He couldn't live on the West Coast. She couldn't live on the East Coast. And neither could ask the other to give up their dream. That wouldn't be such a big problem if either of their jobs allowed time for leisure travel. But by the sounds of things at the party, Mia would have her nose to the grindstone. And Rafe would be either playing or practicing nearly every day for eight months of the year.

This was screwed, plain and simple.

The SUV stopped in front of the hotel, and reality rushed in. They only had days left together. Once they went their own ways again, everything would change. They'd be friends, but it would be different now. A thin layer of awkwardness would always exist between them. Neither would know exactly where their friendship boundary lay, so both of them would stand back a little further, in fear of stepping over.

Next time he saw her, maybe this summer, she'd be dating some new hot surfer dude, all buff and bronze. Rafe and Mia would pretend their time together never happened. They'd laugh and talk about how they'd been friends forever, how they knew each other inside and out, but they wouldn't. Not anymore. Because this time together had already changed them both. Rafe would hug her when he left, like he always did. Smile and wave as if he were the carefree bachelor that fit the rumors. But inside, he'd be leaving the most important piece of himself behind.

"God." She exhaled and covered her eyes. "I just wish time would stop."

Instead, the car stopped, and they both had to get out and face reality.

Rafe thanked the driver, offered him a tip, and opened the door, offering his hand. He glanced toward the hotel as the wide glass doors opened and a gaggle of his teammates wandered out. Thankfully, Kilbourne wasn't with them.

"Shit," he muttered, dropping his hand before Mia had time to take it, then stepped back, putting space between himself and the car.

"Savage," a few of the guys said in unison. Then Tierney asked, "Where you been, man?"

Before he could answer, Mia stepped out.

All five guys slowed, their gazes a mix of suspicion and you-dirty-dog. Then shared looks to confirm they all believed the same thing—that he and Mia were getting it on.

"Oh, hi, guys," Mia said easily, as if she didn't notice. "Where are you headed?"

"We're going to meet Tate and a few other guys over at Sweet," Hendrix said, a wicked smile growing on his face. "We'd ask you to join us, but it looks like you already have a private little party—"

"Ty," Mia cut him off with a don't-start attitude. "Knock it off or I'll give Kimberly a call, and she'll knock it off for you as soon as you get home."

A couple of the other guys laughed and shoved Ty's shoulder.

"Lighten up," Isaac said. "I was just kidding."

"No, you were being a prick," Rafe told him. "And if you want to win the Cup, you won't shoot your mouth off about something you know nothing about to Tate and fuck up the balance we've got going."

That wiped the smile off everyone's face.

The guys continued on their way, with Isaac offering, "Don't stay up too late, kids."

"And you guys stay out of trouble," Mia said. "You know I'll hear about it if you don't. And you know all your wives and girl-friends like me better than they like any of you."

That brought a little joviality back to the group, and Rafe followed Mia into the lobby. "You are so damn sassy."

She shot a half smile over her shoulder. "They'll be *so glad* when they find out I'm going to be across the country."

At the elevator, Rafe stepped up close behind Mia and leaned forward to press the button, purposely brushing his body with hers. He slid his hands into his pants pockets but stayed so close at her back, their heat mingled. Their magnetic fields pushed and pulled.

"You know this whole team has the deepest respect for you, right?" he said, his voice low. "The way you call them on their shit. They may not like it, but they respect you for it."

"Some do. Some don't. Either way, I don't care. They can say what they want when I'm not around, but no one's going to pull that shit to my face. Ty's a privileged young brat, born with talent. He'll be a whole different person once he's had an injury and faced his hockey mortality."

She glanced up at him. "Besides, Kimberly really *does* love me, and she's way too good for him. What do you want to bet he apologizes to me before the next game?"

The elevator doors opened, and Mia walked in. Rafe followed, keeping his back to the doors as he tapped the button for Mia's floor. "I love wagers. But I can't wait thirty-six hours for the outcome of a bet I want to win right now."

The doors closed, and they were alone. He'd wanted to be

alone with her for what felt like for-fucking-*ever*. He took one step to close the distance between them and pressed his hands to the bar running along the wall behind Mia. He bent his head until his mouth was millimeters from hers, and when her lips parted and her eyes sparked, a thrill coursed straight through his body. This woman could do so much to him with so little effort.

"Want to make another bet with me? One that we could resolve, say, in the next thirty to sixty seconds?"

"Depends. What kind of outcome were you hoping to get right now, Mr. Savage?"

"You," he said without hesitation. "All you. All naked. All night."

Her breath hitched, and another thrill shot straight through his cock.

"I love that I can make your breath catch like that. And the bet is that you're dripping wet by the time we reach your door."

"We're almost to my floor. And you should be exhausted after the game you played tonight."

"The thought of getting you naked gives me all kinds of energy." He eased his lower body against hers, groaning at the delicious feel of counterpressure to his aching erection. "I want to be in your bed tonight, Mia. Deep inside you *all night*."

Mia scraped in an audible breath and pushed out a lust-filled "Rafe..."

"Yes. I want you saying my name just like that. Over and over." Fire flashed through his veins. "I want you to moan it. And scream it. And beg it." He lowered his mouth as if he were going to kiss her, and used every ounce of restraint he had to let his lips hover over hers. "Are you wet for me, Mia? Because I am *so* hard for you."

"Shit." The word barely emerged audible. Her eyes darted to the numbers on the elevator.

"If you're not wet yet, you're going to be when I tell you what's in my pocket."

Her gaze lowered to his, her lids heavy. "What?"

He pressed his lips to her cheek. Her temple. Then whispered, "A tie. A crimson silk tie. If you tell me what you want to do to me with that smart, ripe, beautiful mouth of yours, I'll let you have it."

The sound that slipped from her throat almost sent Rafe over the edge. A tight, delicious whimper of desire.

"If I put my hand under your dress and touched your pussy, would you drip on my fingers like icing?"

"You are..." She panted in quick, shallow breaths. "So bad..."

The elevator stopped, and Rafe pivoted away. It would be just his luck for Tate to have come back to the hotel, check in on Mia, and be standing at the elevator doors when Rafe had his hand under her dress.

But the doors opened to an empty hallway. He put his foot in the door's path, leaned forward, and glanced into the hall, looking both ways.

"Get your key out," he told her.

"What?" she asked.

He glanced back. "Your key. Get it out so we can go right into your room."

When she pulled it from her purse, he snapped it up, kissed her hard, and let her go with a little momentum toward her door across the hall.

He pushed the door to her room open and didn't wait for it to close before gathering her close and kissing her again. She responded like she'd been waiting all night for this moment. Her passion acted like a catalyst for an explosion between them. He groaned into her mouth, pushed her against the wall, and kissed her the way he needed her—like he was drowning, and she was his air. He poured all his confusion, frustration, need, desire, want, and love for her into the kiss.

Mia pushed at his jacket until it fell off his shoulders, and he released her waist to let it slide off his arms. He wanted to slow down. Wanted to savor her. But that would have to come later, because this need was white-hot and wild. While she worked at his buttons, he worked on his belt. And by the time she spread his shirt, Rafe bent to slide his hands under her skirt and pull at her panties.

They were both breathing fast and hard when he lifted her and pinned her against the wall with his body. When she slid a hand between them to grasp his cock and position it right where it belonged. Rafe managed to pause a moment there. He moved hair off her face, then tightened his fingers in the strands.

"I've *never* wanted anyone the way I want you, Mia," he confessed, his voice ragged. He dropped his forehead to hers. "This is…"

He didn't have words to describe the depth of need and emotion inside him and just shook his head.

Her nails bit into his shoulders where she'd peeled his shirt back. "Shut up and fuck me, Rafe."

A growl rolled through his throat, and his hips lunged forward, penetrating her in one long stroke. Her cry mingled with his. His brain went white with pleasure. And need took over. The need to drive and drive and drive the intense pleasure between them.

With Mia's legs tight at his hips, her nails digging into his skin, Rafe slammed her against the wall with each thrust. Her cries for more, harder, deeper drove him until she broke, arching against the wall, head dropped back, mouth open.

The feel of her coming, squeezing his cock, her juice raining over him, pushed him to the edge of sanity. Pushed him to demand more. He fucked her until her hands slipped on his sweaty skin. He fucked her with the frenzy of a man who'd found the Holy Grail. With the desperation of a man who knew the prize would be taken from him at any moment. He fucked her until she begged for mercy. And when he came, Rafe's world spiraled.

While they caught their breath, Rafe grappled with the realization that there was no way in hell he could let her go—Tate or no Tate. Joe or no Joe. Riders or no Riders. He needed Mia with him more than all three of those combined.

19

R afe felt like he was glowing when he hurried up the steps to the arena the next afternoon, glancing at his watch as he pushed through the locker room doors with two minutes to spare. He could have a goddamned light stick up his ass, he felt so amazing.

But as he walked the familiar cement hallway in the bowels of the stadium, with the familiar sounds of his team working out and talking echoing off the walls, Rafe was high on his fantastic day with Mia. A day that had given them time to bond. Just the two of them, relating as more than friends. And more than friends with benefits. Today, they'd bonded in a whole different way, in a whole different setting, with a whole different future on the horizon. Now, he just had to figure out how to get two other key individuals to see the same future.

And that shit was not going to be easy.

Or even possible.

Rafe turned into the locker room and greeted a few of the guys changing at their lockers, tossed his own bag down, and pushed off his shoes as he unzipped the duffel.

"'Bout time." Tate dropped to a seat on the bench beside

Rafe's and leaned back, wiping his face with a towel. His hair was damp, and a dark gray sweat stain marked the front of his light gray tee. "Where the hell have you been all day?"

Rafe's defensive instinct was immediate and automatic, and he had to consciously, purposefully tuck it away and relax. "I told you to come to the party. It would ease your mind about her being so far away if you saw where she was going to live and met some of her friends."

Tate's gaze drifted to the floor, and he lifted a shoulder. "If you say she's good, I know she's good." His eyes darted back to Rafe just as he pulled his shirt off. "Is she? Good?"

Rafe's mind immediately went in a whole different direction than Tate meant. And for the first time, it wasn't even completely sexual. Mia was good for Rafe in every way. She always had been. Rafe just wasn't convinced *he* was good for *her* in every way. Definitely not living across the country. And especially not if he cost her these important relationships.

Rafe nodded and told him the truth. "She is."

"So what did you do today?" Tate asked, clearly miserable over the topic, but compelled to know.

"We drove down the coast—man, what a gorgeous day. Stopped at a popular beach spot for lunch. I let her walk around, shop, sort of get the feel of the place, you know?"

When Tate nodded, Rafe went on, leaving out all the hand-holding, all the smiles, all the sweet caresses. All the kissing and laughing and dreaming. He left out walking barefoot in the sand, chasing her in the cool ankle-deep surf while she laughed at him over her shoulder, picking her up off her feet and twirling her around until her hair and skirt flew out behind her.

"We stopped by the apartment, talked with Cynthia, her roommate, again. Then I dragged her to a department store and got her what she needed so she wouldn't have to worry about the logistics or the finances of it when she got here. You know how she is. I had to argue with her and call it her housewarming, birthday, and Christmas present all wrapped into one *and* agree to let her pay me back at least half—which was a total lie on my part—before she relented."

"Bet that got ugly. Good call, bro."

"We took the drive to and from work to see what that was like. Did a little research on public transportation and the price of cars..." Rafe trailed off and cut a look at Tate where he bunched the towel in his hands, thoughts turning in the wheels of his head. "You're taking this move awfully hard."

"I just wish she'd talked to me first. Between you, me and Dad, we could have found her something closer."

Another thought Rafe had been tossing around entered his mind again. He braced his hand against the locker, took a breath, and just said it. "You think you might be connecting Mia leaving with Lisa leaving?"

Mention of his ex-wife brought Tate's head up, and if eyes could throw daggers, Rafe would be a dead man. "That's stupid. The two don't connect at all. What are you trying to say?"

Rafe lifted his hands in surrender. "Just that it might bring back some of the same feelings, which could be making this harder for you than it should be."

"When did you become Dr. Phil? I noticed you and Mia patched up your yearlong silence fast. You two are suddenly inseparable. Want to tell me what that's about?"

The accusing tone burned straight down Rafe's spine. "Forget I said any—"

"He's doin' her." Kilbourne walked through the locker room from the direction of the gym, wiping his face with the hem of his tee.

Both Rafe and Tate frowned at him and his random, monotone comment to no one in particular, almost as if he were talking to himself. He reached his locker and turned his head, looked between them, then lifted his chin toward Rafe and settled his gaze on Tate. In that second, Rafe knew what he'd meant, but he couldn't react fast enough to keep it from spewing from Kilbourne's mouth a second time.

"He's doggin' her because he's doin' her, man. I told you weeks ago." He opened his locker. "Shit, nobody listens."

Fury launched Rafe the twenty feet between them. He grabbed Kilbourne by the bicep and flipped him around, slamming him back against the lockers. "Stop talking shit. That's his sister and my friend. And she's been nothing but nice to you. You don't talk shit about family here, you got that?"

The cocky bastard looked Rafe right in the eye and said, "It's not okay for me to talk shit about her, but it's okay for you to fuck her?"

Someone caught Rafe's arm before he even realized his hand was fisted. Surprise cleared the haze of venom, and he found Beckett holding Rafe's fist where it was pulled back to his shoulder and on a trajectory to Cole's smug face. And Rafe hadn't wanted anything as badly as he wanted to pound Kilbourne right now except Mia.

"What the *hell* is *wrong* with you guys?" Beckett's bellow echoed off the walls. He used Rafe's arm to shove him backward, then stepped between Rafe and Cole, glaring at them. "Do you want to win the fucking Cup or not? Because we're not going to win it with our heads up our asses, which is where your heads"—he used a hand to point to each of them—"are right now."

"Kilbourne." Tremblay's bark made Rafe start and turn. "My office. Now. Savage. Hit the ice. The rest of you, try to teach these guys how to act like adults. These are only the most important goddamned games of the season."

Rafe jerked his arm away from Beckett, whirled toward his locker, and ripped his pads from the hook. A weird, icy-hot panic swirled around his ribs. Adrenaline and fury still burned in the pit of his stomach, joined by the innate anger of injustice over having to hide his feelings for Mia and the guilt of both hiding them and still seeing her. And in about sixty seconds, he was going to have to lie about it, because Rafe could feel Tate coming up behind him.

This sucked. The pressure inside Rafe was so intense, he felt like he was going to crack. He had to just...

Tell Tate.

God, he had to just...

Tell Joe.

Fuck, he had to just...

Let Mia go.

The pain that hit him dead center in his chest could only be described as agony. Rafe closed his eyes and rubbed his hands over his face.

"Is there something you need to fuckin' tell me?" Tate's low, menacing, rough voice, shaking with tension, sounded at Rafe's shoulder.

He pivoted on Tate, putting his face within two inches of his friend's and matching his tone. "What the hell do you think?"

"I think you're still playing like a motherfucker on fire when the chick you were screwing is back in DC."

"I think you're looking for someone to take your frustrations out on. We both know I play just fucking fine regardless of who I do or when."

Tate searched Rafe's eyes for a long, extremely tense moment.

And stood down.

But he didn't look happy about it. "I think it's time to get on the fucking ice and take out some of this stress on the pucks."

Tate disappeared down the hall toward the rink, and Rafe dropped to his bench, taking his sweet time suiting up. The guilt and anger and frustration had reached a fevered pitch. The stress of Tate finding out added a little more weight to

Rafe's shoulders every day. And the thought of losing either Mia or Tate ate at Rafe's gut like acid.

As he jerked his shoulder pads over his head and tightened them into place, Rafe knew something had to give, because if it didn't, he'd snap.

20

Consciousness tried to drag Mia to the surface, but she resisted. She didn't know why, only that she wanted to stay right where she was—comfortable, warm, content, and happy. So very happy. Everything about her—inside and out—was at complete and utter peace.

She felt complete.

Complete.

Something about the thought created a burr beneath her blanket of comfort. Mia stirred, repositioning her head on the pillow, searching for that utopia again. What she found was a whole different kind of paradise, hard and warm and erect—again—cradled by the indentation of her ass cheeks. Which was when she felt the familiar, rhythmic tug of her hair as Rafe stroked one piece before he wound it around and around his finger, let it fall, and started over again.

A sleepy smile lifted the corners of her mouth. She parted her lids and searched for the LED numbers on the clock. They read 2:00 a.m. "Baby, you need to sleep for your game tomorrow."

He just hummed softly.

The front of his body cradled the back of hers from shoulders to ankles. He was like a heated blanket. She reached back and took the hand playing with her hair in hers. Threading their fingers, she pulled his arm across her body and hugged it tight.

"What's wrong?" she asked softly. "Something's been bothering you since you got back from practice, and it wasn't any better after you had dinner with the team."

He pressed his face to her neck, took a deep breath, and let out a hum of pleasure, then kissed her there. But he didn't talk, and she realized this was why she hadn't wanted to wake. This tension stole the joy between them.

When he lifted his head, she leaned back and parted her lips in offering. Rafe took them with a moan of relief. He pulled his hand from hers and cupped her face, deepening the kiss with a greedy quality that bordered on desperation. Mia recognized the tactic—drowning himself in distraction.

Mia pulled out of the kiss and reached back to stroke a hand through his hair. "Hey. Talk to me."

He closed his eyes and rested his forehead against hers. Sighing, he loosened his hold, allowing her to roll him to his back and turn to face him. She stretched out beside his naked body, resting her head in her hand and let the other one slide over his abdomen. She followed the ridges there with her fingertips while she waited for him to get his thoughts together.

"Weather's nice here, huh?"

She smiled at his absurdly roundabout way of starting the conversation, but went with it. "Very."

Silence.

"Your boss and coworkers seem great."

"Mmm-hmm."

"I was telling Tate at practice that you were solid, you know? That you have everything you need, that you have good people around you. That you're going to be okay."

She tipped her head to look at his face in the ambient light. He was wide awake, staring at the ceiling. Her heart pulled, and she lifted a hand to his cheek. "I *am* going to be okay, Rafe."

He nodded. "I know. But, Tate, he's taking it hard."

"Are you sure it's *Tate* who's taking it hard? I haven't seen much of him while we've been here, and I haven't been hiding from him."

Still, Rafe didn't look away from the ceiling. "I think it has something to do with Lisa."

A protective instinct surged inside Mia. She lifted her head and sat up straighter. "What about Lisa?"

Rafe shook his head. "I just think you moving away is pulling up some painful stuff for him. I think he's associating the two and associating your move with some of the junk he's still carrying around from Lisa leaving him."

Mia's gaze blurred over Rafe's chest. Her teeth clenched. "That bitch." That got Rafe's attention, and he finally turned his head toward her. "And Tate's just as much to blame. He was blind and stupid. I tried to tell him while he was still dating her. Tried to tell him early in their marriage. But he's so damn loyal. Always believes the best of everyone."

Rafe heaved a sigh that ended on a groan, and he lifted a hand to rub at his eyes.

A stab of guilt sliced Mia's heart. "Shit, I'm sorry, Rafe."

"No." He laughed, the sound completely humorless. "You're right."

Mia squeezed her eyes closed. With her heart already aching, she curled her legs and sat up. "Rafe, maybe it's time to end this chapter of our story."

His head jerked toward her, his eyes sharp and surprised. "*What?*"

"This stress isn't good for you. It's affecting your sleep, your concentration, your relationships, your mood, and eventually, it will affect your game. No one can afford that. Not you, not Tate, not any other member of the team. This damn Cup has been a dream of yours and Tate's since you've been kids—"

"No." Rafe rolled toward her and gripped her thigh with one big hand. "My dream has always been to get paid to play hockey. I was living my dream at nineteen. I've never cared *how much* I got paid to play. And I don't give a shit about trophies or titles or my name engraved on a piece of silver on a cup."

Mia frowned, confused. "But Tate always said—"

"Tate is... Tate is...smart and driven and a leader. He's honest, dependable, and generous to a fault, and he's the best friend I'll ever have. But we both know Tate sees things in black or white. Everything is his way or the highway. And he's so caught up seeing things his way, believes that his way is so two hundred percent right for everyone, he doesn't even realize there's another way to see it."

"Okay, I'll agree with that. But I still don't get—"

"Tate wants the Cup. And Tate loves me. So Tate wants the Cup for me too."

Mia frowned. "Maybe I'm still half asleep, because that's not computing."

"Tate wants to share all the good things in his life with the people he loves. He loves you and me. Which is why—"

"We have Joe."

"And why I got to take lessons with Tate and the private hockey coach Joe paid for. And why I got tutoring with Tate and the math tutor Joe paid for."

"I get what you're saying."

"And I *do* want the Cup, just as bad as the other guys do. But I want it for Tate. I want it for the guys on the team who need it to fulfill some dream they had skating on a remote pond as kids in Canada or Russia or Sweden. So, yeah, I want that cup, and you can bet I'll bleed for it, but it's not *my* dream."

Mia was thinking about dreams. About Rafe having achieved his personal dream so young, yet going on to use his talents to help other people fulfill their dreams. And damn if she didn't fall in love with him again, right there on the spot.

With her heart so full it ached, she leaned down and kissed him gently, letting her lips linger on his. He stroked her hair off her face, and when she pulled back, she smiled. "I can't tell you how lucky I feel to have you in my life. You are such a special man."

He stroked her cheek with his thumb and held her gaze until she curled into his arm and pressed her head to his shoulder.

They'd gotten way off the subject of their relationship, and Mia didn't know how to bring it back around to ending it, or if she even should right now.

"What would you think of me spending the summer here?" came from him out of nowhere.

She processed that for a split second, but when she only came up with *what the hell?* Mia sat up. She looked at him, opened her mouth, but her thoughts tangled somewhere between her brain and her lips. Frustrated, she scooped his T-shirt from the floor where she'd dumped it when she'd pulled it off him earlier that night before Rafe had pinned her to the bed.

Pulling it over her head and jerking her arms through, she rolled to her knees, planted her hands on her thighs, and said, "Where did that come from?"

He shifted to his side, and the sheet fell forward, exposing the curve of his ass and his thickly muscled thigh. "Sounds like you don't like that idea." His tone was guarded and hurt. Brittle. He sat up and swung his legs off the bed, giving Mia his back. "That's fine. Let's drop it."

She lunged for him and dug her fingers into his shoulder. "Don't you dare do that with me."

He turned back, shrugging off her hand. "Do what? I asked

you a question. You answered it. You don't have to read something into everything."

"You didn't just ask me a question, Rafe. You just spun my world on its axis. So don't act all butt hurt when I call you on it."

He heaved a breath, hung his head, and ran all five fingers through his hair. "*Shit.*"

Mia was torn. Half of her wanted to be his best friend, show him compassion, and tell him he could tell her anything and it would be okay. But she'd crossed well beyond friendship with him, and that deep investment held an incredible risk to her heart. She needed him to know he couldn't just say anything and expect her to accept it.

So she fought for a happy medium. "Rafe, it's me. Just talk. It doesn't have to come out right the first time. I've heard every stupid thing you've ever said." That made him huff a laugh. "Just start somewhere, and we'll talk it out until we get it straight."

He dropped back to the bed. Quiet seconds lingered that twisted Mia's insides into a pretzel. By the time he turned to sit sideways, Mia had a fist pressed against her belly for counterpressure.

"There's nothing to straighten out. I try to find ways to make this work, but every path I take ends in a brick wall. I figured I should ask if you were even interested in the idea before I kept denting my head. I mean, it's your new life and all. Maybe you want to start fresh, no ties. I mean, I could understand that, I guess."

"The idea of, what? Having you in LA this summer?"

His gaze met hers in the most adorably hopeful look, she wanted to jump in his lap and kiss him. "Yeah."

She bit her lip to help herself deal with her very painful reality. "I think that would depend on what you planned to do after the summer. Because I'm over having guys walk away from me. And I'm definitely not up for just falling even deeper in love with you only to get my heart broken even worse when you say *hasta la vista* as soon as hockey season kicks in."

He gave her a curious look, like he hadn't fully understood what she'd said. But he turned toward her a little more. "The season is where I keep hitting walls. All the West Coast games are scheduled together in one week. But the other months, we're playing every second day, practicing on the others. All except for those once-a-month three- or five-day breaks. But you know how the management stuffs those with charity and promotional events."

"Hold on." She put up her hand. "I just need to make sure we're not in parallel universes right now. You're talking about having breaks in play to be able to come visit me?"

"Yeah," he said with that *what else* attitude.

Breathe.

Breathe.

But the giddiness didn't settle.

"Okay," she said, grabbing his arm. "Come here." She didn't relent until she was back on his lap. "Now." She took a breath, cupped his face, and said, "Tell me exactly what you want, Rafe."

"What I've always wanted," he said, his voice soft, matter-of-fact. "You. I just want to find a way to be with you."

Those giddy flutters kicked up in her gut. Something had definitely happened at practice today. "And what about Tate?"

Unease hazed Rafe's eyes, but Mia also recognized a familiar determination. One that she trusted. One that allowed her to relax and release all her reservations. Tate was as loyal as Rafe was dependable.

He met her eyes, then skimmed her face. "I can talk to him after the season's over, two weeks at the longest." He shook his head, his expression grim. "It won't be pretty. He may hate me for a while." Rafe went quiet, but his hands continued to move over her back. Finally, he shook his head. "I don't know how Tate or Joe will feel about me, and I can't control that." He lifted his gaze to Mia's and cupped her face. "What I do know is that I can't face a future without you loving me."

Mia's breath caught, and a little gasp choked in her throat. She pressed her forehead to his and doubled her arms around his neck. His arms mirrored hers around her body, pulling her close.

He forced the air from her lungs, allowing her to pull in fresh air. And she used it to murmur a shaky "I love you," at his ear, then laughed tears of relief. "I love you so much."

Rafe turned his head and found her mouth with his, and Mia tasted a fresh wave of emotion and desperation.

He pulled back, dragged the shirt she'd pulled on over her head, and stroked his hands over her skin from hips to shoulders. "Show me, baby."

21

Rafe raced off the ice during a line change near the end of the first period. On the bench, he purposely ignored the curious gazes of his teammates, leaned his shoulder against the wall, and followed the game while his breathing and his heart rate slowed.

His line mates, Tate and Ty, dropped to the bench and grabbed water bottles. Tate threw Rafe a towel, and he wiped the acrylic shield on his helmet.

Paul, one of the developmental trainers, stopped next to Rafe. "Chippy game already."

"Yeah." He tossed the towel at Tate, and when he looked back, Rafe said, "Water?"

The water bottle flew. Rafe caught it and squirted the cold liquid into his mouth. He felt Paul's gaze on his face, scrutinizing, like he was trying to crawl inside Rafe's head.

He knew he was acting different today. He was *feeling* different today. But there wasn't anything he could do about it. Even if there was, he wouldn't, because he was playing the best hockey of his life.

But he wasn't feeling high today. Not like he had in

previous games after making love to Mia and playing like Gretzky. Correction, after fucking Mia. Maybe that was the difference. Last night, he and Mia had made love. And today, Rafe was playing like Gretzky and Crosby combined. On drugs.

And, ironically, it wasn't because of the sex. Yet it was.

Rafe was fully aware that while the act of sex itself was a fantastic stress reliever and energy inducer, it was no magic wand for great hockey. But making love with Mia and hearing those words come from her heart had shifted the foundation of Rafe's life. And he'd been all in...until he'd shown up at the stadium. And been greeted so enthusiastically by Tate and the rest of his team.

Facing them all, knowing he would very well also soon shift the foundation of all their lives—and not for the better—had put a huge dent in his post I-love-you euphoria. Everything in Rafe's life had suddenly gained significance—and fragility—making him intensely in the moment. Hyperaware of his relationship with Tate, his interactions with every teammate. Which had extended to the game. To every micromovement of every opponent and the puck on the ice.

That made Rafe lightning quick. It enabled him to anticipate things before they happened. Allowed him to cut off plays, block shots, steal passes, and make the only two goals in the game thus far.

Now, on the ice, Beckett slammed the Ducks' defenseman against the boards and slapped the puck to Maddox, who sprinted toward the opposition's goal.

Rafe took the empty spot on the end of the bench beside Tate and rested his burning thighs, trying to keep his head in the game. He'd be going back in soon and needed to be informed when he did.

"You're white-hot again tonight," Tate said without taking his eyes off the ice.

The barely there insinuation in his friend's tone made Rafe's stomach pinch. "Gettin' lucky."

Tate's head turned toward Rafe. "With who?"

Rafe frowned at him and found accusation in his friend's familiar eyes. The look cut deep. Panic trickled through his gut. "I meant in the game, dumb shit."

"You believe in skill, not luck."

The crowd surged with hope, and they both refocused on the game. But Rafe's icy panic melted into a pool of dread.

He had the overwhelming sensation of being trapped. Trapped between his two best friends. Trapped between the two people he loved most.

And terrified he could lose them both.

"First line." Tremblay's words brought Tate, Rafe, and Tierney to their feet with two minutes left in the first period.

Rafe and Tate stood at the open door. Hawkins straddled the half wall leading to the rink, waiting for the second line to get close before they pushed onto the ice.

Just as they shoved off, Tierney smiled at Rafe. "Let's go for the hat trick. You've got two minutes."

As soon as Rafe's blades touched the ice, his mind cleared of all his scattered thoughts. Noise from the stands, the announcers, the stadium, faded. All he heard was the swoosh and scratch of skates and sticks. The swat and smack of the puck. The call of voices between teammates.

And that strange haze that had infiltrated his brain since he'd walked into the stadium earlier in the day settled over him. Rafe's body moved on the ice automatically, the way other people walked without thought. He saw the rink and everyone on it within a 180-degree view at once. Read body language in split-second increments and reacted.

With the clock sliding toward the minute mark, the Ducks' forward, Drew Dekker, caught a rebound off Tierney's skate blade and sprinted toward the Rough Riders' goal. Rafe had seen the rebound and Dekker's position to catch it a second in advance, and he was already swinging that direction when Dekker gained control of the puck. By the time the Duck lifted his head to assess his path to the goal, Rafe's stick was already on a trajectory for Dekker's.

He tapped the stick, stole the puck, and continued in a smooth slide, then sprinted toward the Ducks' goal with his complete and utter focus on the goalie and every subtle move of his head, body, and limbs. Rafe kept his mind open until the very last split second, and when the goalie put more weight into his left foot, that was the side Rafe shot toward, aiming for the net's upper corner with pinpoint focus.

In his head, Rafe swore he heard absolutely nothing but the *clack, clack, swoosh* of the puck as it hit the top pipe, the side pipe and finally the net.

Fucking A.

A stream of adrenaline mixed with triumph and joy. The first real spurt of joy he'd felt since he'd left Mia's bed that morning.

Rafe laughed and glided into the corner, turning back toward center ice. But he didn't get far before his other four teammates body slammed him in a group hug while a few baseball hats—about one percent as many as in their home arena—flew onto the ice. With the buzzers and bells and mixed response from the Anaheim crowd, Rafe didn't hear much of what the guys said. But Tremblay pulled them off the ice for the last thirty seconds of the period.

And as he followed the others through the small doorway into the box, Rafe glanced toward the stands for the first time since the game started. Mia's and Joe's seats were just a few rows up and to the right of the bench, and when he scanned past the fans waving their hands and taking pictures, he found Mia. Her smile was waiting for him. And the sight of it, filled with something very different, something intimate and special, something he'd never seen there before, made him feel like a flock of birds had been released in his belly.

He stepped onto the rubber mat of the box, and something hard hit him in the chest. Rafe's attention tore back to the bench. Tate pushed Rafe so hard, Rafe stumbled back. He almost tripped right back onto the ice through the open doorway, but caught himself on the half wall at the last second, saving their team from a penalty.

"*What the fuck?*" Rafe yelled, half-pissed, half-confused. Then the look on Tate's face registered—fury. You-betrayed-me-in-the-worst-way rage. I-want-to-kill-you ferocity.

And Rafe's stomach took a free fall.

The final buzzer for the period filled the stadium.

Tate leaned in until they were nose to nose and rasped, "Yeah, Rafe, *what the fuck?*"

And Tate checked Rafe's shoulder hard, slamming him against the wall as Tate turned, leading the team into the locker room for the break.

Rafe stood there a second, his mind racing as the other guys filed by. He felt their strange looks, felt the tension vibrating among the players. And he hated it. He just didn't know what to do about it.

Tremblay stopped beside Rafe, bit out a short "This isn't the place to screw around. No matter how good you're playing."

Then fell in with the guys and disappeared through the hall.

All the warmth and joy Rafe had just felt looking up at Mia iced over. He couldn't bring himself to glance at her. Even knowing she'd seen the confrontation. Especially knowing she'd seen the confrontation.

Beckett was the last in line and gripped Rafe's shoulder. "Something I need to know?"

Rafe felt sick as he met Beckett's gaze. "I have a feeling everyone's going to know soon, whether they should or not."

He turned into the hallway with Beckett following and used the short walk that should have been filled with triumph and excitement to shore himself up for pain—both physical and emotional. The kind of pain he suffered when he'd played a truly shitty game. Ironic he'd be subjected to it when he was playing his best.

The coach was already talking when Rafe turned into the open space outfitted for the visiting team. Rafe immediately searched for Tate and found him pacing in front of his locker space that adjoined Rafe's. With one hand rubbing his mouth, his fingers distorting his lower lip like a cartoon character, Tate scowled at the floor as if he were contemplating setting it on fire.

"That's the way to win battles, Rafe." Tremblay's words pulled Rafe's gaze from Tate. But the coach was already redirecting his words to the team at large. "Go right at them. Simplify the game. We've been the better team throughout the playoffs, and we just need to hold on to it. Don't rattle, just keep playing our game just the way you're doing it. Nothing changes here, boys."

Everyone offered their version of agreement in a hoot or shout or affirmative, and Tremblay turned for his office. He smacked Rafe's shoulder on the way past. "Way to attack the net, kid."

"Uh, yeah," Rafe said, pulling his gaze from Tate again to glance at Tremblay, muttering a distracted "Thanks, Coach."

His mind drifted back to Tate and what in the hell he was going to say to calm him down as he watched his coach disappear down the hall. Rafe could lie. Tate was only making an assumption based on a look he'd seen between him and Mia. But that would only make coming out with the truth later more hurtful. More damaging.

What a cluster—

Rafe caught movement in the corner of his eye, but before

he could turn his head that direction, Tate shoved Rafe against a cement block wall.

Air surged from of Rafe's lungs. He let his helmet and stick fall to the floor but didn't drop his gloves. The force wasn't anything new, but force in this setting stunned him. More so because the man using Rafe's jersey to hammer him repeatedly against the wall was his best friend. Only Tate didn't look anything like the friend Rafe had always known. His eyes were so dark, they were almost black. His expression so tightly etched with fury, he looked a decade older. But it was the pain there that cut Rafe. A pain he had only seen hints of since Lisa walked out on Tate. One he was realizing now ran a hell of a lot deeper.

A river of regret as black and thick as tar opened down the middle of Rafe's chest. "Tate," he rasped, "come on, let's talk about—"

Tate got a grip on Rafe's shoulder pads and slammed him back so hard, Rafe's vision blurred. Anger joined the regret inside, creating a volatile pain. Now he dropped his gloves, but he held it together. For Tate. For Joe. And for Mia.

He took a breath. "Tate—"

Tate jerked him nose to nose and with gritted teeth said, "*You're fucking her.*"

The locker room went quiet. Icily, eerily silent.

All the sickness in Rafe's gut twisted. He wanted to lie so bad, it was all he could think about. "It's not...". *Don't. Don't lie.* "It's not like that."

Tate released his jersey with one hand, and that hand landed in Rafe's gut as a fist. His stomach clenched behind the force of it. The shock of it. All his breath rushed from his lungs on a grunt, and his eyes watered. "Shit," he wheezed. "Tate, listen—"

"It's either like that or it's not. And I saw the way you looked at her."

Another punch landed closer to his kidney. The pain buckled him, and Rafe shoved Tate back with another curse. But Tate was livid. He slammed Rafe against the lockers again and smashed a cross to Rafe's mouth.

His head snapped sideways. Pain cut through his cheek, jaw, mouth. Blood squirted over his tongue. Again, not exactly new to Rafe. The real pain came from knowing Tate was on the delivering end. Knowing it came out of fury and hate. A deliberate intent to inflict pain. Not an adrenaline-induced burst of anger over a play.

"*Hey!*" Beckett's voice came from across the room. "Knock it *off.*"

Everything inside Rafe surged toward fighting back. He wanted to reach for Tate's jersey, jerk him around, pound him wherever Rafe could reach. But he didn't. Couldn't. Wouldn't.

All he could do was protect himself as best as he could until Tate backed off.

When Tate hauled back to take a right hook to Rafe's face, he blocked with his hand only to catch a gut punch from Tate's left. And when his other arm dropped automatically toward the pain, Tate's fist was there to ram his knuckles into Rafe's eye.

The force slammed Rafe's head back against the concrete wall. Pain stabbed his skull. Another punch whipped his head sideways.

"*Tate,*" Beckett yelled, closer now. "Back off. *Right now.*"

Beyond that, Rafe lost track of things. His head split with pain. His gut ached. When he tried to focus, everything blurred and spun.

"What the *hell* is going on?" Tremblay's booming voice rattled Rafe's brain.

Suddenly, Tate was off him. Tierney's voice came quiet near Rafe's shoulder. "Are you still with us, man?"

"Yeah," he breathed. "I think."

"Get the doc," Beckett told someone.

"He's bleeding pretty good from the back of his head," Tierney said. "Throw me a clean towel."

Rafe forced his head up. It swam and threatened to float off his neck. He searched the room with his blurry vision for Tate. Found him standing ten feet away, flanked by Tremblay and Beckett, shoulders sagging, hands on hips, head hung.

"I love her, man," Rafe said. When Tate's head came up, Rafe said it again. "I really love her."

"I love her too, but I don't fuck her."

That sparked another flare of anger. "She's your *sister*."

"She's *your* sister too, asshole. She's family. *We're* family. *You don't fuck family.*"

"I told them." Kilbourne's voice came from somewhere in the room. "Why doesn't anyone listen to me?"

Tate turned and lunged, but Beckett caught him and shoved him across the room the opposite direction. "You're testing my patience, Tate."

"Deal with this *outside* the rink," Tremblay told them. "Back on the ice. Everyone."

Tate turned away, pushing through the rest of the team toward the rink. The team doctor crouched beside Rafe while the other guys filed through the tunnel. Leaving Rafe to wonder if instead of finally finding the woman he was meant to be with, he'd finally screwed up the best family he'd ever had.

22

This had been the longest hour and a half of Mia's damn life.

She paced the exterior tunnel leading from the stadium to the team parking lot, waiting for someone to emerge from the locker room. She'd been down here for forty-five minutes. Rafe hadn't come back out onto the ice after the first period, and he wasn't answering her texts or voice mails. Mia was so worried, she wanted to chew the hinges off that damn door to get inside and check on him.

Rafe's hat trick had been wasted when the Rough Riders tanked in the second period, ultimately losing to the Ducks four to three.

The first family members wandered into the tunnel, and dread tightened Mia's belly. She didn't want to make this tension—tension that had obviously become ugly between Tate and Rafe—public.

She uncrossed one arm and rubbed her forehead. Maybe she should wait for Rafe at the hotel. But if he needed to go to the hospital, she wanted to go with him. Tate sure wouldn't go, and she didn't want Rafe to be alone.

"Hey."

The soft, worried, female voice startled Mia and brought her head up. She found Eden there.

"Sorry," Eden said, her gaze worried. "What happened to Rafe? Why didn't he come back after the first period?"

She shook her head. "I'm not—"

The hard pop of the metal door echoed through the cement tunnel like a gunshot. Mia swiveled toward the sound as Tate stormed out the door, his dress shirt untucked, blazer flapping open, no tie, bag slung over his shoulder, head down.

Any hope Mia had been holding on to evaporated.

She offered Eden a quick "Excuse me," before cutting into Tate's path.

He stopped short, and the look he leveled on her—eyes dark, nostrils flaring, mouth tight, pain and disappointment and anger draining the light from his expression—stabbed her heart and dragged her back an entire year. To the days after Lisa's betrayal.

"I think he's associating the two and linking your move with some of the junk he's still carrying around from Lisa leaving him."

"What did you do?" she asked, her stomach filling with dread.

He huffed something that was probably meant to be a sarcastic laugh but didn't come close. "You and Rafe are the ones *doing* everything."

"Where is he? Why didn't he come back after the first period?"

Tate's jaw flexed with the grind of his teeth. The look in his eyes, so dull, so cold, gave her an eerie tingle. "Don't call me when he hurts you. When he leaves you like all the others."

Fear bloomed in the pit of Mia's stomach. "Tate, I'm not—"

"Leaving you" never got out of her mouth. Another boom sounded, followed by Rafe's voice. "*Tate.* Talk to me, you fucking coward."

"Good luck with that," Tate said, tipping his head toward Rafe before sidestepping Mia and continuing on even as Rafe started toward them in a pained stagger, hand pressed to his side.

Mia got two steps toward Rafe when she heard Joe's voice behind her. "What in the hell is going on here?"

Mia looked over her shoulder. And when she saw his expression, she saw so much similarity between him and Tate, an icy chill filled her stomach. Joe took hold of Tate's arm as if his son was three, not thirty, and dragged him to where Mia stood and Rafe approached. And when Mia looked at Rafe again, she gasped.

"Holy *shit*." She scanned the cuts on his mouth, his cheek, his eye. The bruises on his chin, his cheek... And spun on Tate, launching herself at him. She pounded both hands against his chest. "You *fucking* asshole." The fact that he didn't move even a millimeter only added fuel to her infuriation. "What the hell is wrong with you?"

"Stop it, Mia." Joe's curt order shocked her to a stop. With his gaze on Rafe's face, he threw Tate's arm away with a sound that was part sigh, part disgust. "Did you do that to the man who's been your best friend for two decades, Tate?" When Tate didn't answer, only glared at Rafe, Joe barked, "*Tate*, I asked you a question."

"Yes, sir."

Joe pried a pained gaze off Rafe's face and stared at his son for a long time. Tate never met his father's eyes. His gaze was pinned to the ground, holding on to belligerent anger. The pain reflected on Joe's face seemed to radiate through the group. They all stood silent, reflecting in the disgrace they'd created among themselves.

She and Rafe might not have gone about it the right way, but Mia wouldn't go back and change her decision. After last night, after knowing how it felt to be truly loved by Rafe, she knew without a doubt she'd never want to go through life missing out on that.

Then Joe turned to Rafe. "Rafe, did you deserve that beating?"

Rafe's lips compressed, eased, compressed. He shifted on his feet. His knee bounced. Head dipped. Never once did he meet anyone's gaze. And Mia's heart fell to the pit of her stomach.

She pulled in a breath to answer for him. But Joe held up a hand to her, index finger raised.

Mia pressed her lips together and crossed her arms.

"Rafe?"

He cleared his throat. Winced. And rasped, "Yes, sir."

The knife in Mia's heart dragged down the center of her body, filleting her open. Her lips parted to ask him exactly what the hell that meant, but Joe spoke first.

"*We. Are. Family,*" he said, his voice rough and livid. "This" —he gestured to Rafe's face, speaking to Tate—"is not how family treats family. I don't care what he did or what he thinks he deserves. I expect better of you." Then he addressed Rafe. "This is a talk I never thought I'd ever have to give you in my lifetime, Rafe."

Mia was watching the bottom of her world slide out from under her. She dropped her arms, fisted her hands, and looked at the three men standing there. All three of them breaking her heart.

"Do *any* of you care about *me*?" That brought all their gazes to her. And it was so too little too late. "You all seem awful caught up in this friendship bullshit." She gestured to Tate and Rafe. "And this father-son bullshit." She gestured to all the men. "Where do I fit into this puzzle? Or am I still just that dangling little leftover who will forever be an afterthought? Secondary to friendship or a convenient tool to winning fatherly approval?"

Joe angled toward her with a confused frown. "What are you—"

This time, she was the one to lift her hand to Joe for quiet, while giving them both one last chance to do the right thing— both apologize for being assholes and show their love for her— as a sister to Tate and a lover to Rafe—was more important than some bromance they'd clung to since puberty. "Either of you?"

Joe glanced at the guys. When neither Tate nor Rafe spoke, Mia's heart broke. For the millionth time.

"Well, that's just perfect." She looked at Tate and smiled through the tears in her eyes. "Bet that happened even faster than you thought it would. Only it wasn't just him." She made a careless gesture at Rafe. "It was *both* of you. You *both* abandoned me. How lucky can a girl get?"

"Mia?" Joe asked, concerned and confused, his hand on her shoulder. "I don't understand—"

"I'm done." She turned away from the men who would obviously always choose each other first, and looked at Joe. "I won't accept anything less than 150 percent in *any* of my relationships anymore. And this time, *I'm* going to be the one to walk away."

She kept her head high and her pace steady as she finally put the past behind her.

23

R afe tried to doze in the ER, but no matter how he positioned himself, he couldn't get comfortable. Something hurt almost everywhere. But he'd refused the painkillers, because, well, the physical pain was a distraction from the far more debilitating emotional pain slicing away at his insides.

His head felt like a watermelon. Rafe forced his eyes open to look at his watch, but when he lifted his arm to put his wrist in front of his face so he didn't have to move his head, pain stabbed at his ribs.

"God, I hate the ER," he groaned, gritting his teeth until he could read the time. One a.m. "Everything takes so damn long."

Rafe closed his eyes and rested the back of his hand on his forehead. He'd only returned because he'd discovered the team doctor had missed another cut on the back of his head. And he'd only discovered the doc had missed another cut because he'd been yelling at Tate and the blood had come gushing out all over the back of his shirt. And he'd only been yelling at Tate because the asshole had been walking away—again—as he'd been trying to talk to him after Mia had left.

Rafe winced. That sensation of being kicked in the gut returned. His eyes stung.

He had no idea what he was going to do now. And it wasn't the hockey Rafe was worried about. He'd played with plenty of guys he'd hated and who'd hated him. Tate could go on hating Rafe until the end of time if he wanted. If it interfered with the game, Tremblay would just change lines or keep them off the ice at the same time or trade one of them. Rafe didn't give a shit anymore. It was too late to care anyway.

But he didn't know how he was going to live with *Mia* hating him. And he didn't have to see her or talk to her or interact with her. Ever. Yet every time he thought about the hurt on her face when she'd all but begged him to claim her, and he'd kept his mouth shut.

The sting developed into tears, and Rafe turned his hand over, pressing his fingers to his closed lids. "Fuck."

The slide of the curtain sounded on the metal rings, and Rafe gave a mental eye roll. If he had to turn down painkillers one more time...

"So." Joe's voice surprised Rafe, and he lifted his hand from his eyes, blinking to focus. He'd brought Rafe to the hospital, then gone in search of Tate once Rafe was settled in the ER. Now, Joe strolled to the side of the gurney, leaned folded arms to metal railing, and quirked a humorless, lopsided grin at Rafe. "You and Mia."

Dread, shame, and self-disgust for all the pain he'd caused coalesced in Rafe's gut. His eyes slid closed again, and he let his hand fall back over his eyes. "Should have known. That *fucker*."

"That fucker says you love her," Joe said. "That true? Love her as in you're in love with her, not as in you love her the way we love her."

Rafe exhaled, his overwhelming emotions making the effort shaky. "Yes."

"Look at me, son."

He licked at his swollen, burning, throbbing lips, moved his hand to his forehead, and met Joe's eyes. "Yes, I love her. I've been in love with her for...God, I don't even know how long. I just couldn't..."

"Because of Tate."

Rafe nodded and lowered his gaze. "And...you."

Joe was quiet. "Yeah," he said finally. "I can see why that little girl is so pissed with all of us."

"She's not pissed at you."

"She should be. She's right. She's so sweet and amiable. Always just wanted to be part of the group. Just wanted to be included. To be loved. And we've all been so concerned with our relationships with each other, she's been popped around between us like a ping-pong ball."

Rafe wiped his eyes. "I don't want to drive a wedge into your family, Joe—"

"Our family, Rafe. *Our* family. You are as much a part of this family as Mia and Tate." He sighed and smiled a little. "I knew you were special the first time I met you. And it had nothing to do with hockey and everything to do with the way you and Tate clicked. I always thought you two acted a lot like twins. I've never felt obligated or pressured to do anything for you, Rafe. And I've never regretted one minute or one penny invested in any of you kids. Everything that you and Tate and Mia have done over the years is a source of great pride to me. Pride I thrive on. Pride I brag about at every opportunity. So, don't think for one minute that your part in this family is even a sliver smaller than Tate's or Mia's."

More emotions spilled in and overloaded his circuits. His system couldn't process them all, and he shut down, numbing them down to a point where he could function without imploding.

"Thank you, Joe."

Joe reached over the side and covered Rafe's hand with his

own. "The only way I could be disappointed in you is if you didn't go after what really makes you happy. And I think Mia makes you happy."

Rafe frowned, confused. "But Tate, the team...shit, the play-offs." Their loss that night filled Rafe's mind, swamping him with guilt. "God, what a mess."

Joe smiled and patted Rafe's hand with his own. "I like to see it as a challenge. And if there is one thing I know about Rafe Savage, it's that he excels at facing challenges."

24

R afe didn't feel up to any challenge as he walked the hall toward Mia's hotel room several hours later.

Joe had brought him back to the hotel from the ER, and Rafe had passed out in his room sometime around three a.m.

Only seven a.m. now, he knew it was too early to be pounding on Mia's door, but he couldn't sleep. And he couldn't stop thinking about her. Couldn't stop spinning all his mistakes around in his mind. Couldn't stop trying to find a way to ease the pain he'd caused and repair the damage he'd done.

And when he wound his way around a laundry service cart in the hallway and approached Mia's door with no answers, he surveyed a spot on the floor at the bottom of the wall beside her door and prepared to sit. But when he put his hand against the wall for support to help him get to that spot without falling on his face, he noticed a gap between the door and the frame. Following that space to the door handle, he found it ajar.

Alarm jumped in his chest. He checked the room numbers first, and when he was sure it was hers, Rafe put his fingertips against the door and eased it open. "Mia?"

A female voice with a Spanish inflection returned some sort

of answer Rafe didn't understand, and he opened the door wide enough to find a woman in a housekeeping uniform pulling sheets from the bed.

She smiled at him. "Oh. Hello. Sorry."

"No, it's okay." From the short hallway leading to the room, he scanned the space. All her things were gone. Her suitcase, her computer, all her charging cords.

She was gone? Mia was gone?

"Is your room?" the housekeeper asked in broken English. "You need be here? I go?"

A wave of sadness hit him so hard, tears flooded his eyes in an instant. He blinked fast to hold them back and rubbed a hand down his face. "No," he told her, his voice rough. "Thank you. It's fine."

Rafe backed out of the room and kept on moving until he hit the wall across the hallway, where he stood and stared at the floor, trying to figure out what the hell was going on inside him.

He'd assumed the texts and voice mails he'd left after talking with Joe at the hospital had gone unanswered because she'd been asleep. But that obviously wasn't the case. And while he knew she had every right to be hurt and angry and even to move on with her life and never look back, he never realized until this moment that he never thought she really would.

He'd also never realized just how devastating that would feel. How very different it felt for him to walk away from someone—even Mia—than to be the one left behind. And how often Mia had experienced that. All because she'd loved Rafe too much to fully give herself to anyone else.

Lifting both hands, he covered his face and rested his head.

Should I just let her go?

The thought twisted the knife in his gut. Rafe couldn't ever remember a time when he'd reached out for Mia when she hadn't been there.

"I won't accept anything less than 150 percent in any of my rela-tionships anymore. And this time, I'm going to be the one to walk away."

She'd made that hard call in the face of extreme pressure. Rafe knew it had to have been one of the hardest things she'd ever done. And now that she'd taken that step and made the break, maybe it would be better for Mia if he just...

"Are you fucking *meditating*?"

The familiar grouchy voice pulled Rafe's head up and to the left. He moved too fast, and his head swam. He pitched side-ways and grabbed the nearest doorframe, catching himself.

"You think you can communicate telepathically with her or something?" Tate prodded in that bitchy, condescending tone he used when he was annoyed and fed up. But at least he wasn't livid. At least he wasn't coming after Rafe, pinning him to the floor, and beating the shit out of him again. "'Cause if you get down on your knees and start chanting, I'm calling security."

"Shut up."

A room door between them opened, and an older man looked out, his face scrunched into an irate scowl. "Both of you shut up. People are still trying to sleep."

And he slammed the door.

"Not anymore," both Rafe and Tate said in unison. Then laughed at the same time.

And just like that, the ice was broken. But the chunks were still floating between them, cold and sharp. And Rafe didn't even care. He just wanted Mia. Only he hadn't figured out if going after her was the right thing to do.

Rafe walked past the complainer's room and leaned his hip against the wall between Grumpy's door and Mia's. His lifelong friend stood there, far more contrite today. Joe had a way of pulling both him and Tate back to earth quickly. But their fights had always been with others, never with each other. And their fights had never been this extreme, this hurtful, or this personal. Rafe didn't know what would happen to their friendship, which was another painful spot in his life.

"We were going to tell you—" Rafe started.

"After the season ended," Tate finished. "I know."

So he'd talked to Mia. That part was good, though Tate didn't look relieved or happy or even any more settled.

Rafe added, "And we didn't mean for it to—"

"Become anything," Tate completed his sentence again. "Mia told me she seduced you and why." He paused only a split second before his face compressed into a scowl and his hand whipped out with a rigid finger pointed at Rafe's nose. "But you still should have said no."

Rafe lifted both hands in surrender. "I should have. I can't count how many times I've said that to myself over the last couple of weeks." A moment of awkward silence existed before Rafe asked, "So, did you two—"

"Make up?" He huffed a humorless laugh. "Hardly." Tate looked at a spot beyond Rafe's shoulder. "In time maybe…"

That didn't bode well for Rafe's chances at forgiveness. His heart dropped even lower.

He pushed off the wall. "I'm gonna go pack. Catch an early flight back. Maybe I can think of something in the next seven to ten hours to say or do that will convince her to at least sit down and talk to me—"

"When did you become such a girl?" Tate asked, giving him a disgusted look. "What's all this talking shit. 'Let's talk about this.'" He lifted his voice to imitate a female. "'I wanna talk about that.'" His voice dropped to his pissed tone again. "What happened to the guy I knew before Mia got ahold of your balls? The guy who took action when he wanted something? The guy who just shut up and went after it?"

Tate dropped his arms and straightened from the doorframe. "You keep that attitude, and we're gonna have to change your last name from Savage to Pussy."

Rafe laughed, relieved to see the return of Tate's good-natured insolence.

"Go on. Get out of here," he told Rafe. "But if you want to do that talking bullshit, you'll have to do it over the phone from the East Coast, 'cause she didn't go back."

"What?" Rafe's attention laser focused again. "Where did she go?"

"To her apartment here. Said there was no reason to go back. Called her boss last night and told him she'd start work early." Tate turned around and started down the hall toward the elevators. "See you back at home." But then he stopped and looked at Rafe again. "Oh, and I think this goes without saying, but I'm going to say it anyway because I'm not going to leave anything left unsaid between us from here on out." He turned deadly serious again. "You cheat on her, you bail on her, you hurt her in any way, you'll answer to me. And when you *really* answer to me, you'll need to retire, because last night will look like a fucking picnic."

He walked away and disappeared down another hallway, but Rafe wasn't thinking about Tate's threats. He was consumed with the realization that she'd already made up her mind. She'd already turned her back on the possibility of working it out with Rafe. She'd already given up on him.

Mia was gone.

25

Mia scrolled through images of filming shots from Cynthia on her phone, enlarging a few to study the construction detail. She was exhausted from too little sleep and too much crying, and the sun and wind on the beach weren't helping her burning eyes. But she was desperate for anything to keep her mind busy, and she'd done as much moving in as she could handle.

She wasn't going back to the apartment until Cynthia called her and told her UPS had picked up everything she and Rafe had bought on their one-day shopping trip together.

Tapping one image closed, Mia shaded her eyes, scrolled through the costumes, and opened another. Before she could magnify it, a text pinged her phone from Faith, Grant's girl-friend: *I have at least a dozen people who want jerseys like mine. So do all the other girls. And I had brunch with Ted at the Crofts' this morning. When he heard you'd approached Silver with your designs and not him, honest to God, you'd think someone just told him the Riders lost the playoffs.*

Mia laughed, but it hurt. God, she was going to miss every-one. Sure, they were still close now, but she knew how time came between people. Distanced people. And knowing she would eventually lose this hurt.

She dug her toes into the warm sand, tossed her blowing hair over her shoulder, but when she went to respond, she didn't know what to say. So she ended up sending Faith a sad emoji.

Miss you. When will you be back? Faith asked.

"Ah crap." Mia dropped an elbow to her knee and her forehead to her hand. She hadn't thought about that when she'd made the decision to stay.

She hadn't said good-bye to anyone in DC. And once she started working here... By the sounds of it, Mia wouldn't get a break until they had to legally give her a break, which would be two weeks' vacation every year and a few holidays.

Shit.

She might need to push back her start date a day or two. Sneak in a quick flight back east just to see the girls and say good-bye. Sure, Rafe and Tate would hear about it, but Mia would be gone by then. She just wanted to see a few people personally before she didn't see them again for, hell, probably a year. Tina, Eden, Faith, Sarah, Amy, Rachel, Lily...

Amy, Rachel, Lily.

Her heart broke a little more. They'd be so different in a year. Mia wouldn't know their sizes or their color preferences like she did now. How could she make outfits for little girls whose tastes changed on a whim when she saw them only once a year?

Would they even remember Mia in a year?

Then she thought of another year without seeing Rafe. Thought back over how miserable she'd been this last year...

A fresh wave of loss tumbled through her and the tears she'd been fighting for hours rose up in her throat. She let her gaze drift to the ocean.

"Suck it up," she murmured to herself. Everyone moves on.

If one of the players got traded, they'd be leaving just like she was leaving. No one was going to watch out for Mia but Mia. That was abundantly clear. It was her own damn fault it had taken her so long to see it.

Mia filled her lungs with the fresh sea air and forced a perspective change. The water was so blue. The waves so serene. The sun so warm. The air so mild.

She could be happy here.

She *would* be happy here.

She was losing friends and family back east, but she would gain new friends here. Find new opportunities. And, maybe, someday, even create a family of her own.

Until then, work would help fill this hole inside her.

Eventually.

So why were those damn tears choking her again?

"Hey."

The voice so close behind her when she thought she was alone startled Mia. In the split second between registering the voice and turning, she knew who she would face before her eyes met his. But knowing and seeing were two different things, and Mia's heart still banged hard against her rib cage. Then it raced and fluttered and squeezed. All her thoughts came to a dead stop, and confusion reeled her brain in a whole different direction. She looked behind him toward the road as if that would explain what he was doing here.

"You are one difficult woman to find," he said, lowering to the sand beside her in slow, pain-filled movements. "Do you realize how big this beach is?" Once he settled, he dropped the running shoes he was carrying. "Or how small you are? Even when Cynthia gave me an idea of where you were going, it was still like that whole needle-in-a-haystack thing."

She angled toward him, wincing at the way his injuries looked as the healing process began. That was never a pretty sight. "You went to my apartment?" She shook her head. "*What* in the hell are you doing here? You should be landing in DC right now."

"But you're not in DC."

She lifted her hands. "So?"

"So that's why I'm not in DC."

What the hell? Mia pressed her hands to the sides of her head and forced her brain to stop spinning. "I'm not fighting with you, Rafe. I don't have the interest or the energy."

"Thank God for that, because neither do I."

A bubble of anger burst inside her. "Look, I can't do this. I don't want to drag this out. I just want us to get on with our lives."

Rafe pulled his knees up and wrapped his arms around them, failing to hold a groan back when he moved. But when he turned his head and leveled that silvery gaze on her, his eyes were clear, his expression, even marred with bruises and cuts, relaxed. Far different from the man she'd seen last night.

"Yeah," he said with a slight nod and a thoughtful tone. "That's what I want too."

The knife in her gut twisted a little, but Mia huffed a laugh. "Then you're in the wrong place, buddy. Get your ass on the next plane east."

"Eventually." He heaved a little sigh. "But this is where I want to get on with my life. With you."

He reached out with one hand and pulled a windblown strand of hair off her forehead, then cupped her cheek. His hand was warm, his fingers and palm rough, and his touch brought memories and feelings flooding back. Mia couldn't keep her gut from clenching with want or her eyes from fluttering closed, but she clung to the image of every man in her life walking away to find her strength.

"I'm sorry, Rafe. That isn't—" The words *"what I want"* hung up on her tongue, because they weren't true. It was exactly what she wanted. But it was also what she knew he couldn't give her, and she had to amend her words to make them accurate. "That doesn't work for me."

She turned her head and lowered her knees to ease from his reach. "I meant what I said last night. I've been settling all my life, and I'm not willing to do that anymore. I know hard limits are going to create situations that require sacrifices and that I'm facing loss." That all too familiar pang hit her in the throat again, and she pulled a stuttering breath. "But, it's time."

He nodded. "I know." Dropping his hand to the sand, he leaned into it. "It took me too long to figure it out. And I'm sorry it caused such a mess with Tate and Joe. I'm sorry I hurt you. Caused you so much stress."

Somehow, this wasn't helping. "Look, I'm sure from your perspective, this was the right thing to do. And I appreciate the apology and the gesture, but I don't want to see you right now." She had to look away from the flash of pain in his eyes and rolled to her knees, then her feet. "But by all means, tell Joe and Tate you extended the olive branch."

Before she could stand, Rafe grabbed her hand. The quick move cost him. His eyes slammed shut, and pain creased his features, but he kept a death grip on her hand while he breathed through the pain.

And when he opened his eyes, he might have looked angry, but his voice was soft and patient, with just a hint of steel when he said, "I'm not here for Tate or Joe."

A flare of temper threatened. "They're the only people who knew I didn't go back to DC." She pulled her hand from his and lifted both in surrender. "And, look, it's *fine*. It is what it is. I understand—"

"No, you don't." He rolled to his knees with a grimace and took hold of her biceps. Deliberately looking into her eyes, he said, "I'm here for *you*, Mia. I talked to Joe when I went to the ER last night, and he gave me his blessing. When I went to your room this morning, Tate told me where you were. You know he wouldn't have done that if he didn't want me to find you. He would have let me get on that plane, waited until we were somewhere over Iowa, then looked at me and said, 'Oh, by the way, Mia stayed in California and never wants to hear from you again.'"

She knelt there on the sand, her mouth hanging open. He was right. That was exactly what Tate would have done.

An uneasy flutter tried to break out, but Mia repositioned her grip. "What did Joe say?"

"He said the only thing that I could do to disappoint him would be to not go after what makes me happy. And he already knows you make me happy."

That made Mia want to sag into a puddle in Rafe's arms.

Reality check. Joe and Tate weren't their only problems.

She shrugged out of his hold and got to her feet. Rafe struggled to his own.

"That's..." She released a breath and tucked her hair behind her ears. "That's great. I'm glad you all worked it out and patched things up. But that doesn't change anything for you and me. I'm done with these dysfunctional relationships, and we both know you never stay with one woman." She shrugged. "It's fine. It's just who you are."

Rafe exhaled and nodded. Shoved his hands into the back pockets of his jeans. "It was who I used to be. Until you. Before you, I never wanted to stay with one woman."

Oh God. Those were dream words. From a dream man.

If only he meant them.

She crossed her arms and heaved a sigh. God, she was so tired. "Rafe—"

"Tate gave me some good advice, believe it or not." He laughed, the sound filled with irony. "He told me I've been letting too much talk take the place of action. And he was right. So, I went back to doing me." He brought his hands around in front of him, and one held a small box. He met

Mia's eyes again, serious and soft. "I'm going after what I want."

She still wasn't following what he was saying. Until he dropped to one knee in the sand again, opened the box and lifted it toward her.

"Mia, I love you. I want you. I need you. Marry me."

Her mind hit a wall. Her gaze jumped between the ring and his face at least half a dozen times while her mind spun and spun but went nowhere. While her lips formed words but nothing came out. Her heart lodged in her throat, cutting off her speech and blocking her air.

"Rafe— What— That's—" She took a step back, hands stacked over her pounding heart. "*What?* You can't be serious."

But, *da-yum*, that ring, sparkling in the sunlight, looked *very* serious.

"You know me. You know I wouldn't ask if I wasn't serious."

And he just stayed right there on his knees, offering the ring.

Hysteria trickling in. It bubbled in her gut and fizzed along her nerves. "Then you need to go back to the hospital for another head scan. *Rafe.* Married? You're insane."

"No," he said, level, calm. "I'm in love. With you. I've been in love with you for what seems like forever. What's insane is the idea I could ever love someone even half as much as I love you. What's insane is us pushing each other away because of what other people think or want or say. What's insane is wasting another minute miserable when we can be happy. Together."

She tented her hands over her mouth. Tears blurred her vision.

He was serious.

This was real.

"Holy..."

He grinned. Barely. And lopsided, with his cuts limiting the movement. "I'd rather hear 'yes.'"

"Rafe," she breathed. "What about…"

She looked up and around, almost forgetting where she was. The whole bicoastal issue smacked her in the face. Then Tate's words echoed in her head: *"I told you not to give up your own place,"* and something that felt the way she imagined PTSD would feel vibrated in her chest.

Was this just another mistake waiting to happen? If she gave up this job, this apartment, this life for a man, and he changed his mind…

"I know what you're thinking." His words brought her gaze back. "But I'm still here." And he was. He hadn't moved an inch. "And I'm not leaving, Mia. We can catch a flight to Vegas and elope tonight if you want. No prenup, no negotiations. You get all of me. One hundred and fifty percent. You keep this job, this apartment with Cynthia. I'll fly in as often as I can. Do my charity work and interviews from here instead of DC. I'll spend the off-season here. We can get a little place of our own to stay at when I'm in town. When you get time off, you can fly back to DC to see everyone. A lot of couples manage on far tougher schedules. In two years, when my contract comes up, and I'm a free agent, then we can…" He grinned again, lifting one brow. "Negotiate."

Mia burst out laughing.

But as soon as the energy was spent, the seriousness of the situation flooded back in. And she *could not believe* she was standing here considering saying yes to a marriage proposal from Rafe Savage.

"And," he said, "I think you might also like to know that I got a call from John Silver about an hour ago. Sounds like he and Dad hit it off and they've been talking. John made some inquiries with NHL and they've agreed to discuss contract options that will allow you to start your own line of jerseys. Of course, that includes a cut of the profit to NHL and the individual teams, but Dad's a negotiating shark. He'll get you a good deal.

Mia was going to hyperventilate.

Rafe winced and pulled his extended arm back. "Sorry, it's still right here." He held the ring closer to his body. "I just can't keep my arm out for that long. I also heard," he said, "that Ted was—"

"Upset that I offered the jersey idea to Silver first," she finished for him. "I just heard."

Rafe nodded. Shrugged. "Right now, the world is looking like your oyster, baby. Stay here and work in Hollywood, live with all your family back east, and run your own company." He shook his head. "It doesn't matter what you choose, I'll be with you all the way."

She piled her hands over her heart. "Oh my God."

Holy shit. This was terrifying. A fist of fear tightened around her heart.

"I know, baby," he said. "It scares me too." He lifted the ring again. "But I'm still here. This is still here. Neither of us are going anywhere."

She sipped a breath and held it. Then finally pushed more words out. "This is forever for me, Rafe. Ever since I was a little girl, I knew when I got married, it would be forever."

A slow grin spread across his face. A big, deep joyous grin that mirrored itself inside Mia.

She laughed, her heart filled, and she stepped into him, ignoring the ring for the moment. "What are you thinking right now?"

She cupping his face and stroked her thumb over the multi-colored bruises marring his skin.

Rafe turned his head, kissed her hand as best as he could with the cuts on his lips, and met her gaze with those silvery eyes. "I'm thinking that forever sounds *perfect*."

EPILOGUE

Six months later.

Mia pressed her hands to her cheeks, smushing her cheeks. "Aye, aye, aye, this is like herding cats."

Rafe chuckled and ran a hand down her back. "You just couldn't settle for models."

She was standing in a photo studio, surrounded by everyone she loved—Rafe, Tate, Beckett and Eden, Grant and Faith, Tina and Jake Croft, and Beckett's sister, Sarah. The cats requiring herding in this situation were the three little angels modeling the beginning of Mia's children's line of jerseys—Lily, Amy, and Rachel.

Sarah and Tina were doing their best to get the girls to stop playing and pose for the camera, but, man, when those three got together...

"Did someone give them giggle juice this morning?" Faith asked.

"I think their heads have grown a little too big for their bodies," Sarah said, finally getting the girls to hold in a pose long enough for the photographer to snap three split-second images before Amy poked her finger in Rachel's armpit and all three girls melted into giggles again. She sighed. "I'm sorry. All this attention has them thinking they're *all that*."

"They're so adorable, you can't even get mad," Mia said, then asked the photographer, "Tom, can you get some shots of them playing? I think those will look just as cute in the catalogue."

The older man chuckled. "I think that's a smart idea."

He spent the next fifteen minutes snapping more photos while the girls acted like they'd been infused with honest-to-goodness fairy dust.

When Tom stopped shooting, looked back through the photos, and smiled, Mia slumped with relief.

"Yay!" she told everyone. "Almost done. We just need a few group shots."

Tina and Sarah handed corralling duties over to the men before joining Faith, Eden, and Mia in front of the camera for several poses.

"Now that's what I'm talkin' about," Beckett said, grinning at the women.

"Ogle on your own time, please," Mia told the men at large.

"Oh, I do," Beckett assured her. "And I will. Just keep making those lip-smackin'-sweet jerseys, Leighton."

Laughter rippled through the group.

Mia had definitely gone a little racy with her rollouts. Deep necklines, bosom-flattering designs and accents, and curve-hugging fabric were only some of the sexy elements she'd added to her designs. She also had mesh, lace, and even a touch of leather incorporated into this smokin' hot line.

By the time Tom finished with the group shots, Mia was exhausted. She's been working eighteen hours a day nonstop to get the first dozen jersey designs created and ready for production.

"I'm starving." Mia stood from the box where she'd been kneeling and stretched her back. "Is anyone else starving? Lunch for my *fantabulous* models is on me."

Agreement made the rounds, and the others discussed lunch options while Rafe slid his arms around Mia and kissed her forehead. "Congratulations, baby. You worked your ass off for this."

She grinned up at him, still fizzing inside. The photo shoot was the last step in the preproduction phase. Now, the jerseys would go into mass production and be on sale in stores wherever Rough Riders' apparel was sold throughout the US.

"It's pretty exciting." And she couldn't stop smiling. "The only thing that would have made it better was having the Cup at the center of our photos."

"Oh, man, I didn't even think of that. Damn, that would have been amazing." He shrugged. "Next year."

She nodded. "Next year for sure."

His gaze dropped to the open neckline of her halter-style jersey, and he hummed. "Speaking of starving, I've been running on famished since you started these crazy hours. Maybe we should skip lunch and hit the sheets instead."

She laughed and slid her arms around him, loving the warm, hard feel of him. "You do know how I like it."

Rafe lowered his head and kissed her. A sweet I-love-you, I've-never-been-so-content-in-my-life, lingering kiss.

"Rafe and Mia," Tom said. "Can I get one shot of you two together?" When they both looked at him, he shrugged. "Good to have on hand for biography pieces."

Rafe took her hand and wandered toward the set. "Hope you're going to be Photoshopping this, Tom."

"Just you, honey," Mia told him. "I'm perfect."

Rafe slapped her butt, making her laugh.

At Tom's direction, Rafe sat on one of the blocks and took Mia in his lap.

"Okay, perfect. Now, just act natural. Pretend the rest of us aren't here."

Rafe barked a laugh that made his eyes sparkle. "We'll scar the kids for life."

But this was easy for Mia. The way he looked at her made her feel like the only person in the room.

He lifted a hand to her cheek. "Have I told you how proud I am of you?"

"Mmm, maybe. Once or twice or fifty times." She tilted her head and kissed him. "Have I told you how much I love you?"

His grin was quick and full. "Maybe once or twice, but I look forward to hearing it thousands and thousands and thousands of times over the next fifty years."

They kissed again.

"Okay," Tom said. "Got it."

But Rafe didn't stop kissing her.

"We're good," Tom said. "It's a wrap."

Still, Rafe kept kissing her.

"That means break it up." Tate's snarky tone cut into the magical moment. "If you need some help...I'm right here."

Tate's sarcasm drew laughter from their friends and family and even Mia. But Rafe sighed and rolled his eyes. "Have we talked about moving to the Bahamas yet? 'Cause I'm ready. Like today. Like now. We don't even have to pack. We can just buy what we need when we get there."

Mia was laughing.

"That's called a *honeymoon*," Tate said. "Honeymoons require *marriage*."

Rafe dropped his forehead to Mia's shoulder and whispered, "Let's sneak away in the middle of the night."

Making Mia burst into giggles.

"Let's get something to eat." Tina came over and rousted them both. Hooking an arm through each of theirs, she started toward the door. "The natives are getting restless." On the way out the door, she turned a conniving little grin on Mia. "Now, what would I have to do to get one of those sequined numbers?"

ABOUT THE AUTHOR

Skye Jordan is the *New York Times* and *USA Today* bestselling author of more than thirty novels.

When she's not writing, Skye loves to learn new things and enjoys staying active, so you're just as likely to find her in the ceramics studio as out rowing on the nearest lake or river.

She and her husband have two beautiful daughters and live in Oregon.

Connect with Skye online

Amazon | **Instagram** | **Facebook** | **Website** | **Newsletter** | **Reader Group** | Tiktok

ALSO BY SKYE JORDAN

ROUGH RIDERS HOCKEY SERIES

Quick Trick

Hot Puck

Dirty Score

Wild Zone

PHOENIX RISING

Hot Blooded

Shadow Warrior

Hell Hath no Fury

Wicked Wrath

FORGED IN FIRE

Flashpoint

Smoke and Mirrors

Playing with Fire

WILDFIRE LAKE SERIES

In Too Deep

Going Under

Swept Away

NASHVILLE HEAT

So Wright

Damn Wright

Must be Wright

MANHUNTERS SERIES

Grave Secrets

No Remorse

Deadly Truths (Coming Soon)

RENEGADES SERIES

Reckless

Rebel

Ricochet

Rumor

Relentless

Rendezvous

Riptide

Rapture

Risk

Ruin

Rescue (Coming Soon)

Roulette (Coming Soon)

QUICK & DIRTY COLLECTION:

Dirtiest Little Secret

WILDWOOD SERIES:

Forbidden Fling

<u>Wild Kisses</u>

COVERT AFFAIRS SERIES

<u>Intimate Enemies</u>

<u>First Temptation</u>

<u>Sinful Deception</u>

Printed in Great Britain
by Amazon

32558277R00142